Louise Allen has been immer_____
history for as long as she can ____
that landscapes and places evoke powerful images
of the past. Venice, Burgundy and the Greek islands
are favourites. Louise lives on the Norfolk coast
and spends her spare time gardening, researching
family history or travelling. Please visit Louise's
website, www.louiseallenregency.com, her blog,
www.janeaustenslondon.com, or find her on
X @LouiseRegency and on Facebook.

Also by Louise Allen

The Earl's Mysterious Lady
His Convenient Duchess
A Rogue for the Dutiful Duchess
Becoming the Earl's Convenient Wife
How Not to Propose to a Duke
Tempted by Her Enemy Marquis

Liberated Ladies miniseries

Least Likely to Marry a Duke
The Earl's Marriage Bargain
A Marquis in Want of a Wife
The Earl's Reluctant Proposal
A Proposal to Risk Their Friendship

Discover more at millsandboon.co.uk.

THE LADY WHO SAID NO TO THE DUKE

Louise Allen

MILLS & BOON

All rights reserved including the right of reproduction in whole or in part in any form. This edition is published by arrangement with Harlequin Enterprises ULC.

This is a work of fiction. Names, characters, places, locations and incidents are purely fictional and bear no relationship to any real life individuals, living or dead, or to any actual places, business establishments, locations, events or incidents. Any resemblance is entirely coincidental.

Without limiting the author's and publisher's exclusive rights, any unauthorised use of this publication to train generative artificial intelligence (AI) technologies is expressly prohibited. HarperCollins also exercise their rights under Article 4(3) of the Digital Single Market Directive 2019/790 and expressly reserve this publication from the text and data mining exception.

® and TM are trademarks owned and used by the trademark owner and/or its licensee. Trademarks marked with ® are registered with the United Kingdom Patent Office and/or the Office for Harmonisation in the Internal Market and in other countries.

First published in Great Britain 2025
by Mills & Boon, an imprint of HarperCollins*Publishers* Ltd,
1 London Bridge Street, London, SE1 9GF

www.harpercollins.co.uk

HarperCollins*Publishers*, Macken House, 39/40 Mayor Street Upper, Dublin 1, D01 C9W8, Ireland

The Lady Who Said No to the Duke © 2025 Melanie Hilton

ISBN: 978-0-263-34529-2

08/25

This book contains FSC™ certified paper
and other controlled sources to ensure responsible forest management.

For more information visit www.harpercollins.co.uk/green.

Printed and Bound in the UK using 100% Renewable Electricity
at CPI Group (UK) Ltd, Croydon, CR0 4YY

To Cheffie with love and mince pies

Chapter One

1st October 1815

'No,' Lady Thea Campion said. 'Absolutely, definitely, no. I will not marry the Duke of Leamington.'

Her parents regarded her with blank astonishment written all over their usually impassive faces.

'Foolish girl,' her mother said, producing a faint laugh as though humouring a stubborn child. 'This is no time for funning. You know perfectly well that you have been betrothed to Avery Vernier since you were in the cradle.'

'I know no such thing,' Thea retorted. 'It was a family joke, the kind of thing the old aunts chuckle about: "Dear child, won't she make a wonderful duchess?" I cannot be betrothed to him, I do not know him.'

'You have met, surely you remember,' her mother said. There was no amusement in her voice now.

'When I was, how old? Ten? Yes, I remember him—a nasty, bullying lout of a boy, all ears and big feet and big opinions of himself to match. I did not like him then. I do not *know* him now.'

He called me Twig.

That had rankled ever since. Yes, she had been a tall, skinny child, all angles and elbows, topped with a mop of red hair that had now matured into the much-admired colour of well-polished mahogany.

But that horrible boy had said she looked like a twig with one autumn leaf left on the end of it. *'I'll call you Twig,'* he'd said with a laugh that cracked in the middle because his voice had not yet finished breaking.

'But surely you understood,' her mother tried again.

Her father simply looked thunderous. Earls were not used to being thwarted and certainly not by their daughters. Daughters were raised to be dutiful.

'It was agreed between us and the late Duke and Duchess soon after you were born,' Mama said. 'It was spoken of as you were growing up, I am sure of it,' she added vaguely.

'Yes, as a *joke*. Why did I have a Season if you had already as good as married me off? Why are we making plans for my second Season now?'

'Naturally you had to learn how to get along in society, to acquire some town bronze. His Grace could hardly marry a girl straight out of the schoolroom. And your first Season was delayed because of dear Mama's death, and then you had measles.' She broke off as if to contemplate the wilfulness of her daughter in catching such a juvenile complaint. 'So naturally it is important that you have as much exposure to good company as possible.'

'I fail to understand what this is about.' Her father finally spoke. 'You sent all those young men along to me to have their suits refused without giving them any encouragement—and there must have been at least six of them. Why was that if you did not already know yourself to be promised, eh?'

'Because I did not want to encourage any of them. I did not *want* to marry any of them. They were perfectly pleasant young men, but that was all. But they were persistent, so I told each of them to apply to you.'

Thea stared at her parents in exasperation. This was so typical of them. They never expected to have to explain anything to anyone, and their word was law in the household.

Their children, of whom Thea, at just past twenty-one, was the eldest, spent a decorous half hour with their parents every day before dinner when they were growing up, attended church with them twice on Sundays and were occasionally summoned for disciplinary interviews when they transgressed. Then, when they reached an age when they could be trusted to behave with decorum, they dined with them with all due formality.

Exchanges consisted of social conversation or directives. Questions and opinions were not encouraged. This, Thea knew from exchanges with her friends, was perfectly normal in aristocratic households, and she did not expect anything else. But not to have informed her that she had been betrothed for all of her twenty-one years, to have just assumed that she had absorbed the fact as anything but a family joke…

For a moment Thea was speechless, then she told herself that, unless she resisted, she would simply be swept along on the relentless tide of her parents' will.

'No,' she said again, firmly. 'I do not wish to marry the Duke and therefore I am not going to marry the Duke.' Her father was turning a worrying shade of crimson, so she asked hastily, 'Where is he, anyway? If he does want to marry me, which I very much doubt, why isn't he here asking me himself?'

'Of course he wants to marry you, foolish girl.'

'I am quite sure he wishes to marry the daughter of the Earl of Wiveton. Our ancestry is ancient, our connections unrivalled and my dowry is impressive—but I have trouble believing that he wants to marry *me*, Thea Campion, someone he met once when she was ten and he was, what? Fourteen? Sixteen? If he wants me, why hasn't he called before now?'

'The Duke, who is now twenty-six years of age, has spent a year at the Congress of Vienna with our diplomatic corps,' her father said. 'With the death of his father on the ninth of June—the same day as the Final Act of the Congress was signed—he was about to return to England. Then the Battle of Waterloo threw the entire area into disarray,'

'That terrible man Bonaparte,' her mother interjected.

'When he finally returned to England, there were all the issues of the succession to deal with and he was in mourning, of course. Now he has set out on a tour of all his estates and is expected back in London by the end of the month.'

Her father's colour had subsided a little as he concentrated on this account, but her mother clearly felt she should continue. 'He has written to inform us of his intention to call upon your father in three weeks' time to formalise matters. He is still in mourning, of course, but the wedding can be arranged for next summer.'

'And was he intending at any point to actually ask *me* if I wish to marry him?' Thea enquired.

'Naturally he intends to meet you, foolish girl. But he has no need to ask, it is all agreed.'

'But not, as I keep attempting to make clear, by *me*.'

Her father's face was thunderous now, and Thea had to curl her toes in her shoes to stop herself backing away. He had never struck her, never administered so much as a smack on the hand, but then, a panicky thought warned her, she had never displeased him like this before.

'You are not trying to tell me you wish to marry someone else? You have not been indulging in some clandestine flirtation, I sincerely trust?'

'Certainly not, Papa. I have not yet met the man I

wish to marry.' Somehow Thea managed to say in a fairly moderate tone, 'Until then, if I refuse to marry the Duke, I fail to see what anyone can do to force me. This is hardly the Middle Ages.'

'In the Middle Ages, undutiful, disobedient daughters were sent to nunneries.' Her mother's voice was so calm that Thea felt a sudden stab of real apprehension that they were not going to take no for an answer.

Her parents exchanged a meaningful look, her father nodded and Mama said, 'If you persist in this nonsense your allowance will be greatly reduced and you will be sent to live with Cousin Elizabeth in Harrogate.'

'Cousin *Elizabeth*?'

Her mother's cousin was twice a widow—Thea's brothers always maintained that she had eaten her husbands in the manner of female spiders—and she employed, and then dismissed, companions at an alarming rate. Or they fled. She was sour, obsessed with propriety and with good works, although only for the benefit of those she considered the Deserving Poor.

'Cousin Elizabeth has had to dismiss yet another unsuitable companion. You will do very well as a replacement for now. I imagine that, after a month, you will find that the prospect of marrying a man holding one of the most elevated positions in society, a nobleman of great wealth, is significantly better than life in Harrogate.'

'And where will you say I am when he arrives on the doorstep in three weeks' time?' Thea asked, trying very hard not to panic.

'I will apologise but explain that, unfortunately, you are having to take the waters after catching the influenza,' Mama said grimly. 'You really leave us very little choice.'

'Which is it to be, Thea?' her father asked. 'Decide. You stop this undutiful nonsense now and agree to receive Leamington, or you go to Harrogate tomorrow.'

'Harrogate,' Thea said, chin up.

At least she was travelling in comfort and had not been bundled onto the stage, Thea thought the next morning as the family's travelling carriage rolled away down Chesterfield Street.

On the other hand, there was far less chance of escape from a closed carriage with a driver and two grooms who had been in the Earl's service for years and, sitting opposite her, Mama's own lady's maid, Agatha Maunday.

She doubted John the driver, or Peter and Tom the grooms, knew why she was making this journey, but there was no doubt from her expression that Maunday did. She was clearly both astounded and deeply disapproving.

Thea shifted on the seat, trying to get comfortable with a purse of money concealed in her stays. It was not a great deal—six guineas and some change—but that was all she had in the way of resources. While her clothes were being packed Mama had removed her jewellery box, remarking, 'You will not be needing these.' That had left her with a pair of pearl earrings, a thin gold chain and a small seed pearl brooch.

Fortunately, the first thing Thea had done when she had reached her bedchamber was to hide almost all of what was left of her quarterly allowance, leaving just a guinea and sixteen shillings in the hope that Mama would believe that was all she had unspent. She had removed the guinea without saying anything.

Now all Thea had to do was to devise an escape plan. But what was there to escape to? And what could she do when she got away? She had no skills other than those any young lady was expected to master and they hardly had much commercial value, not without references to support them.

She could write herself some letters of recommendation, she thought, pondering the possibilities, but only governess, companion or semptress came to mind and she could not see herself being very successful at any of them. Companion perhaps. Not every lady in need of one could be as objectionable as Cousin Elizabeth, surely?

An hour later, she recalled the road book that lived in a door pocket of the coach and drew it out. Following the route might be a distraction.

Thea found Harrogate on the map. Goodness, but it was a long way north. She traced the route with her fingertip, all the way up the Great North Road. Finchley, Baldock, Stamford, Grantham, Doncaster...

Grantham. Grantham was the nearest town to where her godmother, the Dowager Countess of Holme, lived. Thea had six godparents, carefully selected for their position in society, their contacts and the likelihood they would leave her something substantial in their wills. She wrote them all dutiful letters from time to time, exchanged small gifts at Christmas, and that was all she had to do with them.

Except for Clarissa, Lady Holme, the widow of Papa's cousin. She was charming, took an interest in what Thea was doing, wrote long, chatty letters and sent gifts of interesting books. Most of those had to be hidden from Mama because they were novels or tracts by ladies proposing the vote for women and other such scandalous things.

Godmama would not approve of Cousin Elizabeth and she wouldn't approve of Thea being forced into marriage, either, even if it was to a duke.

And they would be driving past her doorstep. Well, within ten miles or so from it. She had two days to think of a plan. Thea lifted the road book, looked out of the window and began to talk. She must seem bright, interested and cooperative.

'This must be Highgate Hill, Maunday. How steep it is! Just think of Dick Whittington climbing it, all ready to give up and leave London, and then hearing the bells calling him back! Now, what is next? Ah yes, Finchley Common. My goodness, do you think we will be held up by highwaymen? There's a tree called Turpin's Oak…'

Three days later Thea was almost hoarse from chattering and Maunday had the glazed look of a woman whose brain had been lightly scrambled. They had stopped for the first night at Eaton Socon at the White Horse and the second at North Witham, about one hundred miles from home and ten miles south of Grantham.

The coachman, she knew, had orders to drive very steadily and to change horses every ten miles or so. He would certainly be prepared to stop at either of the excellent inns at Grantham—either the Angel, reputed to be the eldest inn in England, as Thea told the maid at length, or the very modern George.

They were about a mile from the town when Thea let her voice trail away. She doubled over, gave a deep groan and clutched at her stomach.

'My lady! What is it? What's wrong?'

'Handkerchief!'

Maunday scrabbled for one and pressed it into her hand.

'Oh, I should never have eaten that ham at breakfast. I thought it tasted strange but I assumed it was a local cure… *Oh!*'

'Hold on, my lady,' the abigail said urgently. 'We are almost in the town and the inns are very good, so

I'm told. John said he'd stop at one to change horses. They'll have a room for you and you can lie down. Just hold on. Wherever did I put the lavender water?'

Hal stretched out long legs and leaned back in the deep armchair. 'You have no idea, Godmama, how good it feels simply to stop travelling.'

'I have, my boy.' The Dowager Lady Holme put down her teacup and smiled fondly at him. 'My late husband never seemed to stop in one place for more than seven nights together and I was dutiful enough to travel with him. Dear Reginald has been gone these past six years and now I move at my own pace. But you are almost at the end of your journey, are you not?'

He nodded, 'I had planned to go into Norfolk, but it is not urgent. I am inclined to continue on down to London now. I'm my own master, after all.'

'It will be quiet, the Season has not yet started,' she reminded him. 'But I suppose you are hardly planning to join the social whirl.'

'True. There are some tiresome business affairs,' he said with a shrug. 'Then visits to my tailors, a look in at—'

From the hall the sound of the front door knocker penetrated upstairs to the comfortable seclusion of Lady Holme's sitting room.

'Bother,' she said vaguely. 'But I told Fenwick I was not at home, so we will not be disturbed.'

Barely a half minute later the door opened.

'A caller, my lady. I believe you will wish to speak with her.' Fenwick, an old family retainer, knew when to treat orders as mere suggestions. 'I have shown the young lady to the drawing room.'

'Do not disturb yourself, dear boy.' His godmother waved him back into his chair as he rose when she did. 'I will not be long. Some problem with the tenants, no doubt.'

Hal settled himself more comfortably, considered another cup of tea, realised it must be cold by now, dismissed the idea of finding a newspaper or a book on the grounds that his godmother would return very soon and settled on simply relaxing.

It dawned on him, after perhaps thirty minutes, that whatever the problem was, it did not appear to be yielding to Godmama's usual decisive approach. Should he go and see if it was something he could help her with?

He stood up, flicked his coat tails into order, pulled down his waistcoat and turned to the door as it opened and his godmother swept in.

Her lips moved but no sound emerged. He realised she was mouthing the words *help me* as she looked fixedly at him.

Help her with what? All seemed tranquil outside the room, his godmother looked perfectly well—except for an expression of what he could only describe as concentrated urgency.

He stared at her wondering if she had received a blow to the head or was suffering a seizure. 'Yes, of course I will but—'

'*And be tactful*,' she whispered before turning to speak to someone behind her. 'Ah, there you are, my dear. You will be positively dying for a cup of tea, I have no doubt. It will be here in a moment, but first I must introduce you. Thea, my dear, allow me to present Mr Hal Forrest, one of my many godchildren. Hal, Lady Thea Campion, my goddaughter.'

Somehow he managed a murmur of greeting and a smile. The tall young woman in front of him was not regarding him as though he had lost his wits, so perhaps he had succeeded.

'Lady Thea, an honour.' He bowed, just as an untitled gentleman should when introduced to a member of the aristocracy.

To a very comely member of the aristocracy.

'Mr Forrest, how do you do? I am sure that if we are both Lady Holme's godchildren we must be related in some way,' Lady Thea said with a warm smile as she sank into an armchair and twitched her skirts into order. 'God-cousins, perhaps, if such a thing exists. I am so sorry to have broken into your quiet afternoon, but I have explained to Godmama that it is an emergency. I am running away, you see.'

'From home?' Hal enquired politely, remembering Lady Holme's instruction on tact.

'Oh, no, nothing so unoriginal.' She flashed him

a smile, presumably for his careful lack of censure. 'From my utterly impossible Cousin Elizabeth. I am in disgrace, exiled to the penal colony of Harrogate with my cousin—a veritable gorgon, I assure you—as my gaoler.'

'And what—' Hal fell silent as Fenwick entered, supervising a footman with a laden tea tray and a maid bearing a platter of tiny cakes.

'Thank you, Fenwick. You pour, dear,' Lady Holme said, sitting back.

However hoydenish Lady Thea's behaviour might be in running off—although he had some sympathy with anyone wishing to avoid the stuffy gentility of a spa town out of season—she certainly had the training of a young lady, judging by the assured manner with which she established his requirements, dispensed tea and urged him to sample a cake.

But what had the daughter of an earl—this particular daughter—done to justify being sent to a northern spa town in disgrace when the Season was about to start?

'Tell me, if you are willing to confide, Lady Thea, what prompted your enforced exile to Harrogate?' he asked when they all were all served.

'Oh, I refused to marry a duke,' she said cheerfully.

Hal, who had followed his question with a mouthful of tea, almost choked.

Chapter Two

'You refused to marry a duke?' Hal asked when he could speak again. 'Er...which one?' He had to ask.

'The Duke of Leamington,' Lady Thea said. 'I believe that at present he is the only one of marriageable age who is unattached, under the age of sixty and in his right mind.'

'Thea, dear,' her godmother chided.

'Well, to my certain knowledge, the Duke of Farringdon shares his dinner table with a goat and keeps a troupe of monkeys in his drawing room,' she said unrepentantly.

'Perhaps influenced by the Princess of Wales,' Hal said, fascinated as much by her plain speaking as his mental picture of Farringdon's home life.

'My point exactly—you cannot say that is normal behaviour, given that it is regarded as bizarre even in the wife of the heir to the throne. And the Duke of Perivale attacked his valet with a chamber...that is, an article of bedroom porcelain, and the Duke of Hampton has just divorced his wife, and from what one hears of her side of the story one can only assume—'

'Quite,' their godmother interrupted hastily. 'As you say, Leamington is really the only eligible duke available at present.'

'Available,' Hal echoed faintly, and reached for another cake.

'Well, it is a marriage mart, after all,' Lady Thea said, helping herself to a piece of shortbread. 'And if one is in the market for a duke, one must admit that the merchandise on the shelves is somewhat lacking in variety. More tea, Mr Forrest?'

'Thank you, yes.' He passed over his cup with, he was relieved to see, a steady hand. 'But apparently you are *not* in the market for such a husband, Lady Thea,'

'I have no objection to a husband as such, sir, it is simply that I do not like that one and I greatly objected to being informed that my fate has been decided since birth. It was a considerable shock, believe me.' She took a ladylike bite from the shortbread biscuit.

'Might I ask what is so objectionable about Leamington?' he asked. 'I do not believe I have heard any stories about goats, or misused wives. Or items of chinaware, come to that.'

'I met him once.' Lady Thea demolished the crumbly slice with a snap of her teeth. 'He was arrogant, loud, rude and his feet and ears were too big.'

'Thea, *dear,*' Godmama said with a faint moan. 'How old was he at the time?'

Lady Thea wrinkled her nose as she thought and Hal decided that made her look just a little like a squirrel, with her dark red hair. A very refined squirrel though: tall, willowy, with high cheekbones, a shapely but mobile mouth and expressive hazel eyes. Her height and her colouring should have made her unfashionable—petite, curvaceous blondes were all the rage—but she had style and presence.

'Fourteen? Sixteen?' she hazarded. 'I was ten or eleven.'

'*All* boys are revolting at that age,' Lady Holme said with authority. 'I have five godsons and they all went through a phase of being noisy young hooligans needing to grow into their bodies. Mostly they managed to develop into quite civilised gentlemen.' She sent Hal a sweet smile. 'You did, didn't you, Hal dear?'

'I do hope so, Godmama,' he said. 'The Duke may be perfectly acceptable by now, you know, Lady Thea. I gather that you have not met him recently.'

'I have not. Having apparently dealt with the troublesome business of finding a wife at an early age—something I had always believed was a family joke until I was disabused of the notion by my parents four days ago—he then completely ignored me. Other than that one meeting, during which he comprehensively insulted me, I have never set eyes on him again.

'I understand that he has been amusing himself at the Congress, where I imagine Lord Castlereagh found his assistance invaluable,' she ended sarcastically.

'The swine,' Hal said and received in return a dazzling smile that seemed to hit somewhere at the base of his spine. He crossed his legs and enquired, 'Might one ask how he insulted you, Lady Thea?'

The smile vanished. 'He called me…a name. A nickname. I am sure he found it wildly amusing. I did not.'

'I can only apologise on behalf of all of us who have been crass young males at some stage in our lives,' Hal said, with what he was surprised to discover was genuine feeling.

'Thank you, Mr Forrest.' That dangerous smile was back.

'And what do you intend to do now, Thea?' their godmother asked. 'Presumably your cousin is expecting you and will inform your parents immediately when your carriage arrives without you.'

'I must consider my options,' Lady Thea said. 'I will write to Cousin Elizabeth and apologise for any inconvenience, of course, and I suppose I must write to my parents and tell them where I am. I have no desire to place you in a difficult position, dear Godmama.'

'Just how did you make your escape if your own carriage has continued on to Harrogate, might I ask?'

Lady Thea turned back to answer Hal with what was perilously close to a grin. 'When we arrived in Grantham I pretended to be unwell and took rooms at the Angel for myself and Mama's dresser who was accompanying me, telling her I needed to spend the day resting.

'Then, as soon as I heard her settled in next door, I left the money for the rooms on the dressing table, went down with my valise and across the road to the George where I hired a post chaise, telling them that I wished to go to Melton Mowbray. Then I bribed the postilion to turn around once we were out of the town and go in the opposite direction to come here.'

'He can probably be as easily bribed to say where he did take you,' Hal said cynically.

'Oh, I am sure he can be, but I only wanted to make sure I was not immediately followed. Maunday is not a woman of much initiative and I am sure she will have either gone on to Harrogate or back to London to seek instructions. In any case, I must let Mama and Papa know where I am. I do not wish to cause them any distress. Any more distress,' she amended carefully.

'Considerate of you,' Hal said drily and received a reproachful look in return. He found he did not want to make those lovely hazel eyes become shadowed and sad again.

'I do try to be,' Lady Thea retorted. 'But this is my future, my entire life, at stake. I fail to see why I must passively accept whatever fate is decreed for me—this is the nineteenth century, Mr Forrest, not the Middle Ages. Why should I be unhappy for ever, just for the sake of a title?'

He opened his mouth to say something—he was

not certain what—and she swept on. 'How would *you* like it?'

'Men have their choices restricted too,' Hal countered with some feeling. 'The son of the village blacksmith will find himself under considerable pressure to take on his father's trade, likewise the son of a farmer, a banker or a lawyer. The heir to a title has no option but to accept the duties that go with that, and those include finding a bride of equal or near status. He cannot shrug and say he does not want those responsibilities or that he would rather marry a pretty dairymaid.'

Lady Thea produced a sound suspiciously close to a snort. 'Do not tell me that the son of the blacksmith or the lawyer would accept being forced into a marriage with a woman he did not like. And as for your aristocratic heir, he will pick and choose from the flock of sacrificial virgins paraded for him at Almack's.'

'Thea, *dear*,' Lady Holme murmured. Hal suspected that she would be saying that a great deal in the near future.

'I am sorry, Godmama. The gathering of well-bred young ladies of unimpeachable virtue pretending to enjoy the delights of the Season, I should have said,' Lady Thea corrected amiably.

'You find the Season unpleasant?' Hal queried. He had managed to avoid the London Season by going to Vienna, where he suspected the social environment was considerably freer and more enjoyable.

Again, there was that charming wrinkle of the nose.

'New gowns and all the balls and parties can be delightful, of course. But one cannot pick and choose, decide that tonight it is really far too much trouble to dress up and have one's hair twisted into uncomfortable arrangements and be dancing and smiling and watching every word and gesture until the small hours.

'There are times when all one wants is to curl up with a good book, or ride shockingly fast in Hyde Park, and not have pins stuck into one by top-lofty *modistes* or spend the afternoon making careful conversation with young gentlemen who do not interest one in the slightest.

'And,' she added bitterly, 'one is being scrutinised the entire time for the slightest slip. Too long behind the potted palms at Lady X's ball with Lord Y? Shocking. Galloping one's horse in Hyde Park? Outrageously fast. An evening gown that is not of the palest shade? Clearly one is on the slippery slope to ruin.'

'But we gentlemen are stalked by predatory mamas on the hunt for suitable husbands for their daughters,' he countered. 'We must be constantly on guard in case we find ourselves alone in the conservatory, or out on the terrace, with a young lady. We must learn the exceedingly delicate art of flirtation—just enough to bring a flattering glow to a young lady's cheeks, but never anything that might be misconstrued as a declaration.'

'Or you can practice the art on dashing young widows and fast young matrons with less restraint,' Lady Thea said, with a teasing smile.

Now, she really would be amusing to flirt with. He must have betrayed that thought somehow, because she coloured, just a little, then batted her eyelashes at him, clearly intending to mock. It would take a great deal to subdue Thea Campion's spirit. But why would anyone with any sense want to?

The door opened to admit the Lady Holme's housekeeper. 'Lady Thea's room is quite ready, my lady,' she said, bobbing a curtsey. 'I have sent Jennie up.'

'Excellent. Thank you, Mrs Bristow. Jennie is hoping to become a lady's maid,' their godmother explained to Lady Thea. 'She is already quite proficient with hair. Why not have a little rest before dinner, dear? And you can write your letters so they can be sent off first thing tomorrow.'

'Thank you, I will do just as you suggest.' Lady Thea stood, obedient to instructions from her elders, like any well-behaved young lady.

Hal stood too, wondering just how out of character her rebellious flight had been. Lady Thea was certainly quick-witted and spirited, but was she also given to escapades and romps, despite that demure exterior? Was this truly the result of desperation or was her proposed husband well rid of a wilful romp?

He sat again as the door closed behind her and regarded his godmother with some suspicion. 'Just what are you about, Godmama?'

'I am always anxious to assist my godchildren in making the right choices,' Lady Holme said, adopting a sanctimonious expression that did not deceive him for a moment. She was up to mischief. 'I consider that dear Thea would make an excellent duchess, do you not agree?'

'She would certainly make an unconventional one,' Hal said drily. 'One can only hope the duke in question is up to it.'

Thea found her knees felt decidedly weak by the time she had followed the housekeeper up the stairs and along the corridor to the charming bedchamber she had been given.

The rush of excitement, the feeling of triumph at her escape and the relief at Godmama's warm welcome ebbed away, leaving her oddly uncertain.

Had she done the right thing? That nice Mr Forrest had certainly not seemed shocked. Surprised, perhaps, which was understandable, but not horrified. But then she suspected that he was something of a flirt and was quite happy to enjoy the arrival of a pleasantly titillating scandal into his life. Godmama appeared to trust him completely, so she supposed she need not fear any gossip escaping.

She dragged her scattered thoughts together and replied pleasantly to Jennie's enquiries about whether she would care to take a bath now, or closer to dinner time. The girl was clearly desperately anxious to do exactly the right thing and reassuring her helped Thea calm her own nerves.

Yes, she rather thought that a bath would be very pleasant. Jennie had already laid out her wrapper and slippers and had shaken out the one evening gown that was all Mama had thought necessary for her life in Harrogate.

Thea sank into the warm water, liberally laced with a fragrant oil, and gave a fleeting thought to what bath time at Cousin Elizabeth's house would be like. Cold water would feature largely, she was certain—bracing, healthful and economical.

With a barely repressed shudder she turned her thoughts to pleasant, positive, things. She was safe, warm and comfortable, Godmama would be full of useful advice and Mr Forrest should be entertaining company. And she was a safe distance from London. Even if Papa set out the moment he knew where she was, she had sanctuary for at least three days.

Or Mama and Papa might wash their hands of her, she thought optimistically. After all, there was only so long that they could fob off the Duke with excuses about influenza. Besides, although she knew herself to be a very good match, she was not the only titled young lady for him to turn to. He would bestir himself to find someone else, then she could return to London, enjoy the Season and make her own choice of husband. If the right person crossed her path, of course.

What would the ideal husband be like? Thea wondered. She had never given it much thought before. She knew what she did not want when she encountered it, of course. The ideal husband would be intelligent, have a sense of humour that was subtle and kind, and would be pleasant to look at—she mistrusted very handsome men, they were usually too fond of themselves, in her experience.

He must be acceptable in good society, because she had no desire to find herself away from London and all its pleasures. Naturally he would be comfortably off, because she did not think she would be happy without her horses or wish to manage without domestic staff. She had no trust in the romantic idea that true love could flourish in a hovel as easily as a palace. At least, not when one of the couple was used to near-palatial surroundings.

For some reason her imagination provided her with a picture of that nice Mr Forrest again. He appeared to be intelligent, she had seen glimmers of amusement in those rather attractive grey eyes and he was certainly no hardship to look at.

His clothing was not quite perfection, she had noticed. Not this season's and it looked more comfortable than immaculate. Clearly, one of Godmama's godsons was not going to be anything but good *ton*, but he had no title—presumably he was the younger son of an earl or a viscount or someone further down the aristocratic tree—and not enough money to indulge in a fashionable new wardrobe for every season.

Papa would not countenance anyone who was not, at the very least, heir to an earldom, and, with a duke in his sights, probably even a marquess would be considered inferior.

The soap slipped from her fingers and she chased it, splashing water as it slid under her feet. The bath was becoming cool, she realised when she had secured the soap. What she was doing thinking about a man she had only just met, with whom she had exchanged only a few sentences, she could not imagine.

What she should be concentrating on was her letter to her parents, somehow persuading them to let her remain with Godmama while she decided what to do.

Thea climbed out of the bath and was enveloped in large towels by Jennie, almost smothering her in her enthusiasm. 'Thank you, I can manage now. Perhaps you could fetch my wrapper and slippers. I have some letters to write before dinner.'

Dear Mama and Papa,

That was easy enough. It was the rest that was so very difficult.

I write to let you know that I am staying with Godmama at Holme Lacey House. I feel that her advice on my future will be more practical and constructive than that of Cousin Elizabeth as she has a wider knowledge and experience of society. She had invited me to stay for as long as I desire.

I am conscious that my ~~escape change of plans~~ deviation from your instructions must have caused you anxiety and I sincerely regret it, ~~but not as much as I would have regr~~ but I hope that this may help me see more clearly how to plan my future in a way which I hope will meet with your approval.

With my best wishes to my brothers,
~~Your dutiful~~

'Oh, that will not do…'

~~Your obedient~~

'Neither will that!'

Your affectionate daughter,
Thea

She laid the pen back on its rest and stared at the page, trying to find a better, more tactful way of expressing what she meant, but could not. With a sigh, she pulled another sheet of notepaper to her, picked up the pen again and wrote out a fair copy.

Now all she could do was wait and see what action Papa decided to take.

That had taken her over an hour, she realised when the sound of the dressing bell reached her. She folded the page but did not seal it, deciding that it was only fair that Godmama read it before she sent it off.

Dressed in her one evening gown and wearing some of her meagre collection of jewellery, Thea went downstairs with her letter. Godmama was in the drawing room alone, thumbing through a copy of what appeared to be *La Belle Assemblée*.

When she saw Thea, she put the journal down and raised her eyebrows. 'My dear, *whatever* are you wearing? Have I missed the intelligence that the latest fashion in London is to be as dowdy as possible? Or have you joined one of those infinitely depressing dissenting churches?'

'Mama considered that this is a suitable evening gown for Harrogate,' Thea said with a sigh. It was bad enough to be enveloped in a garment of dull maroon which clashed nastily with her hair, but the neckline was high enough to suit a novice nun. 'Here is my letter to Mama and Papa. I have left it unsealed so you can see what I said.'

'Thank you. I will enclose it with my own note.' Lady Holme put it down unread, still frowning at Thea's gown. 'Is that the only evening gown you have with you?'

'I am afraid so,' Thea said, sitting down on the sofa next to her.

'Oh, dear.' Godmama glanced at the clock and sighed. 'It is too late to do anything about it now, but

I am certain my woman can alter some of my gowns to fit you. As it is, I suppose it is not a bad thing,' she added vaguely, puzzling Thea.

As she opened her mouth to ask why on earth she should think that, the door opened and Mr Forrest came in, clad in the black and white severity of evening wear. Thea felt a sudden shiver of awareness. What was it about this man?

Chapter Three

Despite a slight shininess about the cuffs, and the fact that the style was a trifle out of fashion, Hal Forrest's evening suit was beautifully cut, Thea realised when she had caught her breath again. Only master London tailors could produce such elegant simplicity where any fault in the cut, fit or the wearer's body would be ruthlessly exposed. Perhaps Mr Forrest had suffered a financial reverse. Or he might have had a lucky win at the tables, or betting on a horse the year before, and had spent the windfall on a new suit of evening clothes.

Thea did not want to be hustled into marriage, but there was absolutely nothing wrong with her eyesight, nor her appreciation of an attractive man. And Hal Forrest *was* attractive, with that dark brown hair and those grey eyes and that height. He was not exactly copybook handsome—his nose had suffered a break at some point and the set of his jaw gave his face a certain unyielding quality when he was not smiling—but he moved with athletic ease and his shoulders were in absolutely no need of any padding by his tailor, nor his calves by a valet.

He bowed slightly to the ladies and Thea, once more in control of herself, inclined her head in response as he settled into one of the armchairs facing their sofa.

Just what did Mr Forrest do in life? If he was a younger son of a titled family, the options were usually the Army or the Navy, the church, the East India Company, or perhaps estate management.

But he was not wearing uniform and, if he was a clergyman, he did not wear the white collar with the two fluttering white tabs that the clergy normally did. If he was with the East India Company he would be in India or London. So, estate management for his father or an older brother, perhaps? Or he might have an independent income from an inheritance, of course, or a small estate of his own.

Thea managed to speculate while making polite and meaningless chit-chat about how pleasant the evening was now the light rain had passed over and yes, what a charming portrait that was of their godmother as a young married lady.

It smiled down at them from above the fireplace with that hint of mischief that always delighted Thea.

'Do you make a long stay in this district, Mr Forrest?' she enquired after her godmother had made them laugh by lamenting the passing of the fashion for yards of heavy brocade and wide skirts.

'At least a week, I hope,' Lady Holme said firmly before he could answer. 'It is not often that I am able to enjoy the company of two of my favourite godchildren at the same time.'

'Favourite, Godmama?' Hal Forrest said with a teasing note. 'I am sure you say that to all of us.'

'Have you met the Johnstone twins?' Godmama queried with a speaking look. 'Hellions, the pair of them. And, not naming any names, two of the girls in my little flock are as insipid a pair as one might encounter anywhere. I favour intelligence, wit, a cheerful disposition and good taste, and in a few of you, I have it, thank goodness.'

When she mentioned good taste, Thea thought she could almost see the strain on Mr Forrest's face as he studiously did not look in the direction of her gown.

'Mr Forrest must be wondering at your judgement, Godmama,' she said with a light laugh, glad of the opening to explain why she looked such a dowd. 'This is the sole evening gown in my possession at present,' she informed him. 'It was considered suitable for Harrogate.'

'Ah,' he said. 'I shall make a note not to look to that town for an enlivening stay in that case. I imagine that greens and blues are more to your taste, Lady Thea. Or perhaps a more vibrant shade of red.'

'Red? With my hair?'

'The right shade would intensify the colour,' he said, head tipped slightly to one side as he studied her.

It should have been impertinent, but it felt detached, almost as though he was giving his opinion on the shade of a wall hanging, or a variety of rose.

'Far be it for me to criticise a parent,' their godmother said, doing just that, 'but one feels that Lord and Lady Wiveton have overreacted somewhat. It is hardly as though dear Thea is unlikely to make a most satisfactory match, duke or no duke. But I am sure a letter from me and her own note of explanation will allow them to reconsider their stance.'

Thea was not so certain about that, but she was becoming desperate to think, and talk, about something else.

'Of course,' she said with a bright smile for her godmother. 'I am not going to allow myself to worry about it. Have you a wide acquaintance in the district, Mr Forrest?'

Her sudden change of subject appeared to have taken him by surprise and he hesitated for a moment before saying, 'It is quite some time since I was in the area.'

That was not quite what she had asked, but Thea took that as a negative, and a not very informative one at that. 'Perhaps you intend to explore the countryside as it is unfamiliar to you,' she said. 'You do not have any commitments drawing you away? A parish left in the hands of a curate, for example?'

It was blatant fishing, and she could have perfectly

well asked Godmama, but she was curious about Mr Forrest's reticence.

'You take me for a clergyman?' He looked so appalled that she laughed. 'The Archbishop of Canterbury would never make so grievous an error as to allow me to be ordained. No, I own some land, and there is nothing that requires my urgent attention just now.'

'So, a landowner and a sinner,' Thea teased. 'Now I have you neatly pigeonholed, Mr Forrest.'

'Not a *very* great sinner, I hope, Lady Thea,' he replied, his mouth curving into a smile. 'But I am a restless man and I like to travel. Any parish in my care would find itself all too frequently left to an overworked curate.'

She smiled encouragingly, but no interesting tales of his travels resulted, so it seemed that Mr Forrest liked to keep himself to himself. That was certainly his right and just because she had poured out the tale of her own situation to him, he was under no obligation to satisfy her curiosity in return, she told herself firmly.

'Had you heard that Lord Brownlow has been created an earl, Hal?' Lady Holme enquired. 'He has had Wyattville working on Belton House and grounds for years—he clearly expected this elevation. I mention it because I thought you might be interested in the works. Brownlow has no objections to neighbours riding over his lands. Likes to show it off, I suspect,' she added. 'He is creating an Italian garden about which I would like your opinion.'

'Thinking of stealing the idea, Godmama? I am sure Lord Brownlow would be flattered by your interest. I imagine Juno will be rested by tomorrow. Do you care to ride, Lady Thea?'

'I do, but with neither horse nor habit…'

'That will be no problem, my dear,' Godmama said immediately, as Thea had rather hoped she would. 'You may borrow one of my outfits.' She slid her foot to the side against Thea's, glanced down and nodded. 'My boots too. Nero would suit you, I am sure.'

'Our mounts are a Roman goddess and a Roman emperor,' Mr Forrest remarked. 'Clearly, it is meant to be.'

Thea was saved from having to reply to that by the sound of Fenwick the butler clearing his throat.

'Dinner is served, my lady.'

Mr Forrest stood and, very correctly, offered his arm to his godmother. She shook her head and indicated Thea, then swept out ahead of them, the demi-train of her gown swishing over the Chinese carpet.

'Lady Thea?'

'Mr Forrest.' She put her fingertips on his forearm and was escorted into the dining room, where he held her chair for her before taking his place opposite on their godmother's left hand.

As the footman shook out her table napkin for her, Thea realised two things. One, she was hungry, and two, she was tired. Very tired. The tension that had gripped her ever since that confrontation with her parents had left her and with it the energy that had kept her going through her flight.

Perhaps, she thought, as the soup was set in front of her, she could regain the strength to make polite conversation throughout the meal, but she doubted it. The best she could hope for was not to yawn.

Lady Thea was decidedly subdued, Hal thought as the soup and the fish plates were removed in turn and all the young woman opposite contributed to the conversation were answers to direct questions.

She was exhausted now she had found sanctuary, he diagnosed, and concentrated on talking to his godmother so Lady Thea did not feel obliged to join in. On the other hand, he could not neglect her, so he tried to find a balance, with offers to pass the bread rolls and occasional smiles.

How many other young ladies would have the courage to stand up to their parents and refuse the marriage they favoured? And how many of them would not be so dazzled by the prospect of becoming a duchess that they could look beyond that and decide for themselves whether or not they would be happy?

The Duke of Leamington was going to lose a rather extraordinary duchess if he was not very careful. He wondered just how, and when, Lord Wiveton was intending to explain to His Grace that his intended had fled rather than marry him. The excuse of a minor indisposition could only suffice for a short while. It would make for an interesting conversation.

'What is causing you to smile so, Hal?' Lady Holme enquired.

'This excellent beef, Godmama. My compliments to your chef.'

She nodded. 'From our own herd. Fenwick, please convey Mr Forrest's compliments to Anton.'

The food seemed to revive Lady Thea somewhat, but by the time she had taken the last spoonful of lemon posset he could tell that she was flagging. Not that it was obvious. Like all young ladies, she had been trained from an early age to maintain a perfect posture and to stay awake and smiling through everything from a tuneless piano recital to a lecture from a crabby old dowager.

When Lady Holme rose to leave him to port and nuts and Lady Thea following her example, Hal said, 'Will you forgive me if I retire now? I recall that I have letters I should write in order that they may go first thing tomorrow.'

Now he would have to produce something to put out for the post, but, hopefully, Lady Thea would also feel she could retire now too.

'Hal was always tactful, even as a boy,' Godmama remarked as they settled together on a sofa in the drawing room. 'I recall looking out of a first-floor window here—the one that overlooks the maze—and seeing him come across Lady Shawfield and… and someone who was not her husband. He simply turned on his heel and walked away and I never saw him betray by so much as a flicker of an eyelash that he knew her secret.

'And now you can take advantage of that tact and take yourself off to bed too, my dear. You must be very weary. We do not want you to have dark circles under your eyes, do we?' Uncharacteristically, for one so calm and composed, she smoothed her satin skirts over her knee and twitched at a bracelet.

Thea winced inwardly. Her godmother must be concerned about her own part in this flight. But her own letter would soon make it clear that Godmama had done nothing except shelter her. Surely her parents would be grateful for that?

'I have to confess I am finding it hard to keep my eyes open,' she said. 'If you will excuse me, I will go to bed now. Thank you for being so understanding about everything.'

She kissed Lady Holme on one scented cheek and went out, passing Fenwick in the hall.

'I will send up Jennie immediately, my lady,' he said in response to her wishing him good-night.

Thea supposed she must have undressed and removed her jewellery, that Jennie had unpinned and brushed out her hair and helped her into her nightgown, but when she woke the next morning, she had no recollection of it.

The room was dark, but sunlight was visible at the edges of the heavy curtains, so she reached out, groping for the bell pull, and sat up against the pillows. She hadn't dreamt at all, that she could recall, but she felt as though she had spent the night with dark, ominous fantasies filling her mind.

Jennie's arrival with a cup of hot chocolate jerked her into the present and the flood of light as the curtains were drawn, and the need to speak pleasantly to the maid, helped.

'Her ladyship's woman has given me the riding habit for you, my lady. If you would not object to trying it on before breakfast, I can make any alterations immediately.'

Of course, she remembered. She had agreed to ride to Lord Brownlow's estate with Mr Forrest. It was what she needed to blow away these megrims—fresh air and exercise.

'Of course, just as soon as I have finished this and bathed.'

Jennie, speaking through the pins tight between her lips, pronounced the habit too large in the bodice and waist, but otherwise acceptable.

'It will be ready by ten o'clock, I hope, my lady.'

'That would be admirable, thank you.'

Thea encountered Mr Forrest in the doorway of the

breakfast room. As she expected, there was no sign of their godmother, who probably would not emerge from her suite until at least noon.

'Lady Thea.' Mr Forrest stood aside to let her precede him and they sat opposite each other at the small oval table while two footmen poured coffee and explained what was under the row of chaffing dishes on the sideboard.

'I find I am ravenous this morning,' Thea confessed as her choice of a plate of bacon, scrambled eggs, sausage and fried potatoes was set in front of her.

'It is hardly surprising,' Mr Forrest remarked, lifting his knife and fork to attack a similar selection. 'You must have had little possibility of finding a good luncheon during your escape and expending nervous energy is always exhausting, in my experience.'

'Somehow I find it unlikely that you ever expend nervous energy, Mr Forrest,' she teased. 'You seem to me to be a gentleman who is always cool, calm and collected.'

'That is quite deceptive,' he riposted. 'I am like a swan. All is calm above the water but frantic paddling is going on below.'

Laughing, she bent to look under the table. 'No, your webbed feet are quite at a standstill, sir.'

'Have you been able to find a riding habit, Lady Thea? I am very much looking forward to our expedition.'

Mama was most insistent on keeping what she

called a 'proper distance,' which meant always insisting on the use of one's title and condescending to mix with anyone of lower status only on the most formal of terms. But, Thea realised, she was tired of formality, and she had no desire whatsoever to condescend to anyone. Mr Forrest made her smile and there always seemed to be laughter or understanding in those grey eyes. And he was, indisputably, a gentleman, and one whose discretion had been vouched for by their godmother.

'Please call me Thea,' she said. 'After all, I am here escaping from the consequences of being the daughter of an earl.' She held her breath. What would he say? Be shocked?

'Hal,' Mr Forrest responded with an inclination of his head. 'I would be delighted, Thea. May I pass you the rolls?'

'The toast, please, Hal.'

Now she was seriously wondering just who he was, because he had not batted an eyelid and appeared equally at ease using her title or not. It would be perfectly possible to be the grandson of a duke or a marquess and to have no courtesy title, she thought. But then there were the faintly shabby clothes…

Forrest? Perhaps an examination of the Peerage *might solve the question. Or I could always ask him directly, of course.*

But somehow Hal Forrest, friendly and smiling as he was, had the demeanour of a man with a high fence around those aspects of his life that he did not chose to share. Thea felt certain that a blunt enquiry would be met with a politely vague response, leaving her just as baffled as before. Either that, or a snub, and she had no desire to jeopardise this pleasant new acquaintanceship.

I can always ask Godmama. That is the logical thing to do. He is not wearing a wedding ring...

'I am told that my habit will be ready at ten,' she said, dismissing that completely irrelevant thought. 'Will half past the hour suit you for our ride?'

'Certainly, I think it will take us about three quarters of an hour to reach the Brownlow estate. I will tell the grooms when to bring the horses around and have a word with Anton about something to pack in my saddlebags to sustain us until we return.'

'After this breakfast I doubt I will be able to eat until dinner time,' Thea said ruefully, and liked it when he laughed with her and did not make a meaningless protest about her sylphlike figure or some other gallant nonsense.

She liked it even more when Hal did compliment her, with clearly genuine feeling, when the first thing Nero did as they rode out from under the stable yard arch was to shy violently at the stable cat.

'You have an excellent seat,' Hal said when she steadied the gelding from his sideways plunge across the gravel and turned him to face the cat.

Nero snorted and tossed his head and the cat sat and licked a paw with insolent unconcern.

'There, you ridiculous creature. What a fuss about nothing. You see that cat every day of your life. Thank you,' added to Hal as, horse steadied, she turned to ride alongside his big grey mare. 'I very much enjoy riding. I would like to learn to drive a pair as well, but Papa considers that all females must be positively cow-handed when it comes to carriage driving, so I am left with just a pony and trap.'

'Perhaps you could persuade him to study some of the ladies driving in various parks at the fashionable hour. I have observed several real dashers driving high-bred teams with aplomb.'

Interesting. Mr Forrest is not just a countryman, then.

Thea stored that piece of information away, although quite why, she was not certain.

'That is a very fine horse. And large,' she said, looking across at the almost white mare. 'Sixteen hands?'

'Yes. She is half Lipizzaner. The Lipizzaner stud was moved around Europe to evade Napoleon and it seems Juno's dam was lost along the way, became rather too friendly with a handsome Hanoverian stallion and Juno is the result.'

'You were fortunate to acquire her.'

'She was raised from a foal by a friend of mine who later fell on hard times. He would not accept a gift from me, but he allowed me to buy her.'

Thea's silent speculations about that were interrupted by Nero's impatient head-tosses.

'Too slow for you?' she asked the gelding, eying the wide verges that bordered the carriage drive. The horse flicked an ear back, attending to her voice. 'You do not think you can outrun Juno, do you?'

'Shall we see?' Hal guided Juno to the left-hand verge. 'You take the right-hand side. It may be a fair match over this distance: Nero looks built for speed and Juno has great endurance, but she is no sprinter. First one to the lodge gates?'

'Very well.' Thea positioned Nero on her allocated verge. 'One, two, three. Go!'

The gelding surged forward. There was a pounding of hooves to her left, but she could not see the big grey. The wind was in her face, the ground a green blur, and Thea realised with a surge of emotion that she was feeling happy for the first time in days.

This was freedom. This was pure, physical exhilaration and, somehow, the presence of this man she had met only the day before lifted the sensations to a new level. Thea laughed in pure joy.

Chapter Four

Thea could ride as though she were part of the horse. A female centaur. Hal blinked the wind-provoked tears from his eyes and watched the slim figure bent over the black horse's withers as the smaller animal gathered speed, gaining on Juno's slower, but longer, stride.

A gentleman would allow the lady to win, but he already knew that this lady would resent that as condescension. She wanted to race and he...

I want to catch, Hal realised.

Juno responded willingly to the pressure of his heels, the shift forward of his weight. He felt the transition as the mare gathered those long legs and powered after the gelding. With the pair of lodges in sight, Hal drew level. The black horse had no more speed in him, but Juno, whose ancestors had been bred for warfare on one side and carriage work on the other, could keep this up for miles yet.

Ahead of them the gates were closed. 'A tie?' Hal

shouted and saw Thea lift her hand in acknowledgement. Then they were both reining in and they arrived at a trot as the gatekeeper came running out, clapping his hat on his head.

The man swung the great wrought iron gates open, touched his finger to his hat brim and they were through, calling their thanks.

'Do you know the way?' Thea asked as they trotted towards the turnpike road.

'A bit late to ask that,' he said, grinning, 'but yes, I do. We go along this road for a mile, then cut across country, and we'll come to the Bellmount Tower with a view down the eastern avenue in about an hour.'

After their race they took the rest of the journey more slowly, trotting or cantering through fields and along green lanes, the land low and undulating. Thea did not appear to feel the need to talk constantly, or to expect him to entertain her with conversation. Instead they rode in companionable silence, interrupted now and again as one of them pointed out a pleasing view, or they watched a kestrel hovering over a meadow.

It felt easy and companionable and Hal felt a kind of calm that had eluded him for what seemed like years now.

'I think we are about to arrive,' he said as the ground rose in front of them. 'The tower should be up there, I believe. I have seen a print of the grounds.'

They let the horses walk up a track and emerged onto a wooded ridge. Below them the park spread out, the long tree-lined avenue running ruler-straight towards Belton House. To their left the tower rose as high as the trees, a tall, very narrow archway, topped with a room and flanked on either side by low pavilions.

'It must have been built as a viewpoint, a belvedere,' Thea said. 'I must say, I do not feel inclined to try the stairs—that room at the top must be quite three stories up, if not more.'

'Yes, a viewpoint and an eye-catcher from the house,' Hal agreed. 'I wonder if it is open. I could see if I can see the Italian garden from up there.' He dismounted, led Juno over to a fence and looped her reins over it, then came back to help Thea down.

'No need to climb all those stairs,' Thea said. 'We can just ask. If the family is at home, which I doubt, they will invite us in for luncheon. Otherwise, I am sure someone will show us the Italian garden.'

She was right, of course. Any genteel persons, let alone an Earl's daughter, arriving at one of the great country houses would expect to be welcomed. If they were of rank they would be received by the owners. If they were merely respectable, they could expect the head gardener to show them the gardens and, if the family were not at home, the housekeeper would show off the public reception rooms in return for a gratuity.

'I confess I would feel somewhat awkward,' Hal said, then felt considerably discomposed by the feel of Lady Thea in his arms as she kicked her foot from the stirrup and put her hands on his shoulders to let him lift her down.

She was tall and very slender, so he had not been expecting the unsettling sensation of feminine curves against his body as he took her weight and lowered her to the ground.

'Oh,' she said as she landed. For a moment he thought he had held on to her for too long, then he realised that she was embarrassed that she might have caused him discomfort by talking casually of gaining admittance, forgetting the difference in their rank. 'Yes, of course, we don't want a lot of fuss made.'

'Will you be all right here by yourself if I climb up the tower?' Hal asked as the door latch yielded under his hand.

'Certainly. I will stretch my legs and admire the view from down here,' she assured him. 'And I hope there is a flask of brandy in those saddlebags to revive you when you stagger down again.'

His instinctive response was ridiculous, a typical male reaction to female challenge. Hal knew it, even as he took the spiral staircase at a run, which lasted for the first three twists, after which he came to his senses and slowed to a walk. He was heartily glad there was no one to witness his staggering exit into the viewing chamber which spanned the top of the arch, an arch he now considered ludicrously tall. The man who commissioned it must have been an idiot with delusions of grandeur, he told himself as he clutched the windowsill and tried not to wheeze.

He was perfectly fit, he knew. He was able to ride from morning to evening—as he had the previous day. He could walk all day, come to that, and he could hold his own in a boxing salon or a fencing school without disgracing himself. But those confounded stairs...

It wasn't the stairs. He could have walked all the way up them without stopping if he had set a sensible pace from the start, but no, he had to demonstrate his male superiority to a lady who wasn't even watching him and start with a sprint.

The windows opened, he realised, and he took off his hat, unlatched the nearest casement and leaned on the sill, breathing deeply.

'Oh, well done!'

Thea's voice floated up from below and he looked down and waved. Far below him her face stared up at him, and then she laughed and turned to give chase as the ridiculous little tricorne hat she was wearing fell off and was caught by the wind.

Something inside him clutched uncomfortably and he pushed away from the opening. This was no place to suddenly develop a fear of heights. Warily, Hal rested his forearms on the sill and peered down again. His stomach stayed reassuringly in the right place.

Most peculiar.

He studied the landscape spread out before him. It was a mile down the avenue to the house, he estimated. Just to his right he thought he could make out a large rectangle between the house and the church that looked more formal than the sweeping landscaped grounds around it. Probably that was the Italian garden. They could ride down the avenue and then turn off before the house.

If the family were not at home, a pair of well-dressed riders on good horses would attract little interest. If they were at home and strolling about their gardens, then they would be treated to a display of bad manners by two people they hopefully would not recognise. Thea might have no qualms about arriving unannounced, but the thought made the hairs on the back of his neck stand up.

He walked slowly down the stairs again and emerged to find Thea regarding him in mock admiration. 'Why, Mr Forrest, I declare you have not a hair out of place and your breathing is as calm as if you had merely strolled around the foot of the tower. I am most impressed. If I had attempted it I imagine I would be laid out on the floor at the top requiring carrying down.'

'That was probably why it was built so tall,' he remarked as they walked back to the horses. 'The gentlemen wanted an opportunity to gallantly carry the ladies and, at the same time, show off how fit they were.'

Thea gave a gurgle of laughter and smiled down at

him when he had boosted her into the saddle. 'Perhaps I should have tried it.'

Hal fought the temptation to fan himself with his hat. Instead, he mounted Juno and pointed down the avenue. 'If we ride down there to that grove of trees on the right, then cut through there towards the church, I believe we will emerge at the new garden.'

They walked the horses down the first, steep section of the avenue, then let them have their heads. This time Juno's greater stamina showed and she drew away from Nero until Hal reined her in so they were riding side by side again.

Thea looked across and found Hal was grinning at her. She grinned back. It felt good to ride like this with someone who let themselves show their feelings, and did not find it necessary to pretend to be bored by a simple pleasure.

London's *ton* irritated her. It was necessary to be fatigued by everything, to find it all a great drag, to need to chase novelty at every turn or be thought insufferably unsophisticated for enjoying simple pleasures.

They slowed to a canter, then a trot as the house loomed ever closer. Hal pointed and they turned towards a ride cut though a plantation to their right. Water glimmered ahead.

'I could see the lake from the tower. Look, there's the church tower, close to the house. We make for that.'

'Hmm. It is difficult to judge how it will look when it is finished,' Thea remarked when finally they stopped at the edge of what had, until very recently, been a building site. The garden looked stark, a rectangle with a lowered central section containing a pool and fountain. The flower beds were in formal patterns, the planting young and insignificant against the bare earth. A raised flagstone walk ran around the edge.

'It is deserted. It must be time for the workers' luncheon,' Hal said as the church clock struck twelve.

Wheelbarrows and gardening tools stood around and trays of young shrubs were set beside the beds, waiting to be set in place, but there were no gardeners to be seen. Nor were there any workmen on the scaffolding surrounding what looked like an orangery at the end of the new garden.

'Strange how there is this return to formality now. The knot gardens of our ancestors were swept away by the creation of landscaped parks with little temples scattered in bosky groves and winding, informal lakes and waterways. And now here we are, back to creating the artificial. I do not believe that Godmama would find this appealing.' He shook his head as he studied the bare earth. 'And then there's all the cost of raising hundreds of bedding plants each season.'

'Quite. I certainly do not think she'd like it,' Thea said, turning Nero's head away from the new garden. 'Nor do I. I like mystery and romance in a garden, and all this shows is how much money its owner has to create it and maintain it.'

'Then let us find a mysterious grove—hopefully one not infested with earwigs and irritable badgers—and see what is in these bulging saddlebags.'

Irritable badgers?

The man had a diverting sense of humour, Thea decided, as she followed Hal. Or perhaps he was reacting defensively to the word *romance*, which was more likely, now she came to think about it. Most men seemed to consider that romance was the preserve of silly girls, or a weapon for luring the foolish into a compromising situation.

What they found was not a grove but a gently sloping grassy bank beside a large pond, or perhaps a very small lake.

'The grass seems dry, even after yesterday's shower,' Hal said, dismounting and crouching to feel the ground. 'I can't believe how the weather is holding so well. It will all be rain and mist and damp falling leaves before long.'

'And there are no signs of badgers,' Thea said, deciding to take that observation as a joke. 'I refuse to hunt for earwigs.'

She kicked her foot out of the stirrup and slid down before he had a chance to come and help her and led Nero to the pond to drink.

Hal flapped open a rug that had been rolled up behind his saddle and unstrapped the bags of provisions before taking Juno to the water. They loosened the girths and tied the horses so they could graze and sat down side by side to see what Cook had given them for luncheon.

'Two slices of chicken and ham pie; two cheese scones, buttered; two apples and two fruit buns, also buttered,' Thea announced, laying it all out on the red-and-white-checked cloth it had been wrapped in. 'What do you have?'

'Two bottles.' Hal removed corks and sniffed. 'Cold tea in one and lemonade in the other. A knife, two horn beakers and two napkins. All very efficient. What would you like to drink?'

'Lemonade, please.' Thea laid out the two napkins between them and divided the food. 'This is just right after a morning's ride. I am famished, despite that breakfast.'

They ate almost in silence, gazing out over the pond, occasionally exchanging comments when a kingfisher flew past in a flash of cerulean blue, or a deer appeared on the far side, nervously scenting the air before drinking.

It was companionable, and Thea felt no pressure to make conversation. It seemed that Hal did not either. She found it relaxing after the social pressures of London, where silences were awkward and one was expected to chatter on, even if all that escaped your lips was banalities. Which were then answered by even more trite observations or opinions.

When they had finished, Hal gathered up the napkins, flapped the crumbs over the water for the fish and came back to where she sat, leaning back on braced arms, her face tilted up to catch the precious autumn sunlight. He joined her, settling down in much the same position.

One of the bottles tilted and he moved to catch it and set it upright. As he sat back, his hand touched hers on the rug between them, fingertip to fingertip. He went very still.

Thea froze too, a wash of heat passing over her. What was it? They had been touching casually all day—he had helped her to mount, they had passed food and drink back and forth—this had no more significance than those fleeting contacts. And yet he was utterly still and so, she realised, was she, holding her breath, her eyes fixed on a rowing boat tied up on the far side of the pond.

Then Hal shifted position, just a little, the faint pressure was gone and she could breathe again.

Ridiculous. What was that about? He is a perfectly nice man, nothing more. A friend. That touch was completely accidental and yet…

They had both reacted in a most peculiar manner, so it was not only she who had sensed something. Now what should she do?

Behave as though nothing has happened, of course, the rather tart voice of common sense informed her.

Because nothing *had* happened.

Oh, yes, it has, a little inner voice contradicted.

Thea shivered.

'You are becoming chilled. There's very little heat in this sunshine.' Hal was on his feet, packing the remains of their picnic away in the saddlebags, before she could protest that she was not at all cold. In fact, she felt thoroughly—

'Yes, you are right, we should be getting back.' Thea stood up while Hal had both his hands full and could not offer one to assist her.

She rolled up the rug while he dealt with the saddlebags and led Nero to a convenient tree stump so she could mount unaided while his attention was distracted.

'I would have helped you,' he said, turning to see her already in the saddle.

'I like to do it myself now and again,' Thea said lightly. 'It pays to keep in practice in case I am ever out alone and have a fall, or want to dismount for some reason.'

Hal swung up into the saddle without comment. It was a perfectly reasonable explanation, but on the other hand...

What the devil had happened just then?

Their fingers had touched, that was all. And yet he had felt nothing like it since he had attended a lecture at the Royal Society by Humphry Davy and had been invited to touch the apparatus. That tingling sensation… Not painful, exactly, but shocking.

He had read more on the subject, amused himself by rubbing a piece of picture glass with a silk cloth and then watching it make pieces of torn paper dance. Electricity, they called it and, according to what he had read, it seemed to be part of living creatures as well as lightning in the sky.

Was that all it had been? The kind of shock one got from touching a cat's fur in a thunderstorm, or the energy that made those paper scraps dance?

He glanced across at Thea's profile. She seemed completely composed, although not, apparently, inclined for conversation. But she had felt it too, he was certain. She had gone very still and quiet until he had heard a sharp little breath when he had moved.

Hal did not understand it and he suspected that neither did Thea. She had clearly trusted him enough to ride out without even a groom in attendance, and she had shown no reluctance to be helped on and off her horse. And then his touch, respectful as it had been, had involved grasping her waist, infinitely more intimate than a casual touch of the fingertips.

'Thea—'

'Let's gallop,' she said, saving him from what he knew would have been a thoroughly awkward conversation.

She was right: ignore it. He urged Juno into a canter, then gave the mare her head. By the time they reached the crest of the hill and had to slow to negotiate the narrow strip of woodland, Thea was laughing.

'Oh, there is nothing like a fast gallop to clear the mind and put me in a good temper,' she said.

'Were you in such a bad one? I thought you had been enjoying the day.'

'Oh, yes, I have been, very much. No, I was so angry with Mama and Papa, but I am coming to see they really do think they are acting for the best, even if I cannot agree with them. No,' she added ruefully, 'I just have to conquer my feeling about the Duke and my disposition will be perfectly sunny again.'

There was an edge to the last remark that had him looking at here more closely. 'And your feelings for Leamington are what, exactly?'

'They are not such that can be expressed with any honesty by a lady,' Thea said though what sounded like gritted teeth.

Every male instinct was screaming at him to leave well alone, that blundering attempts to comprehend were likely to result in her wrath being turned on his head.

Hal told himself not to be a coward. He owed it to Thea, his new friend, to understand, even if he was offering up his head for a washing.

Chapter Five

'But you haven't met Leamington for years, have you?' Hal observed, rashly, as he realised when Thea glared at him. With what he felt was considerable courage, he continued. 'And then it was a dislike of him as an adolescent youth—and we agreed, we males are all insufferable at that age. I thought it was your parents you were angry with for forcing this match with the Duke on you.'

'I do not like what they are doing, but I can see it is what any ambitious parents in society would do. But that man has shown me nothing but the most arrogant disrespect.'

'He has? But if you have not met as adults, how has this occurred?'

'He treats me like property,' she said, making *property* sound like a swear word. She huffed out a breath and continued in a more restrained tone, 'A duke requires a wife. Yes?'

'Yes,' Hal agreed warily. 'For, er, heirs; to be a hostess; to look after the cares of the tenants and so forth.'

'Indeed. And there are various requirements that must be met: she must be of childbearing age, in excellent health and preferably from a family that has a good record of producing sons. An excellent bloodline is essential. Useful political and social connections go without saying. Acceptable social skills are vital and intelligence is desirable.'

'Yes,' he said again. 'Those would be necessary.'

'The Season will be populated by many young ladies who meet those requirements. So, this hypothetical duke only has to do a little work, a trifling amount of research, to produce a list of suitable young ladies.'

Hal found he was nodding along in agreement.

'Then he must seek them out and decide which best meets his needs, which one he is most compatible with,' she continued. 'This is easily accomplished in the course of the Season. Yes?'

Hal nodded. His response was clearly only a matter of form, because Thea was well away with what could only be called a rant, even though it was delivered in an even, cool tone that had every nerve tingling.

'And should the young lady who is his first choice find herself unable to like him well enough, then she will have the opportunity to make this clear in some firm but tactful manner. At which point he moves on to the second on his list.'

She took a breath.

'That is what would apply to any other duke, or nobleman, seeking a bride. But Leamington does not have to exert himself in this way. He already has a future duchess all ready and waiting. So he treats her as he does his coronet, which is another essential ducal accessory. He leaves her in her box in a secure place until she is required. On the shelf, in fact.

'She is actually less trouble and cost to him than the coronet. That has to be kept in good repair. Its care involves jewellers and a secure place to keep it. Its five gold strawberry leaves must be polished and its velvet cap brushed and free from moth. But this convenient duchess-in-waiting is kept securely, fed and watered, gowned and educated, by her parents.

'There she sits, on her shelf, waiting patiently—he assumes, if he gives her any thought at all—until it suits him to announce he is ready to wed. She costs him nothing, certainly no anxiety or effort. All he has to do is claim her while she is still young enough not to have her gilt tarnished, or to have been attacked by moth.'

'I see why you are infuriated,' Hal agreed, appalled, finally seeing it from her point of view. This proposed marriage was not so much an honour as an insulting refusal to see her as a person in her own right and, if the tables had been turned, he would have been furious too.

'The Duke should have visited frequently over the years and written when he could not,' he said, as much to himself as to her. 'He should have come to know her and allowed her to know him. He should have made it easy for her to refuse to marry him if that was her wish.'

'Exactly.' Thea sounded crisp, but considerably less irritable now. Her outburst appeared to have cheered her considerably, which is more than it had for him.

'Have you thought about how you will deal with this situation now?' Hal asked after perhaps another half mile of gentle cantering.

'I shall refuse to receive him. He will have to be incredibly thick-skinned if he does not take that hint that I do not wish to marry him. My parents will be furious, of course, but they can hardly force me to see him. Or if they do, then I will tell him, *No*, to his face.'

'Might I offer a suggestion?' Hal said. 'Could you not agree to speak with him and then tell him frankly, as you have me, how you feel about his treatment of you? It seems to me that this could have three possible outcomes. One, he might walk away, abandoning his attempt to marry you, but learning nothing from the encounter. This I doubt—he has clearly behaved very badly, but I have no reason to suppose the man is a fool.'

Ignoring Thea's disbelieving snort, he continued. 'Two, he accepts your reproof, agrees to abandon his suit and goes to court another lady, this time having learned a valuable lesson.'

'And thirdly?' She sounded intrigued now.

'He is chastened, but wishes to court you still, and you, deciding that he is not a lost cause, agree to that. You may then make a decision having come to know him better. Whichever of these three occurs, you will avoid further angering your parents by an outright refusal, but on your own terms.'

Silence. Had he spoken too soon while she was still furious and in no mood to heed his advice?

'That appears to me to be very sensible. Thank you, Hal.'

He let out a sigh of relief. He had half expected that she would be annoyed at his interference and had little optimism about her accepting his advice, so this was a relief. He still would not wager much on the third outcome—too much depended on Thea keeping her temper when confronted by her neglectful suitor.

Thea felt a definite lightening of her spirits as they rode on. Hal had set out a plan that covered all contingencies that she could see and which gave her flexibility while appearing to bend to her parents' wishes.

'Thank you,' she said when they were walking back from the stables. 'I appreciate your advice.'

Hal made the kind of dismissive sound that she supposed meant, *Think nothing of it.*

'You came here for a quiet visit with our godmother,' Thea persisted. 'You did not expect to have your tranquillity interrupted by a runaway heiress in need of advice and you have been very patient about it.'

'Patience was not required, neither was tranquillity, if it comes to that,' he said, sounding amused, and she thought what a pleasant voice he had. Deep and warm, yet flexible. It was reassuring although, for some reason, not exactly calming.

Thea sought out her godmother when she had bathed and changed and found her in her little sitting room, her feet on a stool and what looked like a novel in her hand.

'Did you have a pleasant day, dear?'

'We did, and we have viewed the Italian garden, but we will both give you our impressions at tea time or over dinner. I just wanted to tell you that Hal has given me some very good advice about what to do about the Duke.'

'He did?' Lady Holme put down her book and regarded Thea with raised eyebrows. 'And what advice was that, I wonder?'

Thea settled on the sofa opposite, kicked off her shoes and curled up comfortably. 'I explained how angry the Duke made me by taking me for granted and not even having the courtesy to write or visit before now. Hal said he could quite see that I felt I was being treated like some kind of ducal accoutrement. Like his coronet—essential but without feelings of its own.'

'Goodness,' Godmama said faintly. 'How insightful of him. I would never guessed he had that much imagination.'

'Oh, it was my analogy, not his, but when I explained how it felt, being left on the shelf unregarded until required, he understood immediately.'

'And what was his advice?'

'To speak to the Duke and explain my feelings quite clearly. If he still wishes to marry me, and is prepared to court me so I can come to know him and make a decision based on his character, then perhaps I will feel able to accept him.'

'That seems to be excellent counsel,' her godmother agreed.

'You find it amusing?' Puzzled by the twinkle in Lady Holme's eyes, Thea wondered whether she was being teased.

'Not at all. It is just that one does not expect gentlemen to be quite that perceptive.' It looked as though she was about to add something, then closed her lips firmly.

'You were going to say something, Godmama. Please, do not hesitate, I need all the advice I can get.'

'Very well. You have come to like Hal Forrest in a very short space of time. To trust him.'

'Why, yes. But, of course, he is trustworthy—you would not allow me to ride out alone with him if he were not to be relied upon in every way. And are you so surprised that I like him when you clearly do?'

'Yes, he is an admirable young man, of course. It is just that… My dear, let me be frank.'

'Of course, please do,' Thea said, with a sinking feeling in the pit of her stomach. Those words, in her experience, never preceded anything that she was glad to hear.

'Hal is a good man. A gentleman. But it would not be wise to allow yourself to grow too fond of him…'

'I regard him as a friend,' Thea said. She sat up abruptly and swung her feet down to the carpet. This was not a conversation to be having sprawled on the sofa. 'I would not dream of…of flirting or…'

'Naturally not, you are far too well-bred for that kind of thing. No, I mean, do not allow feelings to develop that can only lead to disappointment.'

'You mean, do not fall in love with him?' Thea demanded. 'Well, of course not! Goodness, I have survived one Season without falling for any of the numerous eligible gentlemen I have encountered. Why should I be in danger of developing a *tendre* for this one?'

'One never knows when these things might strike,' Godmama said earnestly. 'I do not suggest for a moment that you would go out of your way to fall for a gentleman who has no title. That would be perverse of you in your position. But Hal is a good-looking and charming young man and I would not be surprised if he did not provoke warm feelings in your bosom. Warmer feelings than would be wise.'

Thea opened her mouth, then closed it again, unsure of what she had been about to say. Best not to say anything for a moment, because she was feeling quite indignant—at least, she supposed that was what it was—and she had no wish to be rude or disrespectful to her godmother. But *really*, she was hardly likely to fall in love, just like that.

It had never occurred to her for a moment that Hal Forrest might be someone she might fall for, not until Godmama had put the idea into her head. And now she had, it was clearly nonsense. He was a very pleasant, attractive, intelligent, amusing gentleman. One who was rapidly becoming a friend. That was all.

All, except that moment by the pond when their hands had touched and the focus of the world around had changed, leaving her confused. It had only lasted a moment, but she had felt unsettled ever since.

It was physical attraction, of course, she told herself. Young ladies were supposed to know nothing about that, although, really, married women must have very short memories of their own youth if they thought that their daughters knew nothing, and felt nothing.

Thea assumed the dutiful, rather earnest expression that she used when Mama was fussing about something. 'I hope I am not so lacking in my understanding of what is expected of me as to fall in love with anyone, least of all a commoner,' she pronounced, a statement that would have completely satisfied Mama.

Lady Holme looked less convinced. 'I do hope so,

dear. So much better to settle for a *suitable* match, one that ensures you live your life in just the way you have come to expect.'

Put like that, a suitable match sounded like a recipe for tedium, Thea thought, suddenly feeling mutinous. What would be wrong with an incredibly wealthy East India merchant, other than a life of luxury and the possibility of exotic travels? Or one of the new breed of industrialists—men who, as Papa had said in tones of disgust, had to buy their land rather than inherit it. It might be fascinating to learn all about steam engines, or cotton mills or coal mines, and to build a house from the ground up with all the modern conveniences.

Not that Hal Forrest was either kind of man. He was simply what she was used to, only with no title, less land and less money.

And less fuss, and less pomposity and more freedoms, an insinuating little voice suggested in her head.

Stop it. He isn't interested in me anyway.

He likes you, and there was that touch...

She realised that they had been sitting in silence for several minutes. 'Yes, well, thank you for your concern, Godmama, but there is really nothing to worry about. I know I have behaved in a most unconventional manner, but I have no intention of making a habit of it, believe me.'

'Of course not. You were always such a good, biddable girl.'

Now, why did that sound like a reproof and not a

compliment? And she really did wish that the notion of falling in love had not been put into her head.

Thea was saved from answering by the butler's entrance.

'Do you wish for tea to be served here, or in the drawing room, my lady?'

'Here, please, Fenwick. And let Mr Forrest know where we are, would you?'

'My lady.'

Did she imagine that faintly pained expression crossing Fenwick's face? Surely she must have done. He was a very superior butler indeed, and she had once seen him deal with an escaped monkey, a hysterical housemaid—bitten by the monkey—and a visiting dowager duchess—the owner of the monkey—without so much as a faint frown appearing on his smooth brow.

It must be her imagination: she really was in a very strange mood today. Probably it was the suspense of wondering how Mama and Papa would react to her escape.

Hal appeared a few minutes later, changed from his breeches and riding boots into the pantaloons and Hessians fitting for a lady's drawing room.

'Now, that,' he remarked as he sat down, 'is not a gown suitable for Harrogate, is it, Thea?'

'No, it is one of Godmama's. The maids have worked miracles altering things for me so quickly.'

'It suits you admirably. The gold in the braid trim brings out the highlights in your hair.'

He said it almost matter-of-factly, but, to her horror, Thea felt herself blushing, as though he had paid her some lavish and rather over-warm compliment.

She *never* blushed at compliments. Why would one? They were always false.

'Goodness, it is quite warm in here, don't you think?' she asked, fanning herself with one hand and then stopping abruptly when she realised she was just drawing attention to her cheeks.

A quick glance in the over-mantel mirror reassured her that they were not crimson as she feared, but even so, they were decidedly pink.

Fortunately, neither of the others appeared to notice anything strange and the footmen arriving with the tea tray and a stand of little savouries and cakes was a welcome distraction.

'Shall I pour, Godmama?' she asked, grateful for something to occupy her.

That worked very well until Hal stood up to collect his own and Lady Holme's cups and then settled back into his armchair.

Really, those knitted pantaloons were exceedingly tight and, when Hal crossed his legs as he had just done, the movement of his thigh muscles was quite apparent.

Ladies—young, unmarried ladies—did not look at men's legs. They were expected to keep their eyes either cast modestly downwards or to look a gentleman in the eye, not look at him drinking tea and think, *Horseman's thighs*.

It was all Godmama's fault, making her think of Hal as something other than a friend.

Then he rose again, lifted the stand of food and brought it over to her. 'Those little savoury puffs look delicious. Do have one and then I will not feel guilty for having two, as I fully intend to.'

She laughed and accepted a puff, almost dropping it when he turned to take them across to their godmother and a whisper of the cologne he must have used after shaving reached her nostrils.

This was ridiculous, she scolded herself. She had admired handsome men before now without getting herself into a tizzy about it. Lord Hardcastle, whose looks were darkly exciting and much admired by all the young ladies, for example. Or Viscount Winstanley, a positive Adonis, all blue eyes and golden hair. Or there was Major Lord Harper, who was ruggedly handsome in uniform, his appeal enhanced by the scar on his right cheek that gave him an air of danger. Any one of them was enough to send fans fluttering amongst the ranks of debutantes, and hers had duly fluttered along with those of all her friends.

But when she had danced with one of those men, or stood conversing with them, she had never felt flustered and *shy*, of all things.

Bother Godmama!

'Thea, dear.' From the gently chiding tone of Godmama's voice, she had already said something that Thea had not attended to.

'I am sorry. I was wool-gathering.'

'I was asking about the Italian garden.'

'Oh, of course. I do not think you would like one, Godmama. I thought it far too formal.'

'It is very new, of course,' Hal said. 'And the planting of hedges and so forth is very sparse as a result. But I suspect it will be rather rigid and also exceedingly costly to maintain. It would keep your gardeners very busy.'

'In that case, I will not be copying Lord Brownlow. It is not the expense, so much, but the formality. I had assumed that an Italian garden would be somehow rather romantic.'

'Not at all romantic,' Thea confirmed. 'When I compare it with your rose garden, I have no doubt which I prefer. There is just a touch of wildness, of mystery, in yours. A sense that nature surrounds you, keeps you safe. That formal garden was all about subduing nature to man's desires.'

'Just at the moment it is far from romantic—very much at the end of its season, I'm afraid. But Fosket, my head gardener, has created what promises to be a delightful winter garden by the old summerhouse. I have had that repaired and made sound. It has a fireplace and I intend using it during the colder months to watch the birds eat the berries and the first snowdrops appear. You must explore it tomorrow.'

'I would like to—if the morning does not bring Papa with it,' Thea said ruefully. She was beginning to get butterflies in her stomach at the prospect of discovering her parents' reaction to her flight.

At least it gives me something to think about other than Hal Forrest, she thought, pouring another cup of tea.

Chapter Six

The first post brought nothing at all from London, although there was a letter from Cousin Elizabeth in response to Thea's letter apologising for any inconvenience caused to her.

'What does she say?' Godmama enquired over breakfast as they all opened their correspondence.

Thea squinted at the closely written black words. It looked as though a particularly angry spider had fallen into the inkwell and then rushed across the page.

'I am a hoyden, a disgrace and must be a source of great anguish to my parents,' she deciphered. 'I am doomed to be... Can it be skinned? Surely not. Oh, *shunned*, by decent society unless I cast myself penitently at the duck's—sorry, Duke's—feet. It goes on in much the same vein for both pages.'

She folded the sheets and tossed the letter down beside her plate. 'And nothing for either of us from Mama and Papa. I do hope that doesn't mean they are coming in person.'

'There will be a letter by the second post, I have no doubt,' Lady Holme said comfortably. 'And, if your parents have decided to come in person, I cannot believe they will arrive before tomorrow evening at the latest. Do you have any plans for the morning?'

Spend it trying not to bite my nails, was the honest answer.

Thea couldn't imagine being able to concentrate on reading anything, she had brought no embroidery with her and they were some distance from a town with shops to browse in.

'The weather has still not broken,' she said. 'I will walk around the grounds, I think. I would like to see your new winter garden.'

'Wrap up warmly, then. The wind has turned to the east, so Fenwick informs me. And you, Hal? What is causing that frown?'

He looked up from the letter he had been reading and grimaced. 'Some legal questions to deal with in this one, and I have no doubt the others also contain decisions for me to make. I have come to the conclusion that owning land is akin to housekeeping—no sooner do you think that everything is set in order than out come all the spiders and the dust miraculously reappears.'

Papa had land agents and bailiffs and what always appeared to be a small army of retainers to manage his estates, but Thea supposed that for someone with less extensive and less prosperous lands a great deal had to be done personally.

She made suitably sympathetic noises and excused herself from the table, taking Cousin Elizabeth's letter with her. It was bound for the small fire in her bedchamber because, somehow, she did not think that a reply would be either welcome or helpful.

Jennie found her stout half-boots, a warm pelisse, gloves and, when Thea rejected a bonnet, a soft Kashmir shawl from the garments that her godmother had pressed on her.

Suitably protected against the elements she made her way downstairs, catching a glimpse through an open door of Hal's dark head bent over some papers on the desk in the late Lord Holme's study.

It would have been a lie to say that dreams of him had not disturbed her sleep, but she had woken with the firm determination to put those warnings from Godmama out of her mind. She was not going to fall in love, not with Mr Forrest and not with anyone else ineligible for a lady of her rank, she told herself, fixing dutiful thoughts in her mind. Life was not one of those novels that anxious mamas kept from their daughters in case their minds were filled with dangerously romantic daydreams. Love was a fantasy.

One of the footmen hurried forward to open the front door for her and she stepped out into the chilly breeze. The old summerhouse that Lady Holme had mentioned as the site of the new garden was around at the back and to the right, as she recalled, but she began by turning left so the wind was behind her.

Gardeners were raking up fallen leaves from the lawns, and a donkey, its hooves in strange little leather boots to protect the grass, was standing patiently in the shafts of the cart they were loading them into. No doubt they would be taken around to the compost heaps behind the vegetable garden to be turned into leaf mould, she recalled from conversations with Ashford, their head gardener at Wiverbrook Hall, Papa's principal country house.

Pleased with recalling this horticultural information, because when she married she would be expected to take an interest in the gardens and grounds of her various new homes, she responded to the men's greetings and strolled on along the paved terrace that surrounded the house.

More men were replacing the flowers that had filled the ornamental urns on the balustrade with small evergreens and she stopped to ask what they were.

'Portugal laurel and holly, my lady. And box and yew. We grow them as little plants like this for the urns, then next year they'll be planted out to grow large in the shrubbery or wherever they're needed,' one man explained, pausing in his task of clipping a plant into a domed shape.

Thanking him, she wandered on, thinking that she had some interesting facts to talk about with Hal. It occurred to her that the day before she had found no need to think of topics of conversation, nor to worry when they fell silent.

But then she had not felt so self-conscious about him, she realised as she rounded the corner to the west front. She supposed there must have been some attraction there, even if she was not aware of it, or she could just have shrugged Godmama's words aside. How mortifying, not to be aware of one's deepest emotions and thoughts.

A window shot up in front of her, and a feather duster was thrust out and shaken vigorously. Thea sneezed, and a flushed and apologetic housemaid leaned out.

'Oh, I'm so sorry, my lady! Shall I send for Jennie? Have you dust in your eyes?'

'It is quite all right,' Thea assured the agitated girl, whose cap was slipping perilously over her forehead. 'Accidents happen.'

She walked on more briskly, trying to think about nice safe matters like the household management of her future home and not the master of said household, whose face ought to be a complete blur and who was dangerously close to acquiring brown hair, grey eyes and a mouth that curved all too easily into a smile.

Glancing to her side as she passed another window, she found herself looking into the study at Hal, who had his head in his hands. As she watched he lifted it, shook it and said something which, with the window closed, she could not hear. It did not appear to be anything for the ears of a nicely brought-up young lady, so she grimaced in sympathy with whatever problem he was thwarted by and walked on. It would not do to be seen staring at him.

As she reached the back of the house, the south front, she could see the roof of the summerhouse ahead of her behind a yew hedge. That must be where the winter garden was. Thea perched for a moment on the balustrade to enjoy the sun, which here was warm on her face, the wind baffled by the bulk of the house.

It was peaceful and the view out across the rose garden and towards the lawns to the ha-ha and the park was tranquil. Really, country life had much to commend it over London.

Then she heard the distant sound of horses and carriage wheels on the front drive and jumped to her feet. Mama and Papa? Already?

The things that she must say tumbled and jumbled in her head. She must be apologetic, yet strong… polite, but firm. She must negotiate—yes, that was the word. Diplomacy was essential. It had all seemed very straightforward yesterday…

Then, with a rattle, the sash of a ground-floor window shot up and a leg appeared over the sill, rapidly followed by the rest of Hal Forrest's body. He looked around and strode towards her.

'Thea. Is the summerhouse open?'

'I have no idea. I was just going to have a look,' she said and found herself being towed along the terrace, down the steps and towards the yew hedge. 'What are you doing? I think Mama and Papa might have arrived.'

'Running away,' he said and, although there was the hint of a laugh in his voice, he looked serious.

'*Is* it Mama and Papa? His bark is worse than his bite, as they say, but my brothers always run away from him when he is angry.' They were jogging towards a gate in the hedge now.

'No, it is not your parents, it is Lord and Lady Chesford. I heard Fenwick announce them.'

'The Chesfords? What on earth are they doing calling at this hour? And why are we running away from them?'

Hal closed the gate once they were inside, and Thea looked around at a rectangular garden with paths dividing it up into regular sections. Much of the ground was bare—presumably for spring bulbs, but there were urns with evergreens, little groups of shrubs, small topiary trees and some charming statues.

'I have no idea why they have called but I am… reluctant to meet them.'

'Reluctant?' Thea stared at him. Anyone less shy she could not imagine.

Hal shrugged. 'I would prefer not have to encounter them.'

Nothing more seemed to be forthcoming and she recalled his unwillingness to call at Lord Brownlow's mansion and his desire to avoid encountering anyone in the grounds.

Perhaps Hal really was uneasy with new acquaintances—although he had shown no sign of it when he was introduced to her. How very strange. But it was not her place to probe, and if he wanted to tell her about it, he would.

'We should be safe here,' she remarked, beginning to wander along the central path leading to the summerhouse. 'Oh, dear, this has suffered over the years, hasn't it? I can recall playing here when I was a little girl.'

The little house, no more than one room, had been designed as a cottage *ornée*, with windows in the pointed Gothic style with leaded panes, a thatched roof, a barley-twist chimneystack and a heavily studded oak door.

Now half the thatch was off and a pile of new straw and a ladder were propped against the wall. One of the windows had been boarded up and most of the wood was in poor condition.

'There's work in hand,' Hal remarked, gesturing to the thatcher's equipment and one window where the paintwork had been freshly done.

They were standing by the front door when they heard voices approaching and swivelled, as one, to stare at the entrance gate.

'…hope you will allow our man to come and talk

to your head gardener while we are away,' said a female voice, clear and penetrating.

'Lady Chesford,' Thea whispered. 'They say she can be heard in two counties when she's on the hunting field.'

'I know,' Hal said with some feeling. 'I have met her.'

'One would not wish to copy,' the penetrating voice continued, 'but it seems such a charming conceit, I am sure he can come up with a different design for me.'

'I…reports… Brownlow's Italian…' Their godmother's softer tones were more indistinct. 'Too formal,' came clearly and, by the sound of it, from just outside the gate.

Hal turned, twisted the handle of the summerhouse door and, as it opened, pulled Thea inside. He closed it silently and went to look out of one of the cobwebbed windows. 'They are coming in.'

'Surely we are safe in here?' Thea looked around at what must be a heap of garden furniture under a dustsheet, a stack of workmen's tools and an upturned bucket.

Safe? Hal was clearly unwilling to encounter the Chesfords again, but why was *she* hiding?

Because I don't want them speculating why I am here and not in London, preparing for the Season, she thought.

Lady Chesford was a gossip, and it would not take much whispering to make bricks out of straw, or mountains out of molehills. What was Lady Thea Campion doing rusticating? Unwell, perhaps? Or removed from an undesirable attachment? Has anyone seen her in the past few months?

Reputation was a very delicate thing, far more fragile than those spiders' webs festooning the windows.

The voices were coming closer. 'Such a charming little house. I wonder what kind of shelter would suit my garden? A Grecian temple seems a trifle cold. A Swiss cottage, perhaps? I see you have a chimney. How large is the fireplace?'

'Curse the woman, she's coming in.' Hal looked around the room. 'Behind that stack under the dustsheet, quickly.'

Fortunately, there was space between the wall and the bulging heap, but Hal still felt exposed. He lifted the edge of the cloth and peered inside. Dusty, and he only hoped for Thea's sake there were no rats or mice.

'Get in,' he whispered, and she wriggled past him without a word of complaint.

Wonderful woman, he thought as he followed her, folding his long legs into the cramped space under an upturned wickerwork loveseat.

'How do you know them?' she whispered.

'Hmm?' He was focused on the voices outside and replied without thinking. 'I have met their daughter, Penelope.'

'Oh. Penelope,' Thea murmured, then, *'Ssh!'*

Which was somewhat unreasonable, he thought, given that she was the one who had started talking.

He could well do without the memories of Lady Penelope, all big blue eyes, fluttering eyelashes and rosebud mouth. It was enough to bring a man out in a cold sweat, and he had certainly needed a good hour and a stiff drink to recover from finding himself in close proximity to her on an otherwise deserted terrace. His retreat had been abrupt and decidedly unmannerly, but effective, and the looks she had cast him afterwards were reproachful.

The door opened, bringing a draught to stir the dustsheets, and several pairs of feet trod into the room.

'There is still a long way to go renovating it, as you can see,' Godmama remarked. 'But I believe once all the gaps have been sealed and the roof lined and the chimney repaired, it will be quite snug.'

Hal was feeling more than a little snug himself. Thea was pressed close against his side, warm and soft, although he could feel the tension vibrating through her.

The cover over them was, he guessed, an old sheet made of worn cotton or linen, and it let the light through from the open door. He turned his head a little and caught her eye as she looked back. Her eyes were sparkling with mischief and he found the laughter bubbling up inside him so that he had to bite his lip and look away to stop it escaping.

What was the matter with him? The consequences of being found like this by one of society's most vocal gossips were horrendous to contemplate. Any desire to laugh deserted him abruptly, leaving him all too aware of another desire, one caused by close proximity to a very attractive female.

Hal made himself concentrate on what Lady Chesford was saying. Surely the wretched woman didn't want to stand in a dirty cottage for half an hour talking? He assumed her husband was with her but, as usual, His Lordship was silent, years of marriage having taught him that attempting to interrupt was useless.

Suddenly Thea gave a soft gasp and stiffened. Hal saw her gaze was fixed on the boards at their feet where a very large, very black spider was marching determinedly towards the shelter of her skirts.

He leaned forward, almost dislocating his shoulder in the confined space, and put his cupped hand over the creature. They didn't bite, did they? He wasn't sure and braced himself not to make a sound if it did.

Now one arm was over Thea's thigh and his whole body stretched across and between her legs. Potential spider bites became much less of a concern in his mind—keeping still and not panting were much higher priorities.

Finally, after what seemed like an hour, but was probably only a few minutes, the door closed, plunging them back into gloom.

Thea wriggled rapidly backwards and he wasn't certain whether she was escaping the spider or if she had sensed his arousal. Hal lifted his hand, the spider scurried away, fortunately in the opposite direction to Thea, and he followed her out.

'Hal, you are an absolute hero,' she whispered. 'I know it is irrational to be frightened of them, but it is the way spiders move, that scuttle and those horrible knees… I think they are still looking at the garden,' she added, with a wary look at the window. 'No, they've gone, the gate is closed. Goodness, what an escape!'

Hal opened the door and she followed him out onto the little raised porch that ran along the front of the cottage.

'Look at the state of you, Hal! Stand still and I'll brush the worst off.'

It was a kind of penance to remain motionless, thinking about icy streams and Latin verbs while Thea ran her fingers through his hair, brushed the dust off his coat tails with the flat of her hand, dusted his shoulders down.

'There. Now you must do the same for me.'

She smelled of dust and orange blossom, cold air and the herbal rinse she used on her hair. The dark red strands coiled themselves around his fingers as he tried to pin back a tumbled curl, and one long hair came away as he brushed a cobweb free. He let it go with regret and it drifted off as the breeze caught it.

Fortunately, her skirts recovered enough when she shook them out briskly and he was spared having to touch those.

'Next time, remind me to dive for cover behind the curtains and not bolt out of windows,' he said, rather more grimly than he had intended, and Thea glanced at him, a little frown between her brows.

'I had not thought you someone to stand so much on their dignity,' she said. 'Or was it the spider?'

'Oh, definitely the spider,' he said. 'Next time, please ask me to rescue you from a fire-breathing dragon or a raging bull and I will do that with pleasure. At least those only have four legs.'

Thea laughed at him, her face alight with mischief, and he felt something shift inside him, just as it had when he had looked down at her from the top of the tower. Not vertigo, but desire and, he suspected, something more. Which was, to put it mildly, inconvenient.

Hal winced inwardly at the word, so wrong to be applied to anything to do with the emotions. Godmama had clearly thought she was acting for the best when she was faced with Thea's unexpected arrival, but now he wondered whether it would not have been better to have told him to leave before he even set eyes on Thea.

But then he would not have come to know her as a friend, would not have been able to give her the advice which, he was certain, would enable her to deal with the question of her marriage in the best possible way. The risk to his own feelings had to be secondary—just so long as she did not come to hate him.

Chapter Seven

Thea smiled at Hal's nonsense and went to open the gate. 'Listen, I hear the distant sound of retreating carriage wheels. We are saved.'

They went inside to find their godmother standing in the hallway looking distractedly around her. 'There you are! Thank goodness. I was in dread that you would come in and I would have to explain what the pair of you are doing here.'

'That was somewhat early for a social call,' Hal remarked as they followed her into the drawing room.

'They are leaving for London and Lady Chesford wanted to return a shawl I had left at Chesford Manor last week. At least, that was her excuse. Actually, she wanted to look at my new winter garden and ask if her head gardener could come and view it. The poor creature—Lady Chesford, not the gardener—is terrified of being behind the trend in anything. Perhaps I should have encouraged her to have an Italian garden instead.'

They laughed and she said, 'And where were you both?'

'Oh, in the gardens,' Thea said. 'We heard voices and thought it best to stay out of the way. We, er, hid.'

Hal sent her an appreciative look, presumably for an explanation which was perfectly truthful and perfectly deceptive. Godmama would have kittens if she knew they had been hiding together under the dustsheet in the summerhouse.

If she had been concerned that Thea might develop a *tendre* for Hal Forrest, then the discovery that they had been positively entwined like that would probably have had her packing Thea off back to her parents within the hour.

And she didn't want to go, not because she feared her parents' wrath, but because she didn't want to leave Hal. But she didn't want to stay either, because otherwise she might find herself falling…

No.

Thea took a deep breath. *Feeling*, that was the word. Feeling more for a man who was not a suitable match for the Earl of Wiveton's daughter, with her magnificent future already lying before her.

On the other hand, Hal Forrest gave her no indication that he felt anything for her but friendship and the kindred spirit of being one of Lady Holme's godchildren. He behaved impeccably, even when stretched out over her body in pursuit of that spider, a most improper position to be in and one which had caused decidedly disturbing sensations in parts of Thea's body that she tried not to think about too closely.

But there had been that moment by the pond… Yet with the passing of time, she became less and less certain that there had been anything, that Hal had frozen into stillness too, that his breath had caught, as hers had. Had she imagined it?

'Thea dear, have you been listening to a word I have been saying?'

'No, Godmama,' she admitted honestly. 'Not a syllable, I'm afraid.'

'I was asking if you would go and see what flowers and foliage Fosket can spare us for the house. He behaves as though I expect him to sacrifice his own blood when I want to pick anything, but at this time of year with less in flower, he is even worse. Perhaps you can charm him.'

'I will try after luncheon, Godmama. He may be mellowed by his own meal.'

Her smile faded as Fenwick entered, a silver slaver balanced on one hand, its surface covered in paper. 'The second postal delivery, my lady.' He placed it on the side table next to Lady Holme's chair.

'Thank you, Fenwick.' She gathered a handful up and began to scan them. 'Two…no, three for you, Hal.'

Thea began to rise to help, but Hal was before her.

He took his post and tucked it into an inner breast pocket without a glance.

'One for me, and this, and this. Ah, this is for you, Thea. From your father, I imagine.'

Hal took it and handed it to her.

Thea looked at it as it lay in her lap. Pandora's box: What would she discover if she opened the lid, broke the seal?

Abruptly she ran her finger under the red wax. The letter was a single sheet and she looked first at the end.

Wiveton. Her father had signed it simply with his title and no words of affection.

Braced now for the worst, Thea made herself read from the beginning.

She had almost been the death of her poor Mama. Her father, scarce able to believe such undutiful behaviour, hardly knew what to write. But her godmother's letter had provided him with some hope that all might not be lost, that the honour of the family, and Thea's reputation, might yet be saved.

She took a deep breath and read on. Lady Holme had graciously suggested that they tell their acquaintance that she was suffering from a mild infection and had asked that Thea visit for a week to cheer her.

She, Thea, would then *Return Home* and do her duty by accepting the Duke if she wished to retain the affection of her deeply distressed parents.

Godmama and Hal were waiting silently, she realised when she looked up.

'It is all right, I think. Godmama's letter has helped, because it gives them a more believable excuse for my absence from London than the suggestion that I had some illness myself. But I am to return within the week and accept the Duke's hand.'

'So what will you do?' Hal asked.

'I will return as they wish, but I will do as you suggested and explain my feelings to the Duke when he calls. Goodness knows what will happen if he then refuses to offer for me, or I decide I simply cannot live with the man. I will have to think of another eligible gentleman and fix my interest with him very rapidly, I suppose.'

'And do you have anyone in mind?' Hal asked, his voice exceedingly dry, it seemed to her.

'I do not, unfortunately. London is full of highly eligible men, many of whom I find perfectly pleasant and agreeable, and none of whom I have the slightest desire to spend the rest of my life with.'

And certainly none I desire to be in bed with. Unlike—

'Difficult,' he said.

'Not necessarily. The Duke might prove to be perfectly amiable,' she said, without a great deal of hope. 'I will reply to Papa's letter immediately and, I suppose, I must set out for London soon.'

'The day after tomorrow?' her godmother suggested. 'You may use my own travelling carriage, Jennie can accompany you and Hal escort you.'

Startled, Thea stared at her. 'But is that entirely proper? And it is a very long way to ride.'

'I shall travel with my own carriage,' Hal said. 'And I will appear to be simply another traveller taking the same road to London. But at the same time I can keep an eye on you and will be at hand if you encounter any difficulties. I only rode the day I arrived here because I felt the need for the exercise.'

'That would be reassuring, thank you,' Thea said.

What else *could* she say? *Please do not. I find you quite disturbing enough as it is*? *Please do, because then we will have a few more days together*?

'Ring for Fenwick if you will, Hal,' Godmama said. 'We must alert the coachmen and grooms, make certain the carriages and horses are ready, and Jennie must begin organising your packing, Thea.'

'But what about Juno?' Thea asked Hal. 'It is too far for her to keep pace with the carriages and their frequent change of horses.'

'Jessup, my groom can ride her down. In fact,' he said, pausing on his way to the bell pull. 'He can start this afternoon.'

'There, everything is settled,' Godmama said after Fenwick had received his instructions and Hal had gone off to the stables. 'Most satisfactory.'

'Indeed, yes,' Thea agreed with a determined smile.

Settled? Once one of her brothers had described

the sensation of being tossed in a blanket by some of his friends and her insides felt just as though that was happening to them.

The moon was full the next evening, breaking through the ragged clouds that threatened more rain to come.

'Autumn is truly upon us,' Hal remarked, making her startle as she stood at the drawing room window, the curtain held back by one hand. 'I'm sorry, I did not mean to alarm you.'

'No alarm, just a little jump,' Thea said, making light of it. 'I was thinking what a striking effect the moonlight is making on the wet garden.'

'The rain under moonlight is like snow,' Hal said, ruefully. He reached up to pull the curtain wider, his fingers warm over hers. 'It looks delightful now, but it makes the journey tomorrow a great deal more unpleasant. I told Jessup to make certain he was well wrapped up and to take shelter whenever he began to feel chilled. He likes to pretend that he's a youngster still, but he's far from it. Not that I can get him to admit it.'

'An old family retainer?' Thea said, aware that she was fishing. Subtly, she hoped. Of course, she could just ask, or consult the *Peerage* and the *Landed Gentry*, both on the shelves in the study. But she found herself reluctant to do so.

What if Hal was in neither? Or the *Landed Gentry*

revealed that he was the son of some country squire who had just happened to deserve Lady Holme's patronage as godmother to his son? Then there was no chance that she would encounter him again in London, no likelihood that he would consider calling—not when he had proved so reluctant to intrude on Lord Brownlow, or to encounter the Chesfords.

'Yes, he worked for my father,' Hal said. 'There's the dinner gong.'

He offered his arm and Thea took it, remembering his voice when he said he had met Penelope Chesford. There had been something there that had made her wonder under just what circumstances, then events had driven the query from her mind.

Penny always cut a swathe through any gathering of men with her blond hair, big blue eyes, petite, curvaceous figure and her apparently irresistible flirtatious technique. She always made Thea feel like a skinny beanpole.

'We have elegance,' she'd said consolingly to one of her friends who had just seen her beau stolen from her.

'So we do,' Maria had replied bitterly, 'but now she's got my James and she'll drop him tomorrow. Not that I'd want him back if he is such an idiot as to fall for her.'

What if Hal had been another of the 'idiots' who had fallen for Penny? He would be in good company if he were, and if he had been considered ineligible by her parents and snubbed, then that would be a very good reason for wishing to avoid them.

And no, that was not something she could ask about. If he wanted to tell her about himself, he would so. She must not pry, she resolved firmly. Hal was her friend, nothing more, and a temporary friend at that.

Lady Holme's travelling carriage was, more accurately, a chariot, a vehicle for two to sit in comfort, looking forwards as one did in a post chaise, but with a coachman on the box driving the team and therefore no postilions. The view was not as good as in a post chaise, but the interior was considerably more luxurious, and Jennie the maid was rendered speechless by the shock of discovering that she was sitting on plush crimson upholstery.

The doors were painted with Lady Holme's coat of arms, contained within a lozenge shape to signify her widowed status.

Hal's carriage, Thea noted, had plain doors and looked like a vehicle that had covered a great many miles in the course of a long life. Drage, their butler, would turn his nose up if that arrived outside the house on Chesterfield Street.

But the horses were good, she noted with interest, and the coachman and groom looked as though they knew their business. Perhaps Hal liked to spend his money on his horses and neglected other refinements such as his clothes or a smart carriage.

Then it was time for final hugs and kisses and thanks from her, and last-minute advice on the journey from Godmama.

Thea turned to find Hal waiting. 'I will be just behind all the way,' he told her. 'I will not stay at the same inns, but find accommodation nearby and I will send a note to say where you can find me. But should our paths cross, it would be discreet if we pretend not to know each other.'

'Yes, I understand. One never knows whom one will encounter on a main coaching route. But we will have a chance to say goodbye properly before we arrive in London, I hope,' Thea said.

'I doubt it,' Hal said. 'Better if we say our farewells now, Lady Thea. It has been a great pleasure.'

She could read nothing in his smile, but then why should she? They had met as house guests, become friendly, shared a rather shocking scrape and taken a long country ride.

Had shared a moment of awareness beside a lake, been intimately entangled, chaperoned only by a spider... Had become friends.

Now they were parting, she for the Season, he for whatever minor landowners did on their estates at this time of year.

'Goodbye, Mr Forrest.' She held out her hand, her gloves still in the other.

Hal took it, turned it and raised it to his lips, pressed

a kiss into her palm, closed her fingers over it and released her.

It was over in a moment and Thea found herself, somehow, outside, standing beside the open carriage door. The groom handed her in, closed the door, said something to the coachman and the carriage began to move. Thea dropped the window glass and leaned out to wave to Godmama, then raised it again and stared rather blankly at the back of the coachman in front of her.

'You dropped your gloves, my lady.'

Thea blinked and realised that the maid was beside her. 'Thank you.' She pulled the thin kid over her fingers, over her hands, sealing in that kiss. What had that meant? Gentlemen did not kiss hands like that, not any more...

'Are you a good traveller, Jennie?' she asked as they turned out of the gates between the flanking lodges.

'I don't know, my lady. I've never been in anything except Pa's cart,' the maid said brightly. 'I expect I am, though. I mean, this is lovely, isn't it? Ever so smooth—it sways just like those rocking cradles.'

'Very smooth,' Thea agreed when the two of them were thrown together as the wheels hit a deep pothole.

'Ooh, my lady!' Jennie said with a giggle.

At least she was cheerful and bright, unlike Maunday, Thea thought. She set herself to enjoy the journey seen through the maid's wide eyes and not to allow her mind to spin, filled with ridiculous speculation.

* * *

The first night was spent at Stilton after a journey of seven hours, including a leisurely stop for luncheon and the regular change of horses. Thea had taken pains not to look around for Hal's carriage as they went, but just as she was alighting outside the Bell in Stilton, she saw it turn into the yard of the Angel opposite across the wide street.

The Bell was the most famous of Stilton's inns and somewhere travellers would stop to purchase the celebrated cheese from the landlord. Now he came bustling out of his front door, wreathed in smiles to welcome a lady arriving in such an elegant equipage.

He had the perfect suite of rooms for Lady Thea, he assured her, ushering her inside. A fine bedchamber, a room for her maid and a private parlour where she could take her dinner quite undisturbed. Her men would be accommodated in comfort in rooms above the stables and at what hour would it please her to take her dinner?

Finally able to get a word in edgeways, Thea ordered a meal for eight o'clock and hot water immediately and was pleased to approve the rooms.

'Very nice, my lady,' Jennie conceded when the door closed on the landlord. 'But you are right at the front overlooking the street. I'll wager it will be noisy in the night with folks coming and going.'

'That's the way of it with inns, and the better they are, the busier they are,' Thea told her. 'One becomes resigned. So long as the bed is comfortable, one just has to stick one's head under the pillow.'

They washed then dined together. Jennie was very stiff and nervous at first, but relaxed as she realised that her table manners were perfectly adequate.

The maid was stifling yawns by the time they had finished and she rang for the waiter to clear the table, so Thea locked the door, changed into her nightgown and sent Jennie off to bed as soon as her hair was unpinned.

She was tired and she ached a little, because however luxurious a carriage and careful the coachman, a long day sitting took its toll. But she was not, she realised, sleepy. She was too restless for that.

Thea looked at the bed, which certainly appeared comfortable enough. Jennie had tested the sheets and pronounced them spotless and dry, and a chambermaid had come while they were eating to slide a warming pan between them, but she knew she would only toss and turn.

Her robe was warm and her feet snug in their slippers, so she prowled into the parlour, studying the rather gloomy prints on the wall, poking the fire, twitching the vase of dried grasses into order.

It was not nervousness about facing Mama and Papa. Or only a little, perhaps. It wasn't even the rather daunting prospect of having to take the Duke to task over his neglect of her. It was the abrupt way she had parted from Hal. But what could they have said that would have made any difference? He had been a friend for a short while, one who had offered her good advice, one who had his own life to live in a world quite different from the universe she was destined to occupy.

If I agree to marry the Duke, she thought.

She could feel herself sliding inexorably towards agreeing and realised that it was Hal's common-sense suggestion about actually talking to the man and expressing her feelings that had made this feel so inevitable.

Before, her determination had been feeding off her anger and instinctive rebellion; now she was going to have to be reasonable, to negotiate. That made her resentful, true, but it also made her feel resigned.

Her reflection in the over-mantel mirror stared down at her and she glared back at it. 'You are an idiot,' she said softly. 'I know what is the matter with you: if Hal Forrest had swept you up in his arms, kissed you passionately and announced that he loved you to distraction, you would have run off with him without a moment's hesitation—and have been sorry afterwards. You don't know how you feel about him, let alone how he feels about you, and now you'll never know.'

Which was probably a very good thing.

The room, with its smouldering fire, was becoming stuffy, so she slipped behind the curtains, perched on the window seat and opened the casement to let in some fresh air.

The rain had stopped some time ago, she realised, and darkness had fallen. The cobbles gleamed wetly with the reflected light from the two inns and, as she watched, three men stumbled into view below her, reeling and flailing at each other, their voices raised.

They were drunk and brawling and had just been thrown out by the landlord, she realised as they stood in the middle of the street, exchanging insults at the top of their voices.

Opposite, Hal strolled out of the front door of the Angel, a pint tankard in his hand.

He stood watching the men who finally staggered off, apparently firm friends again, then looked across, his gaze lifted, probably to look at the famous inn sign of the Bell that stretched out across the pavement, Thea thought.

In the darkness between curtains and glass he couldn't see her, of course, but she lifted a hand in greeting nevertheless.

Hal stared and Thea realised that her white sleeves, and perhaps the pale oval of her face, must be visible in the gloom.

He raised his right hand, as though to wave back, then someone opened the door behind him and two men walked out. Hal turned the gesture into one of smoothing down his hair, ruffled by the breeze down the street, and the men walked away, leaving the door into the Angel open.

As Hal turned and walked away, the light from the room behind sent his shadow, elongated into a bar of black, across the road to the walls of the Bell, and then he was inside, the door closed, and the street was deserted once more.

As he had promised, he was watching out for her, had heard the drunks shouting and had come out to make certain it was nothing that could threaten her.

Warmed by the thought, Thea parted the curtains and made her way to bed, suddenly so weary it was an effort to drag off her robe.

Chapter Eight

'How would you like us to go about the next stages, my lady?' Baggott the coachman asked at seven the next morning. He stood respectfully by her breakfast table in the parlour, hat and whip in hand.

'Are you wishful to break the journey at, say, Baldock, ma'am? The White Horse is a good inn, I can recommend it as being very respectable for a lady. If that is what you'd like, then we can take it easy all the way. Or, if the weather holds and there are no problems on the road, then we can make it to London tonight. But it's near eighty miles and a long day for you.'

'It will be an even longer one for you, Baggott. I can't ask you to drive all that way.'

'Oh, Jim and the lad will spell me, my lady. They're both good, safe drivers, never fear. If the weather turns against us, then we can always stop somewhere else.'

'Then try to do it in the day, please. But I am relying upon you to stop as soon as you are all feeling tired—or before that if necessary!'

The prospect of two more days on the road, with her father waiting fuming at the end of it, was not at all enticing. Best to get it over with. She was tired of uncertainty and muddled feelings and a vague sense of dread.

The autumn weather was kind to them. It was grey and overcast with threatening clouds, but no rain fell. As they passed through the valley of the River Ivel, the horses splashed through floods and Jim the groom leaned down to call through the window that they should put their feet on the seat in case water came in, but they passed through safely and reached the White Horse in Baldock to take a snatched midday meal.

Thea saw the shabby black carriage pass them and stop outside a smaller inn further along the street.

'Well, I'll be b— Er…blowed, my lady,' Baggott said. 'That's—that's Mr Forrest driving.'

'Giving his men a rest,' Thea said, secretly impressed that Hal drove a four-in-hand with such skill. 'Does he know we are intending to do the journey in the day?'

'Yes, my lady. His man came over to ask me this morning. Good hands, he's got.' He slapped his hat back on his head and strode off to the stable yard muttering something that sounded like, 'Only to be expected.' Which made no sense to Thea.

She shrugged and hastened to finish her chicken soup and rolls so they could be on their way as soon as the men had refreshed themselves.

The church clocks were striking eight as Lady Holme's carriage finally drew to a halt in front of the house on Chesterfield Street and Jim jumped down to ply the knocker.

The door opened to reveal Drage, directing two footmen to take the baggage, and he came down to help Thea descend instead of sending a footman, a great condescension on the part of a butler who normally would only stir himself for the Countess herself.

She turned to thank Baggott and the grooms, who were being directed to the mews, and the familiar battered carriage came past at a walk. All she could see of the occupant was one hand resting on the edges of the open window, a glint of gold as the light from the *torchieres* touched the old signet that Hal wore on his left hand, the engraving so rubbed it was impossible to read.

Then it was past and the driver whipped the horses up so it rattled away, around the corner into Curzon Street and out of sight.

Thea put back her shoulders, fixed a smile on her lips and greeted Drage and the footmen. 'Good evening. It is good to be home. This is Jennie, who has been taking care of me. She will be staying for a few nights. Please find her a nice room to herself.'

Then there was no putting it off any longer. Chin up, she sailed through the front door and turned into the drawing room.

They were both waiting for her, Mama on the sofa, her father with one foot on the fender. Of course, Mama and Papa would never cause a scene in the hall in front of the servants.

Thea closed the door behind her and dropped a curtsey. 'Mama, Papa. Good evening.' Her stomach felt as though an entire nest of ants had taken up residence there, but she managed a smile.

'Thea.' Mama at least produced a thin smile in return.

Her father merely frowned at her, then pronounced, 'Dinner will be served very shortly. We will discuss this business tomorrow.'

No. Deal with this now or be powerless for ever.

'There is no need, Papa. I am sorry I upset and worried you both,' Thea said. 'My time with Godmama has given me the opportunity to think about things more calmly. I will do as you say and receive the Duke of Leamington when he calls.'

Not that I am promising to accept him, even if he continues to offer for me after I have had my say.

She waited, doing her best to appear obedient and dutiful. It appeared to be effective because Mama was looking faintly surprised and relieved and her father's frown had disappeared.

'*Hrumph.*' He was trying to look forbidding still,

but the deep grooves between his brows had vanished. 'I am glad to see that you have come to your senses and realised your good fortune, my girl. Now go and change. Your brothers are joining us for dinner tonight.'

'All of them?' Piers was seventeen, Clarence fifteen, Basil ten and Ernest six. Normally only Piers was permitted—or instructed—to eat his dinner with his parents.

'Certainly not,' Mama said. 'Piers and Clarence, of course.'

Thea bobbed another curtsey on the principle that one could never overdo respectful behaviour and made her escape.

Upstairs she found Jennie confronted by Maunday.

'I am Lady Thea's maid.'

'You? A chit from the country?'

Normally Thea was looked after by one of the maids, cowering under the eye of Maunday and too nervous to utter a word.

'Certainly,' Thea said, entering the room and making an instant decision. 'Jennie has been most efficient. I am hoping she will stay on as my lady's maid but, of course, she must make up her own mind about that.'

Jennie's eyes widened with surprise and she stared at Thea, open-mouthed. Clearly her words had simply been defiance in the face of Maunday's sneers. Then she confirmed Thea's good opinion of her by composing her expression and saying politely, 'Thank you, my lady. I am very pleased to accept the position.'

'There you are, Maunday, no need for you to trouble yourself. Thank you for offering your assistance.' Thea stood away from the door in clear invitation for the woman to leave.

'My lady,' she said stiffly and swept out.

'She will be on her way to tell Mama that I have employed a maid without permission, but never fear, when she sees how well you do my hair you will be allowed to remain. If you are sure, that is. Won't you be homesick? And I suppose I should ask Lady Holme before poaching her staff.'

'She said I could stay if you asked me, my lady,' Jennie said. 'Her ladyship knows I have ambitions to be a lady's maid. Which gown would you like? I have ordered bathwater to be brought up immediately.'

Thea suppressed a smile. It seemed she had unleashed a formidable presence on the servants' hall. 'Excellent. There is a dark green gown with lighter green ribbons that should be in the press in the dressing room. What is your last name, Jennie? Now you are the third most important female member of staff, you must have that dignity.'

'I am?' Jennie stopped halfway to the dressing room door.

'The housekeeper, Mrs Holt, then Mama's maid, Maunday, and then you. We have a male chef, so there's no cook in the hierarchy.'

'Blimey. I mean, goodness. It's Eames, my lady.'

'Very well, Eames. And you need not call me *my lady* with every sentence, you know.'

'Yes, my lady. Thank you, my lady.' Jennie, now Eames, beamed at her and retreated to the dressing room.

Nothing the slightest bit troubling was discussed at dinner, naturally, even though there were no guests.

Over soup, Papa spoke with some feeling about the latest problems in the government, and both his sons managed to assume expressions of interest and concern. Piers even asked a sensible question.

Thea, being female, was not expected to have an opinion on political matters.

As they consumed the fish course—a Dover sole in a cream sauce with capers—Mama held the floor with the latest Court news.

The King's health was giving cause for concern, which it always was now, not least to anxious mamas with daughters whose Season would be blighted if they had to go into full mourning for the monarch. As for the Prince Regent, Mama confined her remarks to the intelligence that architect John Nash was starting work on the Marine Pavilion in Brighton. 'One shudders to think what His Royal Highness will demand,' she said. 'His taste becomes even more extreme with each passing year.'

Over the main course, Piers and then Clarence gave

summaries of their day—heavily edited, Thea was certain, and then, with dessert, it was her turn.

'Godmama is much improved in health,' she said, mindful that her brothers would not have been told about the real reason for her journey. 'She sends her best wishes. Although I was not there for long, I did have the opportunity to view Lord Brownlow's new Italian garden and orangery. The building is handsome, although incomplete, but I found the garden somewhat formal.'

That provoked a lecture on the necessity to keep one's estate up to date with the latest innovations and trends by Papa, which left Clarence glassy-eyed with boredom.

Piers, with surprising tact, enquired whether Papa was considering such an innovation at Wiverbrook Hall and Thea was able to consume her Chantilly cream with almond wafers in peace.

When Mama rose to leave the men of the family to their port Thea followed her out, expecting to face a battery of questions about Lady Holme. Instead, she was interrogated about her new maid.

'Maunday says she is some untrained country girl. Where on earth did you pick her up? And why?'

'I certainly did not just pick her up, Mama. Eames has been trained by Lady Holme and she is an excellent semptress, as well as being very good with my hair.'

'She did that style? I assumed that Maunday had dressed it for you.'

'This is entirely Eames's work, I assure you.'

'Hmm... It appears competent enough, and Clarissa is always well turned out, so she would not stand for lax standards in her staff. You may keep the girl for now, although whether she has the experience to attend on a duchess remains to be seen.'

'Thank you, Mama.'

And the Duke 'remains to be seen' as well, not just my maid...

His Grace the Duke of Leamington would call the following day at two thirty, Papa informed her the next morning after breakfast. He had apparently arrived in London rather earlier than expected.

'Yes, Papa.'

'I hope you are now aware of the very great opportunity this is for you and appreciate the benefits to your brothers of having such an influence on their future careers and prospects.'

The sons of a well-connected earl would, naturally, all expect to do well in life, but it was unarguable that the influence of a duke would be exceedingly valuable, whether they wanted to make excellent marriages, or the younger ones secure government positions or perhaps enter the diplomatic service.

'Yes, indeed, Papa.'

The thought that if she turned down the Duke, it

might disadvantage her brothers did concern her, but part of her rebelled at being the one whose own interests had to be sacrificed for the rest of the family, just because she was female. They were all bright boys with advantages that the vast majority of the population could never hope to possess. Piers would inherit the title, of course, and the others would make their own ways in the world, she was certain.

'I am relying upon you to do your duty to the family and to our name.'

'Yes, I know, Papa,' Thea said earnestly. She could only hope that when she met the Duke she could agree to marry him.

Love, she did not expect, that was a lottery, perhaps a fantasy for someone like her. Yet again Thea clenched her fingers over her right palm and pushed away the memory of that kiss.

Liking and attraction were not love, she reminded herself, making herself focus on the prospect of the Duke. There had to be liking and respect. And that respect must come from him too. If he could not accept how much he had neglected her, insulted her by taking her for granted, then, no, she would not marry him.

What she would do if she refused him, she had no idea. Would Papa accept that, allow her to finish the Season in the hope of attracting another suitor? Surely, she wouldn't be packed off to Cousin Elizabeth again, because if she was, then only barred widows and leg shackles would keep her there.

'Very well, run along then. I expect your mother has a great deal to discuss with you.'

Mama did indeed, have much to say. There was the coiffeur who was coming that afternoon to be instructed, there was the lengthy discussions about which gown she should wear, with Eames laying out every single afternoon dress that she could find. There was even the important matter of which piece of embroidery she should be working on while she waited for His Grace, so it could be casually put to one side for him to admire one of her suitably feminine talents.

When the *coiffeur* had finished with her, and Eames had earnestly listened to his instructions on curl papers for the night, there were her nails to trim and buff, her eyebrows to be scrutinised and her jewellery to be agonised over.

At least, Thea thought, the effort to stay patient and pleasant and to appear delighted at the fuss took her mind off tomorrow's encounter.

The next day was hardly any better. Her complexion was inspected, difficult decisions were made about a little powder here, the merest touch of rouge there and perhaps lamp black on the lashes—all to be applied after a light luncheon. She was forbidden from going out in case she became flushed with the exertion of walking and so had to sit calmly while the morning dragged past.

Luncheon was at twelve to allow plenty of time for

dressing and primping and then, finally, it was time to sit in the drawing room, a piece of Mama's half-finished embroidery on a frame and a basket of silks beside her so she could set a stitch or two.

At least she had a partial view out of the window to the street a few feet below, as the house had a half-basement and therefore a flight of steps to the front door. She would have a few moments warning when he arrived.

As the clocks chimed the half hour, a glossy town carriage drew up. A footman jumped down to open the door and Thea caught a glimpse of the top of a tall hat. There must have been someone watching from inside, because she heard the front door open and then the sound of masculine voices in the hallway.

There was another carriage slowing down outside. Distracted, she glanced at what she could see of that, wondering if another caller had chosen to arrive at just the wrong time, then the drawing room door opened and she stood up, sticking the embroidery needle into her thumb as she did so.

The pain was so sharp that she spoke without thought, staring at the figure in the doorway.

'Hal?' she whispered.

He must have arrived just before the Duke. How hideously embarrassing.

'But—oh, my goodness, we are expecting—'

Drage, materialising just behind Hal, cleared his

throat and announced, 'His Grace the Duke of Leamington, my lady.'

Her mother moved past her, sending her a dagger glance and a hissed *'Ssh!'* as she did so.

Thea craned to see past the men who seemed to fill the doorway—Hal, Drage and now Papa. Where was the Duke?

'Your Grace.' Mama came to a halt in front of Hal and…

And shook his hand.

'Lady Wiveton. I am delighted to be here at last. It must be quite ten years, if not more, since we last met. I do hope I find you in the best of health.'

Thea, on her feet, clutched at the embroidery frame for support, convinced for the first time in her life that she was going to faint.

'Do allow me to introduce you to my daughter because, although you have met a long time ago, I believe you will find she has changed out of all recognition since then. Thea, dear.'

Apparently, she had not fainted. Thea found herself walking forward, then took the hand held out to her and dropped her very best and deepest curtsey.

She met Hal's eyes as she rose—somehow without collapsing at his feet—and found she could not read his expression at all. 'Your Grace,' she murmured as he released her hand.

Now Mama was going to order tea and expect her

to pour and make inane conversation, and she didn't think she could manage a word.

To her huge relief, Hal turned and smiled at her parents. 'Sir, Lady Wiveton. I wonder if you will permit me a few minutes private conversation with Lady Thea? As old friends we have a great deal to catch up on.'

'But of course.' Predictably, Mama was already halfway to the door, urging Papa and Drage before her. 'Do ring for refreshments, Thea dear.'

Thea was scarcely conscious of them leaving. She took two steps back away from him so she could see him properly. 'You… You absolute… *Swine*.'

The room began to blur and tilt and she reached out a hand, just conscious of it being take in a firm grasp before everything went black.

Chapter Nine

That could have gone a lot better, Hal thought grimly as he lowered Thea's limp form onto the sofa.

Even as he wondered whether to make things even worse by ringing for a glass of water, she opened her eyes, then sat up.

'You!' she said again, her voice shaky. Then it hardened as her gaze came back into focus. 'You *lied* to me.'

Hal shook his head. 'I did not, although I admit I hid a great deal from you.'

'*A great deal?* And you are still doing it,' she said fiercely. 'You said your name was Hal Forrest.'

As he entered, Hal had noticed a copy of the *Peerage* lying in a side table next to a stack of partly addressed invitation cards. He picked it up and brought it over to the sofa, flicking through the pages until he came to his family's entry.

'See?' He held it out and indicated the place. 'Avery Henry de Forrest Castleton Vernier, sixth Duke of

Leamington. I always hated Avery and I've gone by Hal ever since I was old enough to insist on it.'

Thea waved the heavy red volume away with a flick of her hand. 'That is just a quibble and you know it. You deceived me, you and Godmama both. What were you doing there?'

'Calling on my godmother on my way to the last visit of my tour of my estates before I came down to London,' he said, laying the book down out of reach of an angry woman. The *Peerage* was heavy enough to fell an ox.

'The final estate is really hardly more than a farm in Norfolk, it was no problem to leave that for the moment and stay for a while as our Godmama wanted.'

'I am *so* glad it did not in any way inconvenience you,' Thea said, her icy tone at odds with the heat in her eyes. 'I told you why I was there, why I had run away, and you said nothing about who you were. *Nothing.*' She broke off, her bosom rising and falling with her agitated breathing. He saw the realisation strike her. 'They all knew who you were—Godmama, Fenwick, the other servants. Goodness knows what they must have thought.'

'Godmama told the staff that I was travelling incognito,' he explained. 'They had no idea why you had arrived or that it had anything to do with me.'

Thea closed her eyes, and he suspected that she was reviewing all the things she had told him and, probably, wishing she could sink through the floor while she did so. Or more likely wishing he would be the one to sink.

After a moment, she raised her lids and regarded him stonily. 'It did not occur to you simply to say who you were and *leave*?'

'No,' he admitted. 'By the time I realised what had caused your flight, you had poured out the whole story. I wanted to help and I could see that if I admitted who I was it would have been acutely embarrassing for you.'

'Oh? And this is not?' she demanded.

'I believed that we had established a friendship. An understanding. I thought that when I called here we would have the opportunity to discuss the situation. And I could apologise.'

'For what, exactly?' She was not giving an inch, he thought, admiring her backbone even as he was inwardly wincing.

'In the first place for taking you for granted and neglecting you all those years. Your description of my unthinking behaviour hit home hard, believe me. You have every right to feel angry about that.'

He meant it. Lord, what an unthinking fool he had been to accept that such a thing was settled and that he had no need to bestir himself. What if he had met Thea and found he thoroughly disliked her? What if she had been a shrew, or a selfish, self-absorbed woman who would have had no care for their dependants, their children? And that was just the practical side of the matter: he'd had no right to assume that he could simply command another person's life like that.

Thea's chin went up. 'Oh? I have your *permission* to be angry, have I? Thank you so very much, Your Grace. That might be the case, but I am finding it very hard to forgive your neglect of me before now. You say you are sorry, you have apologised and I am sure that soothes your conscience, but it does not make *me* feel any better about it.'

Hal nodded, accepting that. It was difficult to see how an apology and an explanation of complete thoughtlessness could compensate for the feelings she must have experienced when Thea realised she was expected to marry an almost complete stranger. Although surely she would not have expected to make a love match? Would she?

He pushed that idea aside. He had never had any thought of making such a thing, and she would not have been raised to expect it either. People of their class married for many reasons, but love was never one of them. Now, somehow, that seemed a…lack.

Hal ignored the strange ache in his chest. He was here to apologise, not dwell on his own feelings. 'And I am sorry for not finding a way to explain it all—to confess, if you like—before we left.'

'I assume Godmama advised you not to.'

She had, of course, and he had allowed himself to be swayed by her arguments. 'I am not going to blame her for what I can now see was my error of judgement.'

'Gallant of you, but I imagine she was very happily matchmaking. Do you know, she cautioned me, very seriously, about the dangers of developing a *tendre* for you. That was clever, putting the idea into my mind, sowing the seed. There is nothing like having something forbidden, advised against, for making one start thinking seriously about it.'

Hal winced. He hadn't known about that and there was no safe way to comment on Lady Holme's tactics, so he stuck to why he had kept his silence. 'It would have been exceedingly awkward to travel back together if you had known.'

Thea took a deep breath. 'I am trying to be fair, and it is not easy, believe me. I can see that it would have been difficult to interrupt me at tea that first afternoon. I was tired and emotional and I should not have poured out all that, I should not have spoken to a stranger about the Duke—about you—in such terms. That was my fault. And once I had said all that, I can appreciate that it was awkward to explain who you were. If you had announced who you were at that point I… I do not know what I would have done.'

Hal felt the stirrings of hope. Was Thea going to forgive what he now saw was a colossal error of judgement by himself and their godmother?

'But you *could* have done it,' she said, drowning that flicker of optimism. 'You could have done it the very next day. It would have been embarrassing, but we could have had a frank conversation and agreed how we were going to deal with the situation. I am finding it very hard to understand why you did not do that.'

Because I was attracted to you, was the honest answer, he realised.

He had enjoyed her spirit and her anger, he had come to sympathise and see very clearly where he had been at fault—and he had not wanted to spoil the growing friendship he could feel developing between them even after so short a time. He had seen that it would be no hardship whatsoever to marry this woman.

'I knew that if I came here as myself then it would be a surprise—'

Thea gave a very unladylike snort.

Hal ploughed on. 'A shock then, but I hoped that our friendship would carry us through it. That we could have that conversation I had suggested to you and we could agree to take this slowly. I could court you and you would see…come to see that our marriage would be for the best for both of us.'

Even as he spoke, he could tell that he had made things worse, not better.

'*Court* me? A few bunches of flowers, your escort to the theatre, a drive or two in the park, I suppose. No doubt that would allow me to experience the sensation of my parents being pleased with me for doing my duty. In fact, it would give me the opportunity to *see sense*. That was what you almost said, wasn't it?'

Thea was on her feet pacing now and, even as he felt the lash of her anger, Hal could admire her for holding firm to what she felt was right for her.

He was not going to lie to her, not any more. 'Yes, I almost said that, but I realised it was…inappropriate.'

She stopped, stock-still in the middle of the room. 'It would be very easy to say, *Yes*. But that only makes things easy for the immediate future.' It sounded as though she was talking to herself, speaking her thoughts aloud. Then she turned and there was no doubt she was addressing him now. 'I have the rest of my life to consider—and so do you.

'Do you know, I almost wished that you—plain Mr Hal Forrest with no title and rather old clothes, a shabby carriage and apparently not much in the way of an estate—were just a little more eligible. Nothing fancy, you understand. A viscount perhaps, or heir to something. Then I could imagine our friendship growing and you being someone that Papa might reluctantly accept for me once I had refused the Duke.'

'But, Thea, I am that person. Even to the clothes and the coach—I prefer to be comfortable when I'm travelling, and my decent carriage broke an axle in Northumberland.'

'No, you are not that man. The clothes and the carriage are mere details. You are the man who deceived me, who manipulated me, who made me believe he was my friend. The man who did not have the…the *guts* to explain the situation to me and trust me to discuss it in a rational manner.

'You set a trap for me, Your Grace, and I am not going to put my neck in the snare.'

Something very uncomfortable was happening in the region of his breastbone, and the urge to bluster and protest and explain was an almost physical force. Hal choked it back down.

'In that case,' he said as calmly as he could manage, 'I can see there is only one thing to do. We must—'

'We must *nothing*,' Thea began as the door swung open and her parents entered, both of them beaming.

'Now,' said the Earl, looking exceedingly pleased with life. 'What have you to say to me, Duke?'

'That Lady Thea and I have come to an understanding,' Hal said, ignoring the gasp from just behind him. 'We have concluded that we would not suit and that both of us should now consider ourselves free of any obligation.'

There was another sound at his back that he sincerely hoped was Thea sitting down with a bump on the sofa and not fainting again.

'I hope I need not say that I hold Lady Thea in the highest estimation and that not a word of this conversation, or of my visit here today, will ever be spoken of by me outside these walls.'

Thea was conscious that she was sitting on the sofa and not on the floor, but beyond that, she was in a daze. Hal was giving up? The Duke was walking away?

'My dear Leamington,' her father was saying urgently when the buzzing in her ears subsided enough for her to hear. 'Thea can be a little headstrong, but I am sure you need not heed any girlish foolishness—'

'I have heard none. Lady Thea has been all that is reasonable and this is an entirely mutual agreement. Neither of us feels that we can honourably enter into a marriage when both of us have the gravest doubts about our compatibility. This leaves us both free.'

'But the match has been an understood thing for… for all your lives,' Mama said.

'It was agreed when we were infants and perhaps at a time when the expectations of what makes for a good match are somewhat different than they are today. It is not something that either of us have agreed to as adults.'

'Oh, if she has been speaking of some foolish romantic nonsense,' her mother said, hands fluttering in agitation, 'that can be ignored. Girls today read too many of those dreadful novels.'

'No word about romance has left Lady Thea's lips, I assure you,' Hal—*the Duke*—said smoothly. 'In fact, I can assure you that our discussion has been strictly practical. I should take my leave, but allow me to repeat, this is an entirely mutual decision and I honour your daughter for her modesty, honesty and honourable desire to do the right thing. Lady Wiveton, Wiveton.'

He turned and bowed to Thea. 'Lady Thea. Good day.'

Thea was hardly aware of him leaving, but he must have gone, because she heard the front door close and Mama and Papa rushed back into the room, almost slamming the door behind them.

'What did you say? What did you tell him, you wretched girl?' her mother demanded.

'We spoke of the nature of our betrothal, the fact that we did not know each other. It became clear that there was no mutual understanding between us,' Thea said slowly, picking her way through the quagmire of truth, lies and deception. 'This, as the Duke said, leaves us both free to find matches that will suit us better.'

'Better than a duke?' Mama sank down in a chair and burst into tears. 'What is better than a duke?'

Both Thea and her father stared, appalled. Thea had never seen her mother exhibit the slightest weakness. Temper, yes. Disappointment, all too frequently, but tears?

Her father began to fuss and bluster, but Mama emerged from her handkerchief after a few minutes and waved him away. 'Stop it, Horace, that is no help.' She dabbed her eyes with the scrap of lace. 'What will people say?'

'Why, nothing, Mama,' Thea said. 'The Duke assured us he would say nothing, and we have no reason to doubt his word, surely?'

'Of course.' Her father sat down rather heavily next to her mother and began to pat her hand. 'But what did you *say* to him, Thea?'

'I… I can hardly recall now. But at no point did I say that I *refused* to marry him.' That, she thought, was nothing but the truth. She had made it abundantly clear, but she had not said the words.

If we had met for the first time now, without any of this history behind us, we might well have decided to wed, she thought bleakly. *But then I would not have known that he was capable of deception, of lying by omission, of manipulating my feelings, just to obtain his own ends. So, this is probably all for the best.*

It was not much consolation, because she was horribly afraid that she had been on the verge of falling in love with plain Mr Hal Forrest and now she knew that he did not exist.

Who had it been that she had sat next to beside that little lake? The Duke or Hal? What if she had not frozen into stillness when their hands had touched, but had turned, leaned towards him? Would they have kissed? And then…

'What are you going to do now?' her mother demanded, even more angry now, Thea suspected, because of her display of weakness.

'Why, undertake the Season, of course,' she said, giving herself a brisk mental shake.

And try to work out what I want to do with the rest of my life.

The temptation to lie in bed all morning the next day was considerable but, as she had spent most of the night awake, Thea decided she might as well get up when she heard the clocks strike eight. Possibly her thoughts might be less scrambled and her brain might work better if she was vertical.

Only Piers was at the breakfast table when she went down, which was not surprising. Her father inevitably rose with the dawn and was probably now out riding. Her mother always took breakfast in bed where she would stay until at least mid-morning. Clarence, Basil and Ernest ate with their tutor in the suite of rooms that included a schoolroom.

She could feel Piers watching her as she moved along the sideboard, lifting lids on the chafing dishes and trying to decide what she could face eating for breakfast. Not devilled kidneys, that was certain.

'Yesterday,' Piers began. 'What was all that with Leamington?'

Thea glanced at the footman standing rigidly against the wall. 'If you could just pour me a cup of coffee, please, Thomas. We will serve ourselves. I will ring if you are needed.'

She waited until the door had closed behind him.

'The Duke called to discuss with me whether or not we should marry. We decided not, that is all. And that is absolutely confidential, do you understand? You know what ridiculous rumours get around with only half the facts, so no gossiping with your friends. I would find it very hurtful and it would be damaging to my reputation.'

'That's not the kind of thing we chaps talk about,' he said with a shrug, but she knew he would keep the secret. Piers was fond of her and, as he grew, was inclined to try to act the protective brother, even though he was younger and only just beginning to find his own way in society.

Next year he too would be taking part in the Season, but for now he and his friends were preoccupied with horses, sparring, learning how to cope with a crashing hangover and very cautiously exploring the scary creatures called women.

'So, what are you going to do if you aren't to marry a duke?' he asked after a few more mouthfuls of steak and eggs. 'Mama must be in a shocking state and Papa was looking grim at dinner last night.'

'They are not best pleased,' Thea said with considerable understatement. 'I shall do the Season, I suppose.'

'Haven't you seen all the eligible chaps the first time around?' her less than tactful brother enquired. 'And you've turned ten of them down.'

'Six,' Thea said absently. 'I turned down six. There

are always new faces. People who did not come to London last year, officers from the Army and Navy home now the wars with the French are finally over.'

'Widowers out of mourning,' Piers suggested, pushing his plate away. 'That's a thought. You could find a rich old husband and then be a rich merry widow when he expires from the shock of having a lively young wife.'

'That's horrible,' Thea said. 'Mercenary and callous. Anyway, I wouldn't want anyone to die.' She tried not to think about what being a lively young wife to a wealthy old man might involve. 'But it is true, widows seem to be the only ladies who have any freedom to live their lives as they chose.'

Widows were free from male control unless they were bound by particularly onerous trust conditions, or were financially dependent on their eldest son.

Now Papa controlled her finances, even the money inherited from Grandmama and one of her godfathers. She could touch none of it without his permission until she married or reached the age of thirty, and that was nine years distant. When she married everything would become her husband's except what was protected in the marriage contracts. And without money she had no options, as she had realised when she had contemplated running away from Cousin Elizabeth.

'I shall do the Season, see if there is anyone I would like to marry who wants to marry me—and if not I shall grit my teeth and sit on the shelf enduring Mama's lectures until I reach thirty.'

Or make a better plan. I am not without some intelligence, surely I will think of something?

Chapter Ten

Thea strongly suspected that her mother had spent the morning in bed working through the *Peerage* and making lists of noblemen and their heirs and then ranking them in order so that she could decide who was the second most eligible bachelor in England.

Or possibly Scotland, Thea mused as she sat in the drawing room pretending to be the perfect young lady while her mother entertained callers.

There were some ancient titles amongst the Scottish nobility, and some great landowners, like the Duke of Buccleuch—who was not in need of a wife, Thea was certain. Although after the Jacobite risings, many of the Scottish lords were still tainted by association, even seventy years after Charles Edward Stuart's hopes of overthrowing the Hanoverian King had been crushed at Culloden.

Irish peers she was certain Mama would discount. For some reason Thea had never been able to fathom, Irish titles were considered second rate. Even the Duke of Wellington made a point of saying that being born and raised in Dublin did not make him an Irishman.

'You have been out of town, I hear,' remarked Lady Beale, who was sitting next to her.

'Yes, into Lincolnshire for a very fleeting visit to my godmother, Lady Holme. She was unwell and we were anxious for her, but she was suffering what proved to be a slight indisposition. She is quite well now and was adamant that I return so as not to miss any of the Season. I am very much looking forward to your musicale the day after tomorrow and would have been sorry to miss it.'

That was enough to divert any curiosity about her travels. Lady Beale possessed both a passion for music and a wealthy and retiring husband and could always be relied upon to start the Season very early with the first of her musicales.

'London is still thin of company,' she was saying now as Thea nodded and tried to look attentive. 'But the Italian contralto Mariella di Luca is in the country for only a few weeks and I could not allow her to leave without engaging her for at least one recital.'

Mama was signalling to her that Mrs Malvern required a fresh cup of tea and she went to pour that, receiving a meaningful look from her mother as she did so. She had no trouble interpreting that signal. Mrs Malvern might not be titled, but she had been left exceedingly well off by her late husband and made no secret of the fact that it would all go in time to her favoured nephew, heir to the Earl of Severton.

Obediently Thea delivered the tea and, as she knew Mama expected, took a seat next to the widow.

'Your second Season, is it not?' Mrs Malvern said after a word of thanks.

'Yes, ma'am.'

'My nephew Richard, Lord Severton, will be in London for it this year. He was at the Congress last year.'

'Many distinguished gentlemen were, I understand,' Thea murmured, a memory of grey eyes and a deceptively innocent smile arriving uninvited into her mind.

Mrs Malvern beamed at the description. 'It has given him quite an air of the cosmopolitan,' she said. 'I am sure he will seem sophisticated compared to some of our less well-travelled gentlemen.'

Thea smiled and nodded and continued to circulate until the last of the callers had rattled off in their smart town carriages.

She was gazing out of the window, lost in jumbled thoughts, when Drage brought in the post.

'Excellent,' Mama said. 'Seven invitations. It seems the Season is starting early this year. The dreadful weather must be driving people into town. We will accept all of these.'

'Yes, Mama.'

'And you are going to need a great many new gowns.'

* * *

The quest for new gowns turned into an entire day shopping, with visits to three fashionable dressmakers in addition to calling at shoe shops, various bazaars and a silk warehouse.

Nothing, of course, would be ready for Lady Beale's musicale the next evening, but however much Mama might sigh over her wardrobe, Thea felt herself perfectly adequately gowned in leaf green trimmed with darker green floss around the neck and twisted ribbons at the hem. A new silk shawl in a Paisley pattern in shades of deep red flattered her hair and old garnet jewellery went well with the green.

Thea eyed Mama's reticule as they waited in the receiving line, wondering if it contained a list of the twenty most eligible gentlemen and a pencil in order to make notes as each was encountered.

She was still feeling the weight of parental disappointment and disapproval over her 'agreement' with the Duke, but Lady Wiveton was too skilled to allow any dissatisfaction with her daughter to show in public.

The salon was crowded. Lady Beale's events were always well attended because she never inflicted second-rate performers, let alone amateurs, upon her guests.

Despite the crush it was, she supposed with a sigh, inevitable that the first person Thea saw as she entered was Hal Forrest.

The Duke of Leamington, she reminded herself.

This was not the amiable, comfortably clad, amusing gentleman whom she'd believed was her friend. This was a very lofty aristocrat indeed, clad in the elegance of severest black, corbeau blue and white that only exceptional tailoring added to a fine physique could achieve.

There was a diamond in his neck cloth, the glint of gold from the watch chin across the admirably flat midriff and, as he raised a hand in greeting to a man approaching him, the gleam of the worn old signet ring on his left hand.

Thea reminded herself that Hal Forrest was a ghost, a figment of her imagination, and that only the man on the other side of the room was a reality. And that reality was simply one more name crossed off the list of people she was not going to marry. Duke or commoner, he was an irrelevance now.

She and Mama began to circulate slowly around the room in a clockwise direction, stopping to exchange a few words with acquaintances as they went. Inevitably they became separated. Thea drifted on, spoke to the Misses Chelmsford, amiable brunette twins who she had always liked, then dodged away with a murmured excuse to avoid Lady Helena Linton, who she cordially disliked.

Lady Helena was blonde, pretty and vivacious. She attracted men in droves, but they all then, inexplicably, failed to come up to scratch. Women had no trouble understanding why, because beneath the smiles and charm Helena was coldly calculating and took no pains to make friends with any female who could not be of use to her. She reminded Thea of Penelope Chelford in looks, but with added slyness and malice.

Thea found herself cornered by two of her mother's closest friends, all smiles and sharp, curious eyes. Had Mama let something slip, made them suspect that she had expected a highly desirable proposal? Surely not. Her mother was very skilled at navigating the shark-infested seas of the Marriage Mart and would never give such a hostage to fortune until she was absolutely certain that the betrothal was reality.

The two matrons expressed concern that Lady Holme had been unwell and delight to hear that she was now recovered. And dear Thea had only been away just over a week? What a long way to travel for such a short time.

Thea knew well that if they could concoct some kind of scandal at her sudden disappearance from London they would have done, but not even two weeks? That defeated even their sharp noses for secrets. Besides, Lady Holme was utterly respectable.

Inwardly smiling at their frustration, Thea moved on, aware, out of the corner of her eye, of a pair of broad Bath superfine-clad shoulders on the other side of the room. Hal—*the Duke*—was standing in the midst of a knot of other gentlemen. With any luck he would stay there, presumably answering their questions about the Congress, the shock of Napoleon's escape and Waterloo, and she could drift past unnoticed.

Not that she was trying to hide from him. Goodness no, she thought, making her way through the crowd. She had nothing to be embarrassed or ashamed about. It was just that she needed a little time to accustom herself to this man not being her friend Hal, but someone else altogether.

Devious, entitled, neglectful—

'Lady Thea. How delightful.'

And there he was, right in front of her.

'Duke.' She inclined her head one chilly, and correct, inch. 'You are a music lover?'

'I am.'

That appeared to be the limit of their conversational resources. Thea was aware of being watched with interest. The most eligible man in London and the highly eligible daughter of the Earl of Wiveton making conversation was one thing, and only to be expected and envied. The pair of them staring speechlessly at each other was quite another, and very intriguing. She had to say something.

'You will be relieved to hear that our mutual godmother, Lady Holme, has completely recovered from her slight indisposition,' Thea said brightly, her voice loud enough for anyone standing close to overhear, even against the background noise of a hundred people all talking at once.

'I am glad to hear that our godmother is well again,' he said, equally clearly. 'You have visited her, I gather.'

'Indeed.' Thea inclined her head again. 'For a few days.'

The Duke bowed slightly and they both moved forward at the same time, unfortunately in the same direction. They collided briefly, Hal stepped backwards sharply, trod on the toes of the elderly Admiral Barwick who was standing behind him, then reached out to steady Thea, who had rocked back on her heels.

'I am quite all right, thank you, Duke,' she said coldly before he could touch her, her temper not improved by hearing the titters from onlookers. She was certain she could hear Lady Helena's voice making some spiteful observation.

'Please look to the Admiral, he appears to be in some distress.'

The Admiral, ancient though he might be, had forgotten none of the salty quarterdeck curses of his naval career. Ladies were clapping their hands over their ears and gentlemen were grinning.

Hal helped the old man off to a chair, apologising loudly enough for his carelessness to drown out the worst of the lively language.

'You are acquainted with the Duke, Lady Thea?' It was one of the Misses Chelmsford. Goodness knew which one. Her eyes were full of curiosity, although her interest seemed perfectly friendly.

'We share a godmother,' Thea said lightly. 'I don't

know about you, but I have far too many godmothers and fathers. I suppose it is inevitable that we find ourselves sharing them with acquaintances on occasion.'

'Leamington is surprisingly clumsy,' Lord Cheney remarked on her other side. 'Doubtless he was confounded by your lovely golden eyes, Lady Thea.'

'Oh, I do hope not, Lord Cheney.' Golden eyes? How much sugar did the idiot think she would swallow? 'How disappointing that the only impression I make on a gentleman is such as to make him recoil and flatten ancient admirals! I would much prefer to have them inspired to send me bouquets, or write poetry.'

Everyone laughed, and she reassured herself that she had defused the situation nicely by making a joke, and a rather flirtatious one at that, rather than attempting to pretend she had never met Hal before. The slightest hint of evasion or defensiveness would alert the hunting instincts of the scandalmongers.

Not that anyone would believe for a moment that she would turn down an offer from a duke. Far more likely was that they would assume that she was angling for him unsuccessfully and that he was the one who had done the refusing. And how humiliating would that be?

She skirted the Duke, who was standing by the still-complaining Admiral, met his gaze and offered a completely false smile of sympathy before continuing to circle the room.

Footmen began to move through the crowd, ringing little hand bells as they went. The performance would be starting soon and the audience began to make their way to the seats.

Hal straightened up from the Admiral with relief, his ears still ringing with an inventive collection of nautical expressions.

'I don't believe my toe is broken after all,' the old man announced, seizing Hal's arm to pull himself to his feet. 'You can help me find a seat, young man. Near the front so I can hear what they're playing.'

'Yes, sir.' As they proceeded at a shuffle towards the audience seating Hal scanned the rows for Thea. He had no wish to embarrass her by appearing to seek her out, especially after that collision and the attention it had attracted, but he did want to stay close.

It would be a long game, the one he was playing, and he dare not rush it. He had seriously misjudged his actions with Thea, perhaps irreparably, although he very much hoped not.

For years he had not given her a thought, then, meeting her at their godmother's house it had seemed only sensible not to admit to who he really was until she had recovered from her shock at discovering what her parents intended.

His judgement had been very wrong, and so had Godmama's. Thea, it seemed, placed a high value on honesty and what he had told himself was simply a slight evasion appeared to her to be outright lying and deception.

Persuading Thea to marry him was going to take a great deal of work on his part and forgiveness on hers, but he was determined that he would make it happen. Somehow. He liked her, he desired her, he respected her and he found that the liking was the overriding emotion.

'I left my ear trumpet somewhere. With my cloak, I expect,' the Admiral announced as Hal lowered him cautiously onto one of the fragile gilt-painted chairs. 'Fetch it, would you, my boy.'

It was an order and Hal caught the eye of a footman who was clearly scandalised at the thought of a duke being ordered around like a valet.

'I'll fetch it, Your Grace,' the man said, and hurried off.

'Your Grace?' the old man echoed. 'Who are you, then?'

'Leamington, Admiral.'

'Good gad and so you are. Spitting image of your grandsire. I remember—'

The footman appeared with the ear trumpet to interrupt a thoroughly embarrassing anecdote about his grandfather and a certain actress and Hal was able to slip away, restraining himself with an effort from mopping his brow.

Almost all the seats were taken except three next to

each other in front of where Thea was sitting between two identical brunettes. Twins, Hal realised after a startled moment when he wondered if fretting over Thea was turning his brain and he was seeing things.

With murmured apologies he worked his way along to the first vacant chair and sat down. He was in front of one brunette and, if he turned his head just a little to the left, as though scanning the empty dais, he could see Thea out of the corner of his eye.

Her expression was not encouraging. Did she think he had deliberately placed himself in front of her? Did she believe he had engineered that collision just now?

Hal twisted in his seat and smiled at the twin behind him. 'I hope I am not obstructing your view, ma'am. Assisting the Admiral left the choice of seats somewhat restricted.' He kept his attention firmly on her face.

She blushed prettily. 'Not at all, Your Grace. I can see perfectly well, thank you.'

'Forgive me for addressing you without an introduction. Perhaps Lady Thea would be kind enough to make us known to each other.'

'Of course.' He knew Thea well enough now to recognise irritation behind the sweet tone. 'Miss Antonia, the Duke of Leamington. Duke, Miss Antonia Chelmsford. And on my other side—'

Both twins laughed. 'We have confused you again,' the nearest one said. 'I am the elder by five minutes, so I am Miss Chelmsford. Clara. This is my sister,

Antonia. But we answer to both names, you know, Your Grace, we have had to learn to.'

Hal stood up and turned to shake hands.

'I believe they are about to start,' Thea said repressively.

With a smile for his two new acquaintances, Hal sat down and fixed his attention on the stage. The back of his neck prickled. Was Thea fixing her gaze on him, radiating disapproval, or was he simply fantasying, imagining an interest in himself that she simply did not have?

Instinct told him that her reaction to the discovery of his identity meant that she had stronger feelings for him than she was prepared to admit, but perhaps that too was wishful thinking.

Hal settled as comfortably as a long-legged man could on the spindly little chairs and turned his attention on the dais, where Lady Beale was leading out the Italian contralto to enthusiastic applause. He had heard the singer before, in Vienna, and knew they were due to be royally entertained. Even so, the short hairs on his nape still prickled: it was not easy to forget the close proximity of Lady Thea Campion.

The music was sublime and Hal let himself drift away with it, his eyes unfocused on the wall behind the pianoforte. The first songs were romantic, heartfelt, and he felt again that sensation he had experienced when he had leaned out of the tower, looked down the dizzying space to see Thea's upturned face. Heartfelt…heartache?

What was the matter with him? He had found the woman who would make him an ideal duchess, he had taken a liking to her and he had managed to give her a dislike of him. That was something that could only be rectified by careful planning, strategy and patience. He must show Thea that she could trust him and then he could begin to build on that tentative friendship that had formed before she knew who he was. And after that—

The applause roused him from his reverie and the pianoforte player struck a rousing chord, the music sweeping into something that sounded Middle European, exciting, rhythmic. He had a sudden mental picture of Thea in his arms, dancing to this music, sweeping around the floor, her cheeks rosy with exhilaration, those lovely eyes laughing and excited.

Dancing. That he had not included in his half-formed plans, but he would now. Surely Thea would love to dance? He knew he wanted to dance with her.

He would open up Leamington House, throw a ball, create a stage for Thea to shine on. Could he do that even though he was in mourning? He had respected and admired his father and had been sincerely sorry to have lost him comparatively young, but he could not feel that cutting himself off socially for a year was necessary to show respect. Certainly nobody seemed shocked to see him here.

Yes, he would hold his ball. There would be waltzes and he would make certain that Thea danced two of them with him. And he had another idea, nothing to do with dancefloors, as the singer changed tempo again and began to sing of roses, moonlight and nightingales.

There was a great deal to plan and he could not put off employing a new secretary any longer.

Chapter Eleven

'He was there. Leamington was at the recital,' Mama said the moment the carriage door closed behind them.

'Yes, Mama, I know. I spoke to him.'

Thea smoothed the folds of her evening cloak around her legs, her gloves running over the satin with the softest of whispers.

'And he sat right in front of you. A most marked attention, I thought.'

'He was in front of Clara Chelmsford. And he had very little choice, because old Admiral Barwick was demanding his attention until virtually all the chairs were taken. He actually ordered the Duke to go and fetch his ear trumpet, would you believe?'

In the gloom of the carriage she could see the swoop of a light-coloured glove as her mother dismissed that irrelevance with a gesture. 'Leamington is not avoiding you, that is the important thing. It would be disastrous if he showed displeasure, or even cut you.'

'I am sure the Duke is too much of a gentleman to do any such thing.'

'I suppose you are right. But any *froideur* would be noticed, would be disastrous.'

'We encountered each other and it was perfectly civil,' Thea said firmly. 'There is nothing to worry about, Mama.'

'Other than finding you a suitable husband now you have wantonly refused the most eligible man in the country,' her mother said with a snap.

'Yes, Mama.' It seemed the only tactful thing to say.

'You are dressed for riding,' Lady Wiveton said disapprovingly as Thea came in to breakfast two days after Lady Beale's recital.

'I thought I would go into Hyde Park and take advantage of the sunshine after yesterday's rain,' Thea said as she lifted the cover from a chaffing dish on the sideboard, wrinkled her nose at the smell of smoked fish and moved on to the eggs.

'Well, do make sure you take a groom. Remember we are not in the countryside here.'

There didn't seem to be much to say about that, so Thea nodded and sat down as her mother returned to the pile of letters that Drage had set by her place.

She smiled her thanks to the footman who poured her coffee and was about to raise the first forkful of eggs to her mouth when her mother gave a faint shriek and waved a gold-edged card at her.

'This is wonderful! He is holding a ball!'

'Who is?' Thea asked, putting down her fork.

'Leamington, of course. You must change as soon as you have finished your breakfast and we will go to Madame Lanchester. We will order a new ball gown immediately.'

'When is the ball?' Thea asked, mentally passing in review the two, unworn, ball gowns that were hanging in her dressing room already.

'In two weeks' time.'

'Then I cannot see the urgency, Mama. Do I even need a new gown? We could keep back the amber silk until then: I do think it is very fine. Besides, I have a slight headache, which I am certain a ride in the fresh air will cure.'

'Very well,' her mother said, regarding her beadily across the table. 'It is fatal to be frowning with a headache, which you are. The next thing we know, you will be developing dreadful lines between your eyebrows. Disastrous.'

Thea escaped after her second cup of coffee, wondering just why her mother was so very concerned about the Duke's ball. Obviously, it would be a major society event, but the same people would be there as would be at any other ball. More of them, of course, because who was going to turn down an invitation to the Duke of Leamington's first ball?

Everyone on Mama's list of eligible gentlemen would be attending if they were in London, so perhaps that was what she was so concerned about—showing off Thea to as many of them as possible.

On the other hand, Thea had been out in society for one Season already, so many of those gentlemen would have had plenty of opportunity to become accustomed to her charms.

But not perhaps wearing in the amber silk dress with the gauze overskirt, she thought with an inner smile as she asked Drage to let Hoskins, her groom, know that she was ready.

Upstairs Jennie eased her into her tight jacket, pinned her dashing little tricorne with its veil and green feather securely and handed her gloves and whip. 'Have a pleasant ride, my lady.'

'Thank you. I am sure I will,' Thea said.

She was hoping to find the park relatively peaceful. The most dashing riders, male and female, would have been out early, taking advantage of the hour to gallop in a park where even a restrained canter was often frowned upon. The fashionable crowd would be riding and driving in the afternoon, so that left the middle of the morning quieter.

Of course, there was the added hazard of nursemaids and their charges, often boisterously running about where one would least expect them, small boys chasing ducks and unruly dogs in pursuit of both, but go further away from the Queen's Walk and the reservoir, and it should be quiet enough.

She ran downstairs, the long skirt of her habit

caught up over her arm, and Drage opened the door to reveal Hoskins on his bay hack, holding the reins of Lara, Thea's bay mare.

He swung down from the saddle and came to boost her up. 'Where to, my lady?'

'Hyde Park, Hoskins.'

The air was fresh and damp, holding the promise of rain to come and, when they reached the park, the scent of the fallen leaves that covered the swathes of grass.

'This will be the last fine day for a while, my lady, I reckon,' the groom observed.

Thea noticed him scanning the park, watching for hazards, for loose dogs and dubious characters. It was part of his job to keep her safe and she appreciated his care, while chaffing at the lack of freedom.

But Hoskins knew her well and, as soon as he had decided that it was safe, he dropped back by several lengths and Thea rode on with at least the illusion of being alone.

Lara was fresh and eager to run, and Thea let her canter strongly, holding her back from a full-out gallop.

The speed should have been exhilarating and enjoyable, but after a moment Thea realised that it was bringing back memories that she could have well done without. Riding stirrup to stirrup with Hal, laughing as they galloped, free as birds, across the countryside, enjoying matching horse against horse. Simply being that uncomplicated thing, two people who liked each other learning how to become friends.

She reined back, bringing Lara down to a slow canter, then a trot, the joy of the ride draining out of her. This was foolish. One man had proved a disappointment, but she should not allow that to dominate her life.

It is not as though I am in love with him, despite Godmama's best efforts, she thought. *Now, that really would be something to be sad about. I am simply feeling low in spirits because of the thought of another Season and this time having to think seriously about finding a husband.*

Because what was the alternative? To set up her own household at her age would be a scandal and besides, Papa would never allow her the money to do it. Remain unmarried but living with her parents? Thea gave a decisive shake of her head. She had seen too many unmarried daughters dwindling into their mother's shadows. They were a disappointment, but a useful one when an elderly aunt needed a companion, or a sister-in-law wanted help with a brood of unruly children.

Of course, there were always Good Works. Thea lips twitched at her own mental capital letters. She felt no attraction to supporting missionary societies, and she suspected that fallen women would laugh in her face if she attempted to redeem them. Then there were great causes that she suspected a young single woman with no control of her fortune could contribute little to—the abolition of slavery, the extension of the suffrage—sprang to mind.

But there were also others where she felt she might do some good—education for girls, the encouragement of money-making opportunities for women, for example. Someone had opened a bazaar in Soho, renting out stalls at affordable prices to widows and women in reduced circumstances so they could sell their needlework, crafts and baked goods. Perhaps more of those would be helpful.

Thea was deep in contemplation of a career in charitable endeavours when she saw the grey horse. The large grey horse that was cantering along one of the rides that would converge with hers. Juno.

She reined Lara down to a walk and almost turned her to ride back the way she had come.

But why should I? I have a perfect right to be riding in the park and I am quite capable of exchanging a civil greeting with a passing rider.

Like most accidents it happened in a split second. A wooden hoop bowled out from behind a small clump of low bushes, just where the two rides intersected, and a small boy ran after it.

The hoop was right in front of the grey mare and, at speed, she had no chance of missing it. Forelegs entangled, she went down.

Thea urged Lara forward as Hal somehow got out of the saddle and half jumped, half tumbled towards the child, catching him and rolling him clear of half a ton of horse and four thrashing iron-shod hooves.

Thea slid from the saddle, conscious of Hopkins behind her. Juno flailed to get her legs under her, then scrambled to her feet.

'My lady, you stay clear,' Hopkins called as she slid from the saddle and started forwards.

There was a great deal of screaming happening. Thea left her groom to look after the horses and discovered a nursemaid having a fit of hysterics over Hal, who was still sitting on the ground holding a wailing small boy.

Nobody, by some miracle, appeared to be bleeding, and all the limbs she could see looked straight.

Thea marched up to the young woman, took her by the shoulders and gave her a brisk shake. 'Stop it! You are frightening the child. He is quite unharmed.'

After a moment, the shrieks dissolved into tears, then hiccups.

'What is his name?' Thea asked, more gently.

'Master Anthony, ma'am. I'm sorry, ma'am, but I thought—'

'I'm sure you did. Now, you go and sit on that tree stump over there and calm yourself. I will look after Master Anthony.'

And make certain Hal is as undamaged as he seems.

She walked back and crouched down. Hal, hatless and with a bruise already darkening over his right eye, looked up at her.

'He is not hurt, just frightened,' he said.

Thea nodded. 'Anthony,' she said firmly. 'What is all this fuss about?'

The child lifted his face from Hal's shoulder and stared at her, indignation at her lack of sympathy written large on his tear-blubbered face. 'Big horse fell on me!'

'No, it did not. You tripped it up by accident with your hoop and this gentleman fell on you to keep you safe. Now, does anything hurt? Think carefully.'

The no-nonsense tone was having an effect. The boy obviously made a mental review of his body inside and out and managed a smile. 'I'm all right,' he announced, sounding surprised.

'In that case, you must go and comfort your nursemaid, because you gave her a very big shock and upset her.' Thea took hold of the boy, stood him on his feet and pointed him in the direction of the maid.

'You were very good with him,' Hal remarked absently, getting to his feet. His attention was all on his horse.

'I have several younger brothers,' Thea said, then realised she was talking to the air. Hal and Hopkins were examining Juno.

Which was only right and proper, Thea told herself, as she went to join them.

'Her legs are undamaged, Your Grace,' Hopkins announced, revealing that he recognised Hal.

Thea wondered just how much the Wiveton family's staff at knew about her parents' failed plans.

Hal was running his hands all over the big horse, stopping at intervals to press his ear to its ribs and listen. 'I can't find any damage. Her breathing is clear.'

'Good thing the ground is soft and you were on grass, Your Grace,' Hopkins pronounced.

'Are you hurt?' Thea asked when it seemed she might finally get Hal's full attention. 'You have a nasty bruise over your eye. Did you lose consciousness?'

'No, I know, and no,' he replied, looking at her directly for the first time and smiling. 'Thank you for your assistance, Lady Thea.'

She blinked at the formality, then realised that both Hopkins and the nursemaid were within hearing. 'I could hardly have ridden straight past, now could I?' she asked tartly, then, 'You saved that child's life. Your reactions were incredibly fast.'

Hal shrugged, and she was aware of the play of muscle through his coat, of the breadth of his shoulders.

Stop it. He is an attractive male, that is all. It does not mean that you have to take notice. Or yearn to touch.

Someone cleared their throat meaningfully and Thea realised that Hopkins was holding the reins of all three horses and gazing off into the distance in such an obviously tactful manner that it was positively embarrassing.

Thea turned abruptly and went to the nurse, who had recovered herself and was wiping the child's face.

'Are you able to get home now?' she asked. 'Or would you like me to call at Master Anthony's home and have them send assistance?'

'Goodness, no, ma'am.' The young woman looked appalled. 'We are quite all right now, ma'am.'

She would probably lose her position if the child's parents realised how close to disaster he had been, but it had been an accident, not carelessness, she was sure, so the less fuss made, the better.

Thea shook hands with Master Anthony, who was politely holding out a sticky paw, and went back to find that Hopkins was mounted, his face a careful blank, and Hal was waiting to help her into the saddle.

Yes, Hopkins knows, she thought as she put her booted foot into Hal's linked hands and was lifted up.

And if Hopkins knew, then probably the entire household was aware that she had been supposed to marry the Duke and had refused him. Her parents normally treated the servants as useful items of furniture and were quite capable of holding highly personal conversations in front of them. Thea was very aware of them as individuals with their own personalities. She thought that their staff were all loyal, but she cringed internally at the thought of the gossip any indiscretion would feed.

'Thank you, Duke,' she said calmly, finding the stirrup, arranging her skirts and gathering up the reins in a manner that she hoped demonstrated that she did not require any further assistance. He had been so very careful not to touch her except in the most respectful way that it made her almost more aware of him, if that were possible.

'I do hope you do not have too much of a headache,' she added. 'You are going to have to come up with some convincing excuse for that bruise, unless you wish to be teased for having your horse fall over a child's hoop.'

Hal swung up into the saddle. 'I shall invent some tale of derring-do and a maiden rescued from a hammer-wielding villain,' he said, straight-faced. 'Good day, Lady Thea. Thank you for your help,' he added to Hopkins.

'Now, that, my lady, is a horseman,' the groom remarked as they sat watching the tall figure canter away. It was probably the highest accolade he could bestow.

'Indeed,' Thea agreed. 'But I do not think this is a story that should be repeated, do you? To anyone.'

The groom looked at her, the smile lines creasing his weather-beaten face. 'I don't tell tales, Lady Thea. Not about good men.'

That evening brought, mercifully, no social engagements.

'I suppose we should expect it at this date,' her mother said with a dissatisfied sigh at the thought of an evening spent at the dinner table with her own family.

Lord Wiveton, who would take himself off to his club afterwards in any case, merely grunted.

'I am quite glad of the rest, Mama,' Thea ventured. 'We will get little enough of it once the Season begins properly.'

'I believe that Leamington's ball will signal the start this year, even though it is early,' her mother said. 'And when I think…' She closed her lips tightly and glared at the épergne in the centre of the table.

Thea knew what she had been about to say. *And when I think we could have been accepting felicitations on your betrothal.*

She felt like sighing herself, wishing she had not discovered that Hal was capable of deceit to gain his own ends, that he was a man who would lure her into a friendship under false pretences because what he wanted was a convenient wife and she happened to match exactly the list of desirable qualities for a duke's bride.

She might have decided she liked him when she met him for the first time as an adult, might happily have married him. Perhaps she never would have discovered the devious side to his character.

Although, she reminded herself as she drank her soup, she would have known that he was selfish enough to have left her on her shelf until it suited him to come for her. Just because she was having trouble forgetting the way that he had dived to shelter that child from those thrashing hooves was no reason to forget why she had not wanted to marry him in the first place.

'I am looking forward to the Hamptons' ball tomorrow night,' she said brightly. 'I have high hopes of meeting some new and interesting people.'

'That is true, dear,' Mama said, looking more cheerful. 'Daphne Hampton's nephew Marcus is Earl of Porchester and he is unwed. He was not in London for last Season because he was in the Army and I had quite forgotten him. I believe that the Duke spoke most highly of him.'

'Ha—? I mean, Leamington?'

'No, of course not, dear. The Duke of Wellington. He expressed himself quite strongly when the old Earl died and Porchester sold out. Such a pity—he would look particularly dashing in his regimentals.'

'Better, perhaps, not to be influenced by the false glamour of a uniform,' Thea said. It was difficult enough to judge a man's character without adorning him with that classic beguiler of young ladies—a dashing scarlet coat trimmed with gold braid.

Chapter Twelve

The Countess of Hampton's ball was a glittering affair, immediately pronounced a great success.

Perhaps piqued by the news that the Duke of Leamington was also holding a ball, Lady Hampton had held nothing back. Not only was there an excellent string ensemble, but there were Pandean pipes as well, and the band of her nephew's regiment had been persuaded to play during supper. Rumours were already flying that Champagne was scarce now throughout London, she had bought up so much.

The ballroom had been dressed on a theme of ancient Greece to complement its marble columns and antique statuary. Swags of laurel and olive decorated the walls, white muslin was draped everywhere and small pages in white tunics stood around holding bowls overflowing with grapes.

The background proved an admirable foil for the ladies' gowns, the footmen worked hard to press wine into every hand and even the rain pounding down on the roof of the conservatory which led off the ballroom did not manage to dampen the effect of a sunlit Mediterranean garden too much.

Thea was firmly resolved to enjoy herself, to flirt with any man who attracted her and to secure at least one dance with the Earl of Porchester.

In that she was immediately successful. Her hostess had her husband on her right side and her nephew on her left in the receiving line and Thea was conscious that he was regarding her with interest as he shook her hand.

'Do promise me a dance,' he said. 'I shall come and hope to claim the first waltz as soon as I am free of my duty here.'

Thea found herself smiling back at a pair of amused hazel eyes, an earnest expression and a beak of a nose that the Duke of Wellington himself might have envied.

'I would be delighted,' she said, and meant it. He looked…interesting. Not at all handsome, but very attractive. Honest and straightforward? Who could tell—certainly not she.

Her mood dipped when almost the first person she encountered as she entered the ballroom was Lady Helena Linton looking particularly radiant in powder blue with silver ribbons.

'Lady Thea, good evening. A delightful crush, is it not? My goodness, what an *original* hairstyle. How very, er, dashing of you.'

Jennie, experimenting, had managed to twist Thea's hair into a pile of shining curls with one twisting lock falling to her shoulder. In Thea's opinion—and she was sensitive about her hair, even though it was no longer so very red—it was both stylish and flattering, although perhaps a touch adventurous for an unmarried lady.

'Why, thank you,' she gushed, as though she had no idea it had been meant as anything but a compliment. 'My new lady's maid created it. I was *so* lucky to obtain her services. I expect you have found it difficult to find anyone to give you a touch that's a little out of the ordinary, but it is worth trying.'

And with a warm smile and the guiltily delightful sensation of having been at least as catty as Lady Helena, she moved on into the room.

Marcus Greyson, the Earl of Porchester, found her ten minutes later and ruthlessly disposed of the two young men who were asking her for dances.

'A waltz, of course,' he said when she opened her card. 'Or have I missed them all?'

'No, my lord,' she said, flattered despite herself by his eagerness. 'The second?'

'Excellent. And another, if you please?' he asked hopefully.

'I would be delighted,' Thea said, 'The fourth set? They are all country dances,' and laughed as his face fell.

She strongly suspected that his aunt, on receiving

her favourite nephew back unscathed from the wars, had looked around and had made her own little list of the most eligible young ladies for him. She knew she would feature on it—not that she took any credit for that, one could not be responsible for one's parentage, or the good fortune to be born into wealth—and she thought none the worse of him for working his way through his aunt's suggestions.

At least, she thought darkly, *he is getting on with it and hasn't left some unfortunate young lady waiting for years while he went to war.*

Even as she thought it, she was aware of the sensation of being watched, turned and found herself standing a foot away from Hal.

'Duke.'

'Lady Thea. May I crave the favour of a dance?'

'Crave? How dramatic. You may certainly request one, of course. A country dance, perhaps? The one after supper is free.'

'That would be delightful, thank you.'

Thea found herself somewhat breathless and realised that she had hardly glanced higher than the diamond stickpin in his neck cloth. With what felt like a physical effort she looked up and gasped. 'Oh, your poor face!'

He had made no effort to disguise the bruise that discoloured his forehead and had spread down to give him a magnificent black eye. 'Quite the Beast to cause all the Beauties assembled here to shudder, don't you think?'

'I believe that it would take more than a bruise to discourage young ladies from dancing with the most eligible man in London.'

'True. Even you have accepted a dance.'

'*Even* me?'

'We know that *you* are the one woman who has no time for the most eligible man in London,' he said with an edge to his words.

'I never said that I had no time for you. I said I wouldn't marry you because you are a—' Thea bit off the rest of what she had almost said. They had kept the volume of their exchange conversational but she was aware that heads had begun to turn, perhaps alerted by something in the tone.

She laughed and tapped Hal's arm playfully with her closed fan as though they had been exchanging playful banter and the watchers turned away, losing interest in just another flirtation.

With a faint sketch of a curtsey, she walked on. Did he turn to look after her? she wondered, her spine tingling. There had been anger in that exchange, anger at her rejection that he had not shown before, and Thea found herself shaken by it.

It was all his fault, she told herself. Not hers. She had been in the right, the injured party, the one deceived. She was still in the right and the fact that he could be angry about it just showed how justified she had been.

Viscount Lammerton broke into her thoughts with a request for a dance and accepted the very first with an expression of surprise. He was a little shy, certainly unsure of himself, and had clearly expected to be fobbed off with a set of country dances towards the end of the evening.

Thea liked him, but felt nothing that would prompt her to encourage his tentative advances and scolded herself for being so unsettled by the encounter with Hal that she had offered the opening dance. Her parents would be horrified at the thought of a mere viscount for her and this would probably earn her a lecture from Mama.

She paused to talk to a small group of her friends near the door to the conservatory and, glancing inside, saw that it was a long rectangular room built along the length of one side of the ballroom. It was filled with greenery.

Miss Jameson had noticed that too. 'Perfect for a flirtation,' she said with a giggle.

'Even better for a kiss.' That was Lady Gloria Hunter, who had a reputation for being fast. 'I have been here before, so I speak from experience,' she added with a naughty twinkle. 'And it is very convenient, because there is another door at the far end, so if anyone comes in you can always escape.'

Shy little Miss Wilson blushed rosily and Thea, seeing Giles Duncan approaching, laughed and moved on. He was a prosy young man with a passion for fishing and, apparently, little else, and she had no intention of adding him to her dance card.

Almost at the end of the room she swerved slightly. Ahead of her were Helena Linton and her mother, Lady Linton, their heads together.

Plotting. The word sprang into Thea's mind, startling her. The two women turned and looked at the conservatory door just behind them and then across the crowded ballroom. Instinctively Thea turned too, tried to see whom they were staring at, but it could have been almost anyone.

She gave herself a little shake. Really, it was unhealthy to allow that woman to annoy her. It gave Helena an importance she most certainly did not merit.

The Pandean pipes ensemble ceased to play and retired amidst a smattering of applause as the string players came in and arranged themselves on the dais. People began to shift to the edges of the ballroom, ladies stood with casual elegance near the dance floor so they could be easily seen and the chaperones settled themselves in the grouping of chairs that had been set out for them. From there they would exchange gossip, demolish reputations, be lethally polite to each other and keep a sharp eye on each and every single young lady.

Gradually, as the players finished tuning their instruments, gentlemen found their partners and led them towards the centre and Lord Lammerton appeared at Thea's side, awkwardly offering his hand.

Fortunately, he was a better dancer than one would guess on first meeting him, and Thea found she could relax and fear neither for her toes, nor her hems, despite the first dance being a complex quadrille. His small talk was limited, but the frequent separations of the steps made conversation impossible anyway, so that was no impediment to her enjoyment.

When their dance was finished he led her off the floor and straight into the waiting hands of the Earl of Porchester who must have been watching out for her.

'A vigorous set,' he remarked as Lord Lammerton bowed and left.

'Very,' Thea agreed, fanning herself as the Earl led her to a chair. Fortunately, the orchestra had settled down to a few minutes of what she always thought of as twiddly music, presumably recognising that everyone needed to regain their breath.

'A glass of lemonade?' Marcus Greyson asked. He was already on his feet and gesturing to a passing waiter.

Thea accepted it gratefully and set herself to attend to his conversation, which, considering that he was an attractive and intelligent man with an easy manner, was proving quite difficult. Something was distracting her, niggling at the back of her mind, and she could not quite put her finger on it.

She talked and smiled and laughed and then, when

the music changed with a flourish to announce the next dance, she realised that she must have been showing an unwise degree of enthusiasm. The Earl was smiling into her eyes with some warmth and somehow his manner, when he held out his hand and escorted her onto the floor, was proprietorial.

Now what have I done? Thea smiled brightly as he took her into hold for the waltz. *And a waltz, of all things.*

There was no escaping the intimacy of this dance as there was with any of the others, with their frequent changes of partner, side-steps and promenades.

But why am I worrying? He is a very eligible gentleman and I like him. Why should I not encourage him?

As she thought it, Thea caught sight of Hal on the other side of the ballroom. He was not dancing; instead, he was standing watching. Watching her.

Surely not. Why should he?

Marcus swept her around a corner in an advanced move that had her forgetting Hal and everything else in an effort to remember her steps and keep pace with a very good, and apparently very adventurous, partner.

A very attractive partner, and one who appeared to be finding her interesting too. She would be careful, Thea promised herself. Not let herself be carried away and give too much encouragement tonight. Tomorrow she would see what she could find out about the Earl of Porchester.

She ran through a mental list of her closest friends.

Who knew all the gossip but were loyal enough not to add her interest in a man to the scandal broth?

Gloria, Clara, Paulina—

The music reached a crescendo, stopped, and Marcus swept her to a halt, kept hold for just a fraction too long and then stepped back, bowing.

Thea curtseyed. 'My goodness, that was stimulating!' She flipped open her fan as they walked off the floor.

'Are you engaged for the next dance or would you care to sit it out?'

'I would like to sit, I believe,' Thea said with a laugh. 'It is clear I have not danced at a ball for several months. I had not thought myself so enfeebled as to be glad of a rest this early in the evening.'

'That was a very energetic waltz, I must admit,' he said as they took seats almost halfway along the wall between the two conservatory doors. 'I should have been more moderate, but it is such a pleasure to find myself with a partner who can really dance.'

'It takes two to make a good partnership,' Thea said and then could have bitten her tongue when she saw the warmth in his gaze. He had read far more into that simple statement than she had intended.

I need more time. To what? To get to know him? To recover my trust in men? Or to recover from Hal?

She had turned her head to compose herself and so she saw Hal go through the door into the conservatory, alone. It was a retreat, she thought, sensing something from the blankness of his expression and the set of his shoulders. He was not enjoying this business of being the most eligible, the most pursued, man in the Marriage Mart, of having to make a choice of a duchess when surrounded by eager young ladies and predatory mothers.

You had a perfectly suitable bride, if only you had treated her properly, she thought, looking away and facing Marcus again as the orchestra struck up to signal the next dance.

Over his shoulder she saw Helena Linton. She was moving, not towards the dance floor with a partner, but alone and through the other conservatory door. Behind her, her mother watched, a little smile on her lips.

There was something furtive about the way Helena had moved, something secretive about that little smile.

'Excuse me.' Thea stood up abruptly and, of course, Marcus rose too. 'I must just…er…'

As she'd hoped, he appeared to assume she had a sudden urgent need to find the ladies' retiring room.

'I'll be back in a moment, but please don't feel you have to wait for me.' She hurried off, then glanced back. Tactfully, Marcus had resumed his seat, crossed his legs and was looking in the opposite direction.

Thea pushed open the conservatory door and slipped inside, closing it behind her. Immediately she was enveloped in steamy air, redolent of warm earth, leaf mould and green growing things.

The space was deserted so far as she could see,

which, admittedly, was not far. Lady Hampton had clearly spared no expense on this and, from the heating system to the number and variety of plants, it was lavish.

Thea threaded her way down a path, around a clump of palms and past a statue of a partly clad nymph admiring her reflection in a still pool of water.

Then she heard Hal's voice.

'Madam, I should leave—'

'Oh, do not be so stuffy, Your Grace! You see, I know who you are. I am Helena Linton and I *so* wanted to meet you. My Papa, Lord Linton, is exceedingly interested in the Congress and I know you were there. It must have been fascinating. Do tell me all about it.'

'Certainly, Lady Helena, but not in here,' Hal said firmly.

Idiot man! Stop being polite—just walk away. Walk out now, this is a trap.

Thea hurried around the next corner in the twisting path and found them. Hal must have been sitting on a bench underneath a large flowering plant of some kind and had risen when Lady Helena found him. He was trapped now, with a wall of foliage at his back and sides and, short of barging his way past her, or crashing through the planting, there was no way out.

Lady Helena took a step forward, gave a faint shriek and threw herself at Hal, who, of course, caught her. 'Oh! I tripped!'

Now what am I supposed to do?

Hal had reflexively closed his arms around the woman clinging to him and it looked exceedingly compromising.

'Oh, thank goodness!' Thea said loudly. 'What a relief to find someone. Now I am safe. If that horrible man has followed me… Oh, Lady Helena, I do apologise for interrupting your conversation, but if I could just remain with you for a few minutes, he is sure to go away. Duke, I did not recognise you for a moment with that palm frond in your face.'

Hal, who was admirably fast at taking his cue, swung around, deposited Lady Helena on the bench and strode to Thea's side. 'Lady Thea, has some scoundrel been making a nuisance of himself? Tell me who it was and I will—'

'Helena, dear.' Lady Linton's voice came from just the other side of the palms and Thea realised she must have entered quietly and come some way into the conservatory before calling out. 'Where have you got to, dear?'

She rounded the corner and stopped dead. Thea managed to keep a straight face, despite the older woman's expression. Chagrin, anger and disappointment fought to escape from behind a rigidly smiling mask.

'Lady Linton. Goodness, I am *so* pleased to see you. I had to take refuge in here because Mr… Perhaps I had best not name him as I see the Duke is ready to call him out—anyway, he was making himself most objectionable and so I ran in here and then I found Lady Helena, which was *such* a relief, and then the Duke who had come to her aid because she had tripped…'

Thea prattled on, although it was merely background noise to the wordless drama in front of her. Hal edged closer to her. Helena, left alone on the bench, and a safe distance from him, looked ready to burst into tears of sheer temper and Lady Linton had the appearance of a kettle about to boil over.

'Perhaps you could escort me out, Duke?' Thea said, managing to put a faint quaver into her voice. She put her hand on his arm and he laid his over hers.

'Of course. I will take you to your Mama. What a shocking thing to happen. I do wish you would tell me the name of the swine who was bothering you.'

As soon as the Linton ladies had vanished from view Thea freed her hand, pointed silently to the far door and hurried towards the one she had entered by.

Lord Porchester was where she had left him, patiently waiting. He rose as soon as he saw her.

'I do apologise,' she said, sitting down again. 'A lace snapped,' she added in a whisper, wondering if she could blush to order, then deciding that she was probably flushed enough from that encounter in the conservatory to counterfeit embarrassment.

'Difficult,' he said sympathetically and then glanced up to find Hal standing there. 'Leamington. Good to see you back from Europe. I was sorry to hear about your father.'

'And I to hear about yours, Porchester. May I have the next dance, Lady Thea?' Hal was looking particularly stern.

What on earth was he looking so grim about? She had thought he might have been grateful for her actions just now.

Chapter Thirteen

Hal stood there in front of them, waiting. The Earl, next to her, was clearly expecting her to rise and accept. You did not turn a gentleman's offer of a dance down, unless you asked him to sit it out with you, otherwise you were considered unable to dance for the rest of the evening and could accept no other partners.

'You only granted me the one when we spoke earlier,' Hal added. 'I have been chastising myself for timidity in not pressing for another. Unless, of course, you are awaiting your partner.'

As it happened this next was the only dance free on her card, which was quite deliberate, because she always liked to have a little breathing space. To say that was tantamount to refusing.

Thea stood up. 'Thank you for the dance and your company, Lord Porchester. Duke, I would be delighted.'

He led her onto the floor and she glanced hastily

at her card. It was a country dance and one danced mainly with, or next to, one's partner.

'What just happened?' he asked as they took their places and waited for the rest of the set to form. 'I mean besides my being as foolish as a green girl and wandering into the conservatory, thus laying myself open to as neat a little ambush as I can imagine. I should have learned my lesson about conservatories by now. Was someone really bothering you? In which case, I will most happily deal with him.'

'I saw you enter and I saw the…er…other two parties watching and then one of them entered by the other door.' Best not to mention names out loud here.

Thea bowed politely to the couples joining them and there was no opportunity to speak for a few minutes as the dance started. At last they found themselves standing together at the end of a row, waiting while those at the top of the group set to the opposite dancers.

'I thought it was tended to entrap you,' she said, low-voiced under cover of the music. 'But obviously, nobody would imagine that you had lured two young women in there to have your wicked way with them simultaneously, so I knew all I had to do was appear and their plan was foiled. We chaperoned each other, in effect.'

'You did that for me? Why should you?' Hal asked. He sounded incredulous.

Thea stared at him.

You have to ask? Because I'm a nice person, that's why.

It wasn't all the truth, of course.

He had put himself into a very dangerous position, simply by not thinking, and the reason he had not been thinking about basic self-preservation was because his head had been full of thoughts about Thea.

And she had rescued him. Why should she do such a thing? It could have had unpleasant consequences for her, and she had certainly made enemies of the Lintons.

'You did that for me? Why should you?' he asked.

Thea looked at him as though he had broken into a jig. 'Because I dislike Helena Linton,' she said frigidly. Then she curtseyed to the man opposite her and he realised it was their turn to dance again.

Her expression as she watched him from the other side of the circle was superficially pleasant, but her eyes were cold and, somehow, hurt. He had wounded her by asking about her reason for saving him, he realised. She had done it out of decency, possibly the last flickers of their friendship, and he had questioned her as though he expected nothing good from her.

The lady next to him coughed pointedly and he hurried into the steps he was supposed to perform. Eventually, after an interminable string of bows, twirls, advances and retreats, he found himself back next to Thea.

'I'm sorry,' he said out of the corner of his mouth. 'I should have had no need to ask. Thank you, Thea.'

He looked down to his side and met her gaze as she looked up. Ruefully, she smiled. 'It was true, I do not like her. But I don't think you deserve her, either.'

'A lesser woman would have thought it a very fair revenge,' Hal observed.

'I don't think revenge does anyone any good,' Thea said.

'I can only hope that young lady thinks the same way as you do. I should watch your back for a while, if I were you,' he warned.

Ten minutes later the dance swirled to its end. Thea curtseyed, Hal bowed, and he took her hand to walk her from the floor.

'There is my next partner, come to claim me,' she said when he showed no sign of releasing her.

'Then allow me to deliver you to him. And thank you, Thea. That is twice recently you have come to my rescue.'

'Twice?'

'You saved me from a sobbing infant and an hysterical nursemaid,' he said. 'I am very much in your debt. As though I was not already,' he added under his breath as another man stepped forward. 'Hardcastle. I reluctantly surrender Lady Thea to you. Do not tread on her toes or you will answer to me.'

They all laughed and Thea was led away, leaving him standing looking after her.

'Am I to see you as a rival, Duke?' a deep, slightly amused voice at his shoulder enquired. 'Because you are going to plunge me into deep gloom if you say yes.'

'Porchester.' Hal tried for a light tone. 'Any right-thinking man would be a rival for Lady Thea's hand, don't you think? A lady of beauty, charm and intelligence.'

'I shall have to find an excuse to call you out and dispose of you,' the Earl said. 'But then I would find myself having to flee the country, so that is no answer. And a duke trumps an earl under all circumstances. Perhaps I should simply shoot myself now,' he added in mock despair.

'I think you will find that the lady in question is not much interested in degrees of nobility,' Hal said drily.

'Indeed?' The other man looked at him sharply, the self-mocking expression wiped from his face. 'Do you mean that she has refused—'

'If you are seriously looking to meet someone at dawn on a chilly heath, then I suggest you continue discussing the lady,' Hal said, and smiled.

Porchester took a step back, hands raised. 'Enough said. No offence was intended. To either of you.'

'None taken,' Hal replied with that same cold smile, wondering if the effort it was taking not to punch the other man on the jaw was showing.

Porchester nodded, and strolled off. Hal had no doubt he would continue to show his interest in Thea, but at least the Earl was warned off making suggestions that linked Hal with her. That would do her no good at all. And he was going to see what he could discover about Porchester. His reputation as an officer was excellent and he seemed a decent man, but what was his true character?

If he did not manage to win Thea for himself, then he was going to make damned sure that she did not fall into the hands of anyone who was unfitting of her.

As he thought it, he realised he was losing his confidence that he could persuade her to forgive him, persuade her that he could make her happy. Seeing her now, in her natural surroundings, watching other men looking at her, desiring her, he saw his own chances dwindling.

Being a duke meant nothing if the woman you wanted did not trust you, felt you had betrayed her.

But…she had helped him in Hyde Park, although probably she was more concerned for the child and his horse than she was for him. And here, this evening, she had risked her reputation to rescue him from a compromising trap. Why would she have done that if she did not feel something for him?

Simply because she is a good person, an uncomfortable little voice replied. *Thea Campion would have rescued any man she had seen walking into that am-*

bush and she must have been very tempted to leave you to fight your own way out of it.

Yes, he was going to have to fight if he wanted her—and he did, to an extent that was beginning to haunt his dreams—so he had better stop being in the wrong, or needing her help to get him out of some disaster.

Hal found that he had actually squared his shoulders and smiled wryly at himself, then the musicians stopped tuning their instruments and he looked around for his partner in the next dance, which meant he would also be escorting her in to supper. Lady Gloria Hunter, he reminded himself, looking around for the tall brunette. A lively young lady, he recalled. At least he would have to concentrate on something other than Thea for a while.

Thea found dancing with Mr Claud Philpott quite relaxing. The younger son of Viscount Cheney, he was amusing, unashamedly frivolous and was, Thea suspected, a gentleman who was 'not the marrying sort' as Mama delicately put it.

They wove their way through the London Reel, delighted with each other for being step-perfect, then went in to the supper room.

Claud found a table with another two couples, which suited Thea very well. The evening so far had been too intense for comfort and she wanted nothing more than to eat lobster puffs and drink Champagne and indulge in friendly and light-hearted conversation.

Then she saw that one of the other ladies was Penelope Chesford, the daughter of Lord and Lady Chesford, who had driven her and Hal into hiding in their godmother's summerhouse. And Hal had said, with some emphasis—some *feeling*—that he had met Penelope.

But then he must have encountered a great many attractive women, Thea reminded herself, and most of them in Vienna. Penelope only made her nerves twitch because she looked very like Lady Helena Linton—very pretty, very blonde and with a pair of much-admired blue eyes.

But Penelope, who Thea had to admit was perhaps not the most intelligent of her acquaintances, had none of Helena's sharpness. Instead, quite confident that she was the prettiest girl in the room, as her mother constantly assured her, she was sunny-tempered and kind to her friends and rivals.

'I missed meeting your parents recently,' Thea said to her when they were all seated. 'I was staying with my godmother, Lady Holme, but I was not in the house when they called in on their way to London.'

'Oh, yes. Mama is so interested in Lady Holme's winter garden and old Johnson our gardener is not at all eager on having to create one. I expect he thinks it will mean work when it is cold.'

'I don't think so,' Thea said. 'I think the work is

done in the autumn with the bulbs and then it looks after itself.'

'Oh?' Penelope looked blank. 'Bulbs? I didn't know that Lady Holme is your Godmama. She's godmother to the Duke as well, isn't she? That's where I met him before.'

'The Duke?' one of the men asked.

'The Duke of Leamington,' Penelope said. 'I did like him a lot, but he is rather serious, you know. He doesn't flirt.'

That must have been Hal taking refuge in excessive formality if he found himself cornered by all that blonde enthusiasm, she thought.

She discovered that she was relieved that there hadn't been any kind of attraction on his part.

Although he believed himself betrothed to me, she realised with a jolt. *Of course he would not entangle himself with other young ladies.*

But that left a number of other temptations. Unbidden, a mental picture of glamorous, and very available, widows and fast married ladies came to mind. All kinds of tales had filtered back to London about Vienna and the international society that had grown up around the Congress. One did not expect young men to live like monks.

'Ah yes, Leamington,' one of the men said with a grimace. 'Far too much like competition for my liking.'

'Well, he *is* the most eligible man in London,' Thea

said, making a joke of it because she feared her feelings were beginning to show on her face. 'Surely you have noticed that all the young ladies are pointed towards him like a compass needle finding true north, Mr Haddon.'

That provoked a mixture of laughter and indignant denials and the party became quite lively. Thea felt her balance beginning to return. She did not want to marry the Duke of Leamington, so, really, who he did find attractive, or flirt with, or end up married to, was absolutely of no concern to her.

And then she saw a dark head across the room and recognised instantly, even through the press of bodies in the supper room, Hal's relaxed, easy walk.

I do not want to marry the Duke of Leamington, but I do want to marry Hal Forrest. Because I love him.

It was a shock, one that jolted her into swallowing a piece of pastry unchewed. Thea choked and coughed and was patted on the back and offered water and Champagne simultaneously.

Eventually she recovered herself, dabbed at her watery eyes and apologised. Then she saw, standing behind Mr Haddon, the tall figure of the Duke. He raised an eyebrow in query and their eyes met and she found herself nodding in answer to the unspoken question.

Yes, I am quite all right.

Then he was gone, back to his table, which was the other side of the room. How had he known it was her? Perhaps her coughing and spluttering had been so loud and unladylike that it had attracted attention from right across the room. Or perhaps he was as aware of her as she was of him.

Something like hope blossomed and then faded. Hal was a gentleman and, whatever she had said before he left her parents' house, he would feel obligated to renew his suit if she showed signs of changing her mind. She could flirt with him, offer encouragement, and he would respond and propose again and she would have no idea whether his feelings were engaged in the slightest.

He had been a good friend to her when she had not known who he was and he had still ben that friend when he had agreed so readily not to marry her. She winced at the thought of how unpleasant it would have been if she had been left to fight against her parents unsupported or just how difficult he could make her life now if he chose to.

But that was simply friendship and honour, wasn't it? She would be deluding herself if she imagined anything else might change in his feelings.

'Do you not think so, Lady Thea?'

'I— Oh, I am sorry, I quite missed what you said, Lady Penelope.' Thea fixed a determined smile on her face and set herself to be sociable. She had to get through the evening somehow, and without allowing herself to dwell on the knowledge that she had been so utterly foolish as to fall in love with the Duke of Leamington.

And then she remembered that she had promised him the dance following supper.

Thea had finished supper without either choking on anything else, or, she was fairly certain, allowing her distraction to show.

She had also come to a conclusion about how to behave with Hal. She would be pleasant, friendly, but not flirtatious. If he showed any inclination to flirt with her, then she would respond. In other words, she would not put herself forward, but neither would she repel him. They were friends already, she told herself. Nothing would change that, unless she let it.

Then, surely, if he had any inclination towards asking her to marry him he would let that show and she could offer more encouragement.

Could she marry a man who did not love her? Yes, she told herself firmly. She had never expected love, after all. Hal never need suspect anything and she would make an admirable duchess, she was sure of it.

Or might he suspect? Just how easy would it be to pretend in the marriage bed? She was aware of what happened, improbable and deeply embarrassing as it sounded, but she guessed that it might be a more revealing process in more senses than that of being naked together with a man.

Cross that bridge when you come to it, she told herself firmly.

And then discovered that the man in question was

standing in front of her, his hand extended, ready to lead her onto the dance floor for the promised country dance.

At least we both have all our clothes on, Thea thought and felt herself blush, the blood rushing to her cheeks in a wave of heat.

It was not her imagination—Hal was looking at her with some concern. 'Are you quite well, Thea?' he asked as they took their places. 'We can always sit this out if we go now.'

'Oh, it is nothing,' she said lightly, quailing at the thought of spending all that time sitting talking with him. 'I am just a trifle embarrassed after causing such a scene in the supper room.'

'A frog in the throat?' he asked with a grin.

'A sudden shock when I had just taken a mouthful of pastry,' she confessed, feeling more comfortable now they were standing side by side and he was no longer looking at her pink cheeks.

'What? Who?' he demanded, making her jump. 'Did someone offend you?'

'No, nothing like that. It was all my own fault. *Entirely* my own fault. Now, *shh*.'

Their set formed up, the music began and, thankfully, Thea found herself with no space to think and certainly no time to stand still and talk to Hal. A happy little voice inside was trying to tell her how protective he had sounded when he asked if anyone had caused her to choke and she trampled on it firmly.

Being unrealistic, snatching at every encouraging sign, could only lead to heartache.

After that dance she was engaged for everything, right up to the usual energetic, but simple, *boulanger* that normally ended a ball, sending the dancers reeling out into the night, slightly dizzy and wearily happy, buoyed up by Champagne and flirtation.

'Most satisfactory,' Mama pronounced as the carriage rattled home over the damp cobblestones. 'I think that Porchester is interested. In fact, I am certain of it.'

'Yes, Mama,' Thea said though a yawn. 'I found him very pleasant. And he is intelligent.'

'Which I fear cannot be said for every young man out there,' her mother said with a sigh. 'I had thought about Wilborough's heir, but I spoke to him this evening and I swear his head is full of goose feathers. One does not require an intellectual in a husband, but some signs of intelligence are essential.'

'Yes, Mama,' Thea agreed and fell asleep.

Chapter Fourteen

Thea assumed that she had woken up when they arrived home and had managed to walk from the carriage to her bedchamber without assistance, but she had no recollection of it when she woke. The little carriage clock beside her bed said eleven o'clock, so she had slept heavily for at least eight hours.

But that sleep had not been dreamless, she realised as she lay looking up through the gloom of the curtained room at the fabric of the half-tester above her bed. Wisps of dreams still wove their tendrils though her mind, teasing her to catch hold of them, mocking her attempts to make sense of them.

There had been images of Hal, standing and looking back as though wondering where she was. There was the recollection of a chase through a tangled rose garden until at last she was caught and drawn into an arbour. But who had been chasing her? Who had caught her? She had not been able to see the pursuer's face. Yet the scent of roses seemed to linger.

When she sat up against the pillows and rubbed the sleep from her eyes, the wisps evaporated like mist on a hot morning, leaving her thinking clearly. And the thought that was uppermost in her mind was that she loved Hal. Desired him, wanted him, loved him.

If she wanted him, she could have him. It was that simple and that difficult, because Thea was coming to realise that loving a man who did not love you in return was hard, but that to be married to him might be torture.

She leaned over and tugged on the bell pull. Lying in bed brooding was not going to be any help at all.

Jennie came in almost immediately, bringing hot chocolate and the promise of hot water for a bath just as soon as the footmen could carry it up.

If I were a duchess I would have one of those new-fangled hot water systems installed so the men did not have to carry the buckets. And indoor privies with flushing water.

It was a nice fantasy and it lasted all through the chocolate and the bath and getting dressed, just in time to go downstairs before luncheon.

Mama had declared that all the boys would assemble for the meal. They sat around the circular table in the smaller dining room looking unnaturally well-behaved. Piers and Clarence managed well enough to appear at their ease and to pass plates of cold meats and to offer butter and rolls to their mother and sister.

Ten-year-old Basil and Ernest, six, were considerably less comfortable and kept being rebuked for fidgeting. Thea strongly suspected that both had something dubious in their pockets and could only hope it was toads, which tended to stay where they were put, and not a mouse or frogs, which could escape at any moment to cause havoc.

They dutifully reported on what their morning lessons had consisted of—Latin, Greek and mathematics for the older boys, reading, writing and history for the younger two. Piers would be off to university next year, not that he showed much enthusiasm for it, unlike Clarence, who was a much stronger scholar than his sibling and might, Thea thought, make a career in the church one day.

Having reduced her sons to silence, Mama turned to Thea and began to interrogate her on the subject of each of her partners.

'I am glad to see that you danced twice with the Earl of Porchester. What is your opinion of him? One cannot say he has much to commend him in the way of looks.'

'True,' Thea conceded. She knew what was required of her, so she added, 'But he seems exceedingly fit and healthy and he has a most pleasant and intelligent manner.'

She was then taken through all of her partners, her mother making no comment when she mentioned Hal except to tighten her lips into a thin line.

'I heard very little news of any great interest,'

Mama announced, then proceeded to recount all the gossip from the Chaperones' Corner, carefully edited for young ears, Thea was certain. Not that she need have concerned herself, as the brothers all appeared to be glazed with boredom and were not attending to a word.

'And then that rakehell Randolph Linton has got himself into a serious scrape. Not that even he would be reckless enough to show his face in London, I am certain,' Lady Wiveton concluded.

'Um, what has he done?' Thea asked cautiously, but her mother rose with a slight shake of her head in Thea's direction, declared the meal over and sent her sons off back to their tutor.

When they were seated together in the drawing room, both with their embroidery in hand, her mother said, 'The rumour is that young Linton behaved in a most reckless way when in Yorkshire during the summer, compromising the daughter of a rural dean. He was expected to marry her, of course, although her father cannot have been delighted, as Lord Linton is merely a viscount and is so hale and hearty there can be little expectation of Randolph inheriting for many years, but the wretched young man announced he could do better for himself and promptly left the district.'

'Goodness,' Thea said. 'He is very fortunate that her father is a man of the church and that she does not have a brother to call him out.'

'Apparently, she does, but he was in Ireland visiting relatives and young Linton removed himself to safety before he could return home and challenge him.'

'Dreadful,' Thea murmured, bending over her stitches. Had Randolph known about his sister's scheme to ensnare a duke? If he had, then he could well have felt his expectations would be greatly improved with such a brother-in-law.

And Helena would be smarting even more, knowing that she had not only missed the opportunity to become a duchess but that she had lost that influence to protect her brother. She would blame Thea, that was certain.

Hal had been right to be concerned and to warn her to watch out for Helena's spite in retaliation. She shivered, hating the thought that someone out there would be hating her.

The next three days passed calmly enough. There were no more balls, but Thea was entertained well enough with a musicale, a reception, a dinner party and two art shows, one at the Royal Academy and one in Spring Gardens.

She did no more than glimpse Lady Helena at a distance at the reception and the musicale, and the other woman was not invited to the dinner party and apparently was not much interested in art. It was a relief and Thea began to relax a little about how Helena's spite might show itself.

On the other hand, there was little sign of Hal either. Thea did see him in conversation with one of the artists at the Royal Academy, and at a distance at the reception, where he arrived late and left early, so there was no opportunity to exchange even a greeting.

Was he avoiding her, or was she giving herself far too much importance and the obvious explanation—that he was simply not interested in, or invited to, the same events—was the correct one?

Her composure was not helped by the weather, which blew wet and blustery every day, stripping the trees bare of leaves and piling them in soggy heaps in every corner, or making roads treacherously slippery for horses.

Finally the rain stopped and, after a day of brisk breezes and sunshine, even Hopkins, Thea's protective groom, declared it was safe enough under foot to ride out.

'Should have taken her out meself and shaken the fidgets out of her,' he worried as Lara bounced, shied and fidgeted her way towards Hyde Park that afternoon. 'You keep you heel down good and firm and don't take any nonsense from her,' he warned Thea as they negotiated the traffic.

Despite his grumbling they arrived safely in the park which was, by then, empty of children and their attendants and beginning to attract quite a number of riders and carriage drivers.

Thea chose a different ride for the one where she had encountered Hal and the little lad with his hoop, and kept Lara to a controlled canter towards the Queen's House in the far south-west of the park.

Ahead was quite a knot of riders, perhaps a dozen in all, and Thea slowed to a walk, not wanting to ride off through the longer grass to detour around them, for fear of her mount slipping. She was hailed by the nearest rider facing her, who she saw was one of the Chelmsford twins, and reined in close to her.

'Good afternoon! What a relief to be out in the fresh air again, is it not?' she said and her greeting was returned by several people she knew.

The group opened up, people shifting their mounts in clear invitation for her to move in amongst them. It was not until she had done so, finished greeting acquaintances and turned her mare to face into the group, that she realised she was opposite Lady Helena and a lanky young man who she guessed from the likeness, was her brother, Randolph, the compromiser of the clergyman's daughter.

Her immediate instinct was to make some excuse, back Lara out of the group and canter off, but that would seem exceedingly odd when she had only just arrived and she would be snubbing a number of her friends and acquaintances. Thea looked right through Helena then smiled at Major Lord Harper to her right. From the corner of her eye she could see Helena lean over to whisper something to her brother and he shifted slightly to stare at her.

It was awkward, but she managed to speak to enough people around the group for it not to be obvious that she was avoiding Helena.

Randolph made some remark to Lord Harper, who answered him rather shortly, Thea thought, and wondered if gossip about the young man's behaviour was now widespread.

She had begun to feel she could move on now without it seeming awkward when another rider joined the group.

Lara lifted her head and whickered a greeting to the big grey mare. Hal, who was exchanging greetings with two of the other men, looked across, saw them and rode through the group to her side.

He raised his hat. 'Lady Thea.' His smile was warm and she could not resist the answering curve of her own lips.

'Duke.'

Hal halted Juno when they were stirrup to stirrup, the two animals facing in opposite directions. 'An awkward encounter,' he murmured. 'Who is that with her?'

'Brother,' Thea murmured back. 'A bad lot, I gather.'

Hal continued to ride right around her until he was facing back into the group. 'He looks it. I suggest we do not linger. May I offer you my escort once we have established that we are not being chased away?'

'Thank you,' she said with some feeling. She should be above caring, Thea knew, but she felt increasingly uncomfortable under the hostile gaze of Helena Linton and the equally unsettling assessment of her brother. It felt as though he could see right through her riding habit to her underwear, and his insolent regard made her skin crawl.

Hal was talking to the couple on his other side, and Thea nodded along to the raptures of the rider on her left whose name she could not recall and who was waxing poetical about the bare branches of the trees against the blue sky.

'I have an appointment,' Hal remarked as the chimes of a church reached them across the park. 'I should leave.'

'Goodness, is that the time? I must go too,' Thea said. 'Good day, everyone.' She began to turn Lara.

'May I ride with you to the gates as we appear to be heading in the same direction?' Hal asked, turning Juno with one hand and tipping his hat to the group as he did so.

They rode away, with Hopkins, who had been waiting at a distance, following.

'If that young scapegrace had ogled you for another minute, I'd have had him off that sway-backed roan and punched his front teeth out,' Hal said abruptly. 'Offensive young lout.'

Thea recounted what she had heard from her mother about Randolph Linton and Hal made a sound of disgust. 'With any luck the lady's brother will catch up with him and put a bullet where it will do most good.'

'Thank you for rescuing me. I had an uneasy feeling that if I rode away by myself, he would follow. I have Hopkins with me, of course, but Mr Linton does not look like a man to tolerate interference from a groom.'

'It was hardly a rescue to compare to yours of me at Lady Hampton's ball. I am deeply in your debt for that.'

'What would you have done if I had not appeared?' Thea asked, curious.

'I would have trampled through the greenery to escape, demolishing Lady Hampton's prize exotics as I went,' he said firmly. 'And, if confronted by Lady Linton, I would have refused to accept that Lady Helena had been, in any way, compromised by me. I rather think that, if she chose to make a scene about it, my credit would prove rather stronger than hers.'

'Helen has few friends,' Thea said. 'She has been spiteful to too many young ladies, stolen away too many beaux—and the mothers remember such behaviour. But it would have been an unpleasant scene.'

'Very,' he agreed with some feeling. 'And mud always sticks, however carefully one washes.'

It felt as though they were back on their old friendly terms again. Thea felt an ease in Hal's company that had been missing ever since her discovery of who he was.

'Porchester seems to be showing considerable interest,' he remarked.

Thea, her mind elsewhere, said vaguely, 'In what?'

'In you.'

'Oh. Yes, I suppose so. I expect his aunt has pointed me out to him as an eligible match.'

'I do not think he needs a female relative to decide that for himself,' Hal said drily. 'And I doubt the things that she would consider important about you are what attracts him.'

It took Thea a moment to realise that she had been paid a compliment. 'There are a great many more beautiful young ladies on the Marriage Mart this Season than I. I am too tall, my hair is an unfashionable colour, I am not…um…curvaceous.'

Hal gave a snort of laughter. 'Oh, I agree, you are not an example of what fashion has decreed is perfection for this Season. But what the *modistes* and the leaders of fashion and the hopeful mamas declare is perfection is rarely what a man considers desirable.'

'And I am?' Thea asked recklessly, staring at him. 'Desirable?'

'But of course. You have a mirror, have you not?'

Something was bubbling up inside her. Something she did not understand, a mixture of desire, longing, fear and old resentment.

For some reason the resentment won. 'You called me Twig,' she said indignantly.

'I did?' Hal stared back. 'When?'

'When we met before and you were a horrible boy. You said I looked like a twig in autumn, all thin and knobbly with one red leaf left on the end, and you would call me Twig.'

Juno came to a halt, presumably at a jerk on her reins. Thea carried on past Hal, circled Lara to face the other horse.

'And *that* is why you would not marry me?' Hal demanded. 'Because as a revolting youth, I insulted you? Besides, as I recall, you *did* look like a twig. You do not now,' he added hastily. 'Your hair is a beautiful colour and you are not at all knobbly.'

It appeared to strike him that this was not perhaps the most tactful way to proceed and he shut his mouth on whatever he had been about to add.

'Of course that was not why I refused! I mean, of course that is not why I told Mama and Papa I would not…' Her voice trailed away. 'At least, I recalled that I did not like you, and I hated being ordered to marry someone I had not met for years and every instinct fought against it. It was later that I realised how much I resented the fact that you had made no effort to meet me, court me. Had just taken me from granted.

'And then, of course, when I discovered you had been deceiving me all the time I was at Godmama's house, that was the last straw.'

'I apologise for the Twig,' Hal said. 'But youths are revolting creatures.'

'I am quite well aware of that. I have brothers,' Thea

said stiffly. 'To allow a childish insult to rankle is, of course, ridiculous. I do not know why we are quarrelling about it now.'

'Are we quarrelling, Thea?' Hal said softly.

She swallowed. 'It feels as if we are.'

'I have always thought that there has to be some… feeling between people who quarrel.'

'And I had thought that we were friends. Before.'

'Can we not still be friends?' he asked.

But I don't *want to be friends. I want to be lovers. I want to marry you.*

'Yes, of course we can,' Thea said.

There must have been something in her tone, or perhaps her expression, because the smile was no longer in his eyes. 'But you have not forgiven me, have you? I do not mean the twig comment,' he added. 'No, do not answer, I do not think I have forgiven myself, so why should you?'

That sounded bitter. Thea lifted one hand, perhaps to reach out, but Hal glanced over her shoulder and said, 'Your groom appears concerned. I think I should leave. Good day to you, Lady Thea.' He touched his whip to the brim of his hat and rode away, the big grey mare surging into a canter as though her rider could not put distance between them fast enough.

Thea sat watching as horse and man grew smaller and finally vanished behind some distant trees.

'My lady? You'll become chilled if you stay still

much longer.' It was Hopkins, and she had not even heard him ride up beside her.

What had just happened? Had Hal been close to saying that he still wanted to marry her for more than her 'eligibility'?

Could she summon up enough courage to show him that she wanted him too? Had she enough courage to risk rejection?

Hal told himself not to look back. It felt as though he had broken something and he had no idea what, or how he had done it. Or what he wanted from Thea. For Thea. A friend, yes. A wife? She would be perfect, except for the small matter of her not wanting to marry him.

The idea of an arranged marriage, a 'suitable' marriage, had never concerned him before, not that he had given it much thought, not until he had seen it through Thea's eyes.

So, friendship, yet somehow that no longer seemed enough.

Chapter Fifteen

'Have you been listening to a word I have been saying, Thea?'

'I am sorry, Mama. I was distracted.' She took a sip of coffee and attempted to look alert and attentive.

Mama gestured irritably at a footman who hastened to remove her breakfast plate.

'More toast, my lady?'

'Thank you, no. You may leave us.'

Thea, who would have welcomed another slice of toast because she had no recollection of having eaten anything, waited patiently for whatever pronouncement required the absence of staff.

'This afternoon is the Dowager Duchess of Langridge's At Home.'

'Yes, Mama?' Thea vaguely recalled something unusual about the invitation. 'Her new conservatory?'

'Exactly. It is not so much a space for plants, one understands, as a gallery to display part of the late Duke's collection of Classical statuary.'

'Fascinating,' Thea said, assuming that was what was required of her.

'A dead bore,' her mother retorted. 'However, it is another excellent occasion to meet eligible gentlemen, and there will be more opportunity to converse in broad daylight with no music except perhaps a harpist, and no dancing. I think you will show to advantage in that new jonquil afternoon gown—a ray of sunshine against those cold marble statues,' she added with an untypical burst of lyricism.

'Now, all the people one would wish to see will be attending, given that it is Daphne Langridge and she is related to absolutely *everyone* who matters,' Mama said complacently.

'One can only hope that the weather is fine,' Thea said, thinking that if it was pouring with rain it was going to be exceedingly gloomy in a conservatory and she had no confidence that she could manage to resemble a ray of sunshine under those circumstances. 'It does sound as though it will be a pleasant change from evening entertainments,' she added, attempting to sound positive.

Would Hal be there? She wasn't sure whether she hoped so or not, but she was feeling an increasing urgency, as though her chances of happiness were slipping away from her faster and faster with every passing day.

She tried to tell herself that it was possible to recover from a broken heart, from not marrying the man you loved—people did it all the time, she was sure. And she tried to convince herself that she could be happy with a man she liked but did not love. After all, that was what she had thought after she had refused to marry Hal.

But now there was no such certainty. She liked Lord Porchester and she suspected he liked her well enough to make an offer. But was it fair to marry a man when one loved another, even if one had no intention of being anything but faithful to one's husband?

She couldn't live like this, she decided. It was impossible to answer any offer that was made to her until she knew Hal's true feelings, and that was that, however embarrassing and potentially humiliating it might be if she blundered.

Today. This afternoon. If Hal was attending the At Home she would find some way to talk to him alone and somehow find a way of encouraging him to renew his proposal, but in a way which meant he could pretend not to have understood her if that was no longer what he wanted.

Quite how she was going to do that she was not at all sure: all she could hope for was that inspiration would strike when she saw him.

The Dowager Duchess, on being widowed, had not stood for any nonsense from her son, the new duke, about surrendering Langridge House on Grosvenor Square to him and his wife, a nervous young woman who had no chance whatsoever of standing up to her formidable mother-in-law.

With her son routed to a less imposing property in Bedford Square, the Dowager remained in possession of a substantial mansion with one of the largest gardens in the Square and had ordered the creation of a conservatory built, not only across the entire width of the back of the house, but also on two levels, with internal steps leading down to wings that stretched out along each side of the garden.

It was a magnificent piece of architecture, Thea had to admit, although it did little for the light levels in the ground-floor rooms at the rear.

The late Duke had been an avid collector, and his heir would still have a large collection to enjoy at Langridge Abbey, his country seat, despite his mother calmly removing at least seventy pieces for her own enjoyment.

It had all been arranged with great taste, the statuary placed with care in the main part of the structure, interspersed with seating groups to allow contemplation of the art and small groupings of palms and ferns.

The two garden wings had more plants, creating a series of glades, each with two or three statues and a marble bench.

Those looked chilly, despite the fact that the day was quite bright, so Thea soon wandered back up to the higher level and did her best to follow Mama's instructions and look like a sunbeam while conversing with as many eligible young men as came her way.

Lord Porchester found her studying a nymph looking coyly over her shoulder at an approaching satyr.

'He is very hairy, is he not?' the Earl observed.

'Very,' Thea agreed. 'And look at those cloven hooves. If I were her, I would be fleeing in the opposite direction, not batting my eyelashes at him.'

'Might I hope you will not flee if I invite you to drive with me tomorrow afternoon?' he said with a charming smile. 'My head groom, who is a noted weather prophet, assures me this dry spell will continue for at least one more day.'

'I would be delighted to.' Agreeing to a drive was not undue encouragement, she considered, and they agreed a time, leaving the destination to be decided on the day.

It seemed natural after that to continue exploring with the Earl. The room was beginning to fill up now, becoming quite crowded, with most of the visitors remaining in the main room with its seating and refreshment tables.

Thea was beginning to feel the need for a cup of tea and was about to mention that when a footman approached with a folded note on a silver salver.

'Lady Thea Campion?'

'Yes?'

'This note is for you, my lady.'

'Thank you.' She picked it up, puzzled. Her name

was written in black ink in a masculine hand she did not recognise, and the note was fastened with red wax, but bore no seal impression.

'Excuse me,' she said to Lord Porchester and moved to a nearby seat to open it.

Meet me in the left-hand conservatory wing as soon as possible. I must speak with you.

It was signed simply *L*.

Thea sat and stared at it. *L* for *Leamington*? It had to be. But why this secrecy? Or was it simply discretion and he wanted to talk to her, but did not want them to be seen going off into the depths of the conservatory together?

'Is anything wrong, Lady Thea?' That was Lord Porchester, and she realised that she must have been sitting staring at the note for at least a minute.

'Wrong? Oh, no, my lord. Simply a reminder about something. But I really must go and find Mama in case she is ready to leave. Thank you for your company, and I very much enjoyed your observations on the works of art.'

That provoked a grin from him, which she was tempted to return, despite her preoccupation. His comments had been informed, but sometimes really quite wicked.

Thea waited until he had bowed and vanished back into the crowd, then rose and made her way to the entrance to the wing on the left side. It looked almost deserted, perhaps because it was now in shade and looked rather chilly and uninviting.

Thea trod down the steps and began to weave her way through the palms and statues, meeting no one. It was certainly a good choice for a private conversation, she thought, trying to ignore the butterflies flapping in her stomach.

There were double doors at the far end and still no sign of Hal. Surely he did not want to talk to her in the garden. It was far too damp and chilly to be standing around without outer garments.

She had almost reached the doors, noticing a last small sitting area to her right, when there was a rustle of foliage behind her.

Hal, at last.

Thea had just time to half turn towards the noise when a hand clamped over her mouth and an arm came around her, pulling her hard against a male body, and she was hustled through the outer doors that were being held open, she could have sworn, by Helena Linton.

But it was only a fleeting impression because she was too busy fighting whoever held her. She tried to bite the palm pressed against her lips, but it was held too tight. She kicked and stamped, but her thin kid indoor shoes made no impression.

Then a hand cuffed her hard against the side of

her head, and as she was reeling, trying to keep her balance, the hand was replaced by a cloth gag, some kind of hood was pulled over her head, something—a cloak?—was swirled around her and strong arms scooped her up.

'Keep still or I'll hit you harder next time,' a voice she had never heard before growled in her ear, and she stopped kicking. This was terrifying, but the idea of being unconscious in this man's power was even worse.

Thea made herself go limp and heavy, as though she had fainted, and tried to work out where they were, where they were going. There was a sound like a heavy gate closing, then the smell of horses penetrated the hood. Had she been taken out of a rear entrance into the mews?

Then there was the unmistakeable sound of carriage wheels and hooves on stone and she was lifted up and deposited on what must be a carriage seat. Thea sat up, scrambled as best she could towards where the other door must be, and was caught around the waist, hauled back and slammed down on the seat again.

The carriage lurched into motion as a big hand lifted her skirts. Thea bucked frantically, but the man moved no higher than her ankles, tying them together with something that felt like cloth. A handkerchief, perhaps.

Then he scrabbled the cloak apart, found her hands

and tied those, finally shoving her back on the seat. 'Stay there and stay quiet, if you know what's best for you.'

Thea realised that she had missed her chance to tell which way they had turned out of the mews. Now she was lost as the carriage wove its way through the streets of London.

It was definitely a carriage, not a cart or a wagon, because what she was lying on was well-sprung. Thea forced herself to think. She had been snatched from an exclusive address in fashionable London in broad daylight. She was travelling in a gentleman's conveyance, not a hackney carriage. And there had been that glimpse of a woman holding the conservatory doors open, possibly—probably—Helena Linton.

What was this? It was too extreme for a spiteful prank. Tales of innocent young women snatched off the street and sold into brothels came back to make her feel sick with apprehension. Could that really happen? Would anyone dare do that to the daughter of the Earl of Wiveton?

Whatever awaited her at the end of this jolting, blind journey, she had to be prepared to act, to seize every chance of escape. Now there was nothing she could do, and she was not even sure how many people were in the carriage with her.

Thea made herself go limp, lie still, listen for any clue as to who had taken her and where she was going.

There was no one to help her; nobody would even know yet that she was missing. It was down to her to save herself.

'Good afternoon, Lady Wiveton,' Hal said and noticed the widening of the Countess's eyes as she saw him. 'Is Lady Thea present this afternoon?'

'Why, yes, certainly. I saw her with Lord Porchester, perhaps half an hour ago.'

'Ah, I must have missed her. I will hope to encounter her later.' He smiled and moved on, scanning the heads in the crowded space. Thea was tall enough, and her hair striking enough, for him to see her if she was standing. But there were a lot of seats, of course.

He thought he had looked everywhere in the upper room, but he began to check again. Perhaps she had gone down into one of the garden wings, although one now looked decidedly uninviting in deep shadow.

Something stirred uneasily inside him. Nerves at attempting to find the words to rebuild the friendship that had been between them, and make it strong enough for Thea to allow him to court her—or apprehension about where she was?

But surely, a young lady was perfectly safe in the home of a dowager duchess, surrounded by most of the *haut ton?*

He saw Porchester, deep in conversation with an older man, and strolled towards them, was recognised and exchanged a few banalities before saying, 'I wonder if I could have a word with you, Porchester?'

The other man drifted off to join another group and Porchester was left eying Hal warily. 'Yes?'

Hal kept his voice low. 'Have you seen Lady Thea?'

'Why?' Porchester demanded.

'Get off your high horse. I'm worried. I can't find her. She's not up here, the right-hand wing is full of nattering matrons and the left-hand one is becoming cold and gloomy. I was going to check it when I saw you.'

Porchester, a tall man, promptly stood on the nearest bench and scanned the upper room. 'No sign here. I'll look in the right-hand side, you check the left.'

They split up. Hal ran down the steps into the lower conservatory and began systematically checking, looking down and under benches in case Thea had fainted and was lying there.

He had almost reached the end when Porchester joined him. 'No sign of her there. Surely she would not have gone out into the garden?'

'Not in the shoes she must be wearing, no,' Hal said as he scanned the last few feet of conservatory. Something was knotting in his gut and he made himself ignore it. There was probably a perfectly simple explanation—and if there wasn't, then what would be needed was a cool head.

'What's that?'

He picked up the crumpled sheet of paper and

smoothed it out, swore and handed it to Porchester. 'She must have thought it was from me.' The knots were back, along with a wave of something close to fear.

He ignored the other man's raised eyebrows at the assumption that Thea would know that a note signed *L* was from himself and that she would follow its instructions. 'Someone has taken her.'

The Dowager was another of his godmothers and one he could trust. Hal fought his way through the guests to her side. 'Something serious has happened,' he told her, low-voiced, and she promptly steered him into a side room and closed the door.

'Worrying,' she said when he had told her about the note. 'Ring the bell.'

When the butler appeared she simply said, 'Send all the staff on duty in here now. And hurry, Gibson.'

Through his anxiety Hal was aware that the Dowager would have made a good general. Within twenty minutes she had established that Thea's pelisse, bonnet and umbrella were still with her mother's things, that she was not in the ladies' retiring room and, unless she was very cunningly concealed, not in the rest of the house or garden either.

None of the staff recalled seeing her after Lewis, the under-footman, had delivered the note and that had been given to him by a gentleman he had hardly glimpsed and didn't know. A thin, dark man and quite young, was all he could recall.

Gibson had begun been sending the staff back into the conservatory after their allocated search had been completed when one footman came in to report that Lady Wiveton was asking if anyone had seen her daughter.

'Ask her to join me if you please, Gibson,' the Dowager said. 'This has now become serious,' she added to Hal as the door closed behind the butler.

'I agree. Porchester, we should check the mews. It seems certain that she had been removed from the house.'

The Dowager's head groom was located easily. Yes, he had seen a strange carriage draw up beside the gate into the garden, but had assumed it belonged to one of the guests who had perhaps been taken ill. He'd had no instructions from Her Grace to interfere, so left it alone, being busy with one of the horses that had gone lame the day before. There had been a driver on the box and a groom up behind and he thought that perhaps one or two men had gone in through the gate.

No, he couldn't describe the driver, nor the carriage, other than it was an ordinary travelling coach, black with no crest on the door, but the team did make an impression.

'Not well matched, that I'll say. Very untidy it looked,' he said with professional disdain. 'One bay, two blacks and a chestnut with a white face and three white socks.'

Hal and the Earl returned to the house to find Lady

Wiveton pacing about the drawing room in great distress and insisting that her husband be sent for at once. The Dowager was seeing off the last of the departing guests, none of whom had realised anything was amiss, Hal hoped.

A few minutes later she swept in. 'Wiveton has been summoned. Have you discovered anything?' she demanded of the two men.

'A description of the unknown carriage that left your mews at about the time Lady Thea was missed and, more usefully, information about the horses, which are distinctive. I suggest we send out grooms and footmen armed with coin to question crossing sweepers in the streets around to see if any of them saw that team and which way it was heading. The fact that it is a coach and four suggests that he is heading out of London.'

'But who could have taken her?' Lady Wiveton demanded. 'Or has she eloped?'

'Not unless the note we found luring her to the conservatory wing was an elaborate hoax on her part,' Hal said, which caused the Countess to sink down on a sofa and close her eyes.

'Oh, my heavens. Which is worse?'

Worse? All that mattered if Thea had eloped was that she might face social disgrace, and that could be managed. But if she had been taken… He made himself stop being practical and absorb that fully for the first time. She might be hurt, and she would be terrified, even though, knowing Thea, she would fight not to show it. And who had taken her? And why? When he got his hands on them—and he would—he was going to make them wish they had never been born. He would—

Gibson's entrance jerked him back to the present. *Act, then worry.*

'Your Grace, excuse the interruption, but under the strange circumstances, I wonder if this is related.'

'If what is related?' the Dowager snapped.

'There is a young man, a Mr Dudley. He is enquiring for Mr Randolph Linton. When I told him the gentleman was not here, he told me that he had been informed at Linton House that he was attending this At Home with his sister. He became somewhat agitated when I informed him that Lady Helena had been present, and has now left, but that Mr Linton had not called. It may, of course, be nothing—'

'I think it may,' Hal said. 'At least one member of that family has no cause to love Lady Thea. With your permission, Duchess, I will talk to him.' He hardly waited for her nod before he was out of the door.

Mr Dudley was a stocky young man and Hal decided that he was a gentleman from respectable County stock.

'I am Leamington,' he said, holding out his hand. 'Tell me how I can help.'

'A duke?' The young man's eyebrows lifted, but his handshake was firm and confident and there was no hint of deference in his voice when he said, 'Is Randolph Linton a friend of yours?'

'Far from it. Come in here and explain all about it.' He steered the younger man into one of the small reception rooms and closed the door. 'You have my utmost discretion.'

'The swine attempted to ruin my sister,' Dudley said between clenched teeth. 'I was in Ireland. When I returned home to the Deanery—my father is a rural dean in Yorkshire—and I heard what had happened, I wrote to Linton, told him to expect a visit from me today to demand satisfaction. If the swine is trying to hide from me, then I'll hunt him down like the rat he is. And force him to meet me.'

'I rather think that he had taken action to tie your hands and revenge himself on another lady at the same time,' Hal said grimly. 'If you are prepared to share your story with a small group of people for whose discretion I can vouch, we may secure your satisfaction and save that lady.'

Chapter Sixteen

It was the second stop to change horses. The sounds reaching Thea as she lay tied and bundled up on the carriage seat were unmistakeable. Ostlers shouted orders at lads, there was the jerk as the traces were released and the new team backed in, the clatter of hooves on stone and the background noises of a busy coaching inn.

Two changes, twenty miles and a main route, she decided.

A groom had blown his horn for the gates, which meant that this was a turnpike road, and the previous inn had been bustling too.

Not, then, some country track leading to goodness knew where. If they knew how she had been taken, perhaps the carriage could be traced. If she managed to escape, then it would be relatively easy to discover where she was.

If...if...

She told herself to be positive. If she gave up, there

was no chance of escape unless her captors were incredibly careless, but if she stayed alert, ready to take any opportunity, then there was hope.

The carriage lurched into motion again and Thea drew in as much breath as she could, wriggled her fingers to try to keep the blood flowing and set herself to follow the route.

'I believe that Randolph Linton has taken Lady Thea,' Hal said after introducing Dudley to the small group in the drawing room. 'He received Dudley's letter informing him that he was about to be called to account for his behaviour towards Miss Dudley and decided to take out insurance.'

'But how does that help him?' Lady Wiveton asked, looking confused.

'If he compromises her, he could reasonably hope that she would have to marry him, and he would then find himself protected by being the son-in-law of a prominent earl. Or, failing that, he could hold her until we somehow bought off or otherwise dissuaded Dudley from calling him out.'

'I'd have thought it simpler for him to refuse to meet Dudley. Disgraceful, of course, and downright cowardly, but it is not as though he has much reputation to lose,' Porchester objected.

'I told him that I would horsewhip him to within an inch of his life if he did not agree to an honourable meeting,' Dudley said.

'Ah. Yes, I can see that a sneaking little wretch like that would try some scheme to wriggle out of doing the honourable thing in that case,' the Earl said.

Gibson entered and announced with a discreet cough, 'Some positive news, Your Grace. David the under-footman found a bright crossing lad who saw that team turn north on Audley Street. He had the sense to tail a cab to follow from junction to junction. It headed north again out of London on the Edgware road.'

'Excellent. Make sure he is rewarded for his initiative, Gibson. Well, gentlemen?'

'I'll follow on horseback,' Hal said. The relief of knowing what had happened, what they were dealing with, was almost physical. 'That will be more flexible. When I find her I can hire a carriage to bring her back.'

'I'll come with you,' Porchester said.

'And so will I,' Dudley said in a tone that would not take *no* for an answer. 'My horse is here.'

'Gibson, have the two best of my son's mounts saddled and tell three of the grooms to mount up also. He keeps his horses here, says he's not got enough stabling at his London house,' the Dowager added as the butler strode out, sounding critical and as though it was not her doing that her son was displaced.

'Oh, and you'll want pistols,' she announced. 'Come with me, my husband had a fine collection of weapons.'

Fifteen minutes later, adequately armed to fight a small war, and with a road book in a saddlebag, the three of them rode out of the mews, the grooms at their heels, just as the Wivetons' empty town coach rattled in.

'We've missed the Earl,' Hal said, relieved not to have to explain it all over to a furious and anxious father. The Dowager was the best person for that. 'Ready? Then let's catch the bastard.'

The next time the carriage came to a halt, Thea heard the door open and she was lifted into a man's arms. A big, strong man, she realised, deciding that struggling was not going to work. The cloak was tucked around her and the hood pulled over her face and then she was being carried in the open. They passed through a door, she thought, and unmistakeably up some stairs.

Booted feet hit bare boards, she heard another door open and then she was dumped casually, and painfully, on what felt like a lumpy sofa. The cloak was pulled away and, to her huge relief, the gag removed, by, she saw with horror, but no real surprise, Randolph Linton.

'Untie me,' she said, thrusting her bound hands towards him.

He shrugged and did so, dropping to one knee to free her ankles. Thea kicked him hard in the chest and he rolled backwards onto a thin carpet, swearing.

The big bruiser of a man who had been standing by the door started forward, but Linton gestured him back as he regained his feet. 'I'm sure you feel better for that,' he said, dusting down his coat tails.

'I would feel better for the use of the privy, a drink of water and an explanation of your conduct, in that order,' Thea said tightly.

'Use that.' Linton pointed at a small door. 'Ned, order lemonade for the lady, ale for me. Then wait outside.'

He turned and regarded Thea with a smirk. 'There's no lock on that door and no window, so don't try anything foolish.'

Thea stumbled to her feet, wincing at the pain as blood flowed back after the tight bindings. She walked, with as much dignity as she could manage, to the door, taking her time, trying to look more shaky than she felt, scanning the room for weapons as she went. There was nothing.

The little room held a washstand and a chamber pot and that was all. The door had opened outwards and had no lock. She would just have to take the chance that Randolph was not bent on humiliating her. Hastily, Thea used the facilities, drying her face and hands on the strip of towel that lay on the washstand, then explored the room, which was no bigger than a large cupboard. The utensils were of cheap pottery, none of them had the weight to do anyone much damage and the strip of towel was no use for anything.

She turned to go out, steadied herself on the washstand and noticed how rickety it was. One leg had broken and had been repaired simply with string to lash it back together. Thea put the basin and ewer on the floor and untied the string to find that the broken leg had splintered, and amongst the broken fragments of wood was a dagger-like piece about seven inches long.

Cautiously she wriggled it into the outside of her right garter. If she had to snatch it out again she would probably be left with severe scratches, but she could do a lot of damage with that piece of wood.

Once she had roughly tied up the washstand again she went out to find a glass and a jug of lemonade on the table. Randolph sat opposite with a tankard in front of him. There was no sign of the big man, but presumably he was outside the door. No escape that way, even if she could overpower Linton. How high was the window above the ground?

But she was still feeling decidedly shaky and it would probably be a good thing to sit and drink and allow her wrists and ankles to recover a little. It would do no harm to allow Randolph to believe she would obey him, either.

The lemonade helped a lot. Now her mouth and throat no longer felt like flannel filled with gravel, she could try to see what she could learn.

'You are very relaxed. How far have we come from London?'

'We are just outside St Albans.' He took a long swig from the tankard.

'But still on the turnpike?' The sounds from outside, and the size of the room, made her sure this was a coaching inn and not one on a side road.

'Yes.' There seemed to be no hesitation in telling her where they were, which seemed strange. She must have looked puzzled because he added, 'I have no objection to being found with you. It will be some time tomorrow morning, I imagine.'

'You expect to be found? No, you *want* to be found.'

'Exactly. You will have been nicely compromised and will have no option but to marry me.'

Thea snorted.

'You may not care if you are ruined—not that I believe that—but your father will certainly insist on marriage. It is not as though I am a groom or the dancing master. The Lintons are good blood.'

'But not good character,' Thea shot back.

Marry Randolph Linton? Never.

'You seem to make a habit of trying to ruin unmarried ladies. Your attempt on the daughter of a rural dean was somewhat unambitious, was it not?'

'Good God, I didn't want to *marry* the chit. She was just an amusement. Damnably dull in rural Yorkshire, believe me.'

'I would not believe you if you told me the sky was blue,' Thea retorted. 'So why not try to behave like a reasonable human being and court someone during the Season? You might find someone deluded enough to put up with you, although I must say, I'd pity them.'

'It turns out that the Deanery girl has a fire-breathing brother who is hard on my heels. I may be heir to a title with blood that goes back to the Conqueror, but we have no influence, no connections. You have. A rural nobody threatening your husband is going to be sent packing.'

'You think so? If you are the son-in-law in question, I imagine Papa would be out there urging on the aggrieved brother. He would probably offer to be his second.'

'Yes? Your husband being involved in a duel so soon after the wedding is going to cause considerable embarrassment to your family.'

'My family would probably pay a marksman to give your opponent extra lessons beforehand,' she retorted. 'Ending up as a widow would not be so bad, now I think of it. Why not act like a gentleman and accept his challenge?'

Randolph drained his tankard. 'A lot of nonsense, these so-called affairs of honour,' he said dismissively, but his eyes shifted away from hers.

'Your family really is a disgrace,' Thea said. 'And you have the brains of a feather duster if you think this is going to work. I can't imagine how you thought up such a scheme, let alone worked out how to abduct me.'

Then she realised.

'You didn't, did you? This is your sister's idea. Helena wants me ruined. She knows you are going to run away rather than face that young man, so either I end up married to you, which she will greatly enjoy seeing, or I will be ruined, which will please her even more. She wants to revenge herself on me for thwarting her little scheme with the Duke and she isn't thinking about your interests at all.'

Randolph's face was scarlet, all the confirmation that she needed. 'Shut up, you bitch.'

'And how do you intend to make me? Bring in your hired bully boy because you can't subdue one young woman all by yourself?'

Randolph looked at her through narrowed eyes, then deliberately looked away and stared at the bed. There was a long silence while Thea's stomach plunged, then he said, 'I really didn't think I was interested enough in you to actively ruin you—skinny redheads are not my fancy—but I have to do something to entertain myself until tomorrow.'

'I'll scream the place down.'

'Not if you are gagged, you won't. Or I can let Pitkin have you. He's not fussy, and it will be a nice extra for him. Amusing to watch.'

Thea felt sick. She thought she might overcome Randolph if he became careless, but she had no confidence she could do anything against the lout outside, let alone both men.

'Very well. I will be quiet. I won't say a word. I'll sit

here and behave,' she said hurriedly. She didn't have to pretend to be cowed—she felt it, despising herself.

You cannot fight both of them. This is tactics, the sensible way to stay safe, not cowardice.

Randolph relaxed a little. 'Very wise.'

Thea was beginning to get the feeling that it was not only the threat of being hurt in a duel that frightened him, but any form of conflict. He would not relish rape, even if he threatened it. He was quite happy to seduce innocent young women, provided he did not have to face them afterwards, but a struggling, fighting woman was another matter.

'May I ask one question?' she ventured.

'Ask away, just keep that adder's tongue of yours civil,' he said. 'Pitkin!'

The door opened and the big man looked in. 'Yes, guv'nor?'

'Have them send up some food and more ale. Go and get some for yourself, but wait and turn the key in the door on your side after the maid's left before you go.'

'Aye, guv'nor.' The door closed.

'Well?'

'You say you expect us to be discovered tomorrow morning. What makes you think someone will trace us and, if they do, why they won't arrive until then?'

'They'll be flapping around for an age. Who'll notice you've gone in all that crush? Then we got you out without being seen. It will take them hours to work out what happened. When they do, I've left them a clue to follow, but that will take time.'

'A clue?'

'Nobody but an idiot would set out on a clandestine journey with as noticeable an assortment of horses in the traces as we did. Yes, I reckon tomorrow morning we'll see them here.'

'What time is it now?'

Randolph pulled a watch from his waistcoat pocket. 'Just on eight.'

As he spoke, the door opened to admit a maid with a laden tray, followed by the pot boy with a jug.

Thea tensed. If she jumped up, tipped the tray over Randolph, ran for the door—

The big man stood there like a boulder. She relaxed again. Not possible, and there was a risk that the maid or the lad might get hurt.

Thea made herself eat and drink, ignoring her rebellious stomach. She felt queasier when she realised that time was moving on and, sooner or later, Randolph would be wanting to go to sleep. And there was only one bed, not even a couch. He might say now that he did not want to ravish her, but she had no confidence that he would still feel like that if he woke in the night and she was there, beside him, on the bed.

At least he was drinking ale and not getting roaring drunk on spirits. Or was that worse? If he was very drunk, he might pass out.

She didn't know. All she did know was that she was

frightened and she wanted Hal. But Hal was not here. He did not even know she was missing.

Time passed. Pitkin let in the maid to clear their dinner dishes.

'I'll bring up hot water, shall I, sir?'

'No, leave it.'

'Very good, sir, ma'am.' The girl cast them a curious look, then left. The key turned in the lock and there was a sound that Thea guessed was a chair being dragged across and placed outside the door.

Randolph produced a pack of cards. 'Do you play piquet?'

'I can,' she said indifferently. Actually, she was quite good at it, the result of playing against Piers, who took the very complex game very seriously.

'To one hundred points?' He pushed the pack towards her.

'Certainly.' Thea cut and showed the four of clubs then pushed the pack back.

Randolph cut and got the ten of hearts. 'Your deal.'

'I shall deal in twos,' Thea announced and proceeded to do so six times. She spread the remaining cards, the *talon*, face down on the table.

She picked up her own hand and examined it. As the dealer she must wait for her opponent to make his discards.

Randolph grimaced, then looked at his cards, took

out five and discarded them face down, replacing them from the *talon*.

Thea studied her hand, wondering what was left in the *talon*. 'Three,' she said then dropped them unheeded as there was a bellow of rage from just outside, more shouts and the sound of something heavy crashing against the wall.

The door burst open and three men almost fell into the room.

One was a total stranger, the second was the Earl of Porchester and the third, with blood on his knuckles, was Hal.

Chapter Seventeen

'She is here, thank God,' Porchester said.

'Name your seconds!' Dudley pushed forward, a bristling game cock of a man.

Hal simply said, 'Thea,' and held out his hands.

She started towards him, then Linton pulled a pistol from his pocket and pointed it at the three of them. 'Stop right there or I'll shoot.'

The man was frightened. His finger on the trigger was far too tense for safety and the gun was wavering. The muzzle swung towards Thea and all three men stopped dead.

It wavered back towards them and Hal saw Thea fumbling under her skirts.

'You fool, you haven't even cocked it,' she said in a voice of scorn, standing straight again with something in her hand.

The weapon dipped as Linton looked down at it and she struck with some kind of dagger, plunging it into his right forearm.

Linton screamed, dropped the pistol. By some miracle, it did not go off.

Hal left the others to secure Linton and the gun. Thea just stood staring at him, the weapon in her hand dripping blood.

'Come, Lady Macbeth, give me that dagger,' he said, hoping the teasing tone would cut through her shock.

She shook her head, dropped it on the table, and he saw it was just a long splinter of wood. 'You came for me.'

'I will always—'

'Where is she? Where is my daughter?'

'Papa?'

The Earl came barging into the room, sending Dudley, who had been standing by the door, staggering. 'Thea!' He stared around the room at the four men: Hal by Thea, Dudley steadying himself on the bedpost, Porchester kneeling beside Linton, who was sprawled on the floor moaning.

'Who is the swine who took you?'

'Randolph Linton,' Thea said, gesturing towards the floor. 'He lured me into the garden wing of the Dowager's conservatory, overpowered me, bundled me into a carriage and drove me here. I was tied up and gagged but I have *not* been harmed in any other way,' she added with some emphasis.

'Sit down, Thea.' Hal took her arm and steered her away from the man on the floor and towards a chair.

He nodded towards Dudley. 'Sir, this is Mr Dudley, from Yorkshire, who has a matter of honour to satisfy with Linton. He joined us when we realised that Lady Thea was missing and together we followed him here.'

'Here, take this chair, my lord.' Dudley pushed one towards Lord Wiveton. 'This has been a most anxious time for you. You are most timely in your arrival.'

'Followed you,' the older man snapped. 'My coachman may recover one day. Says he's never driven so hard for so long in all his life.'

He took a deep breath and glowered at them all equally. 'Well, which of you is it to be? One of you has to marry her now.'

'Papa!'

'I am betrothed,' Dudley stated hastily. 'Not that I would not be… Not that my station in life…' He fell silent.

Linton half lifted himself from the floor, muttered something about doing the right thing and Porchester trod on his hand. With a gasp, he subsided again.

'I would be honoured,' Porchester declared. 'Lady Thea has my deepest respect and admiration.'

'To the devil with that,' Hal said.

Over Thea's protest of, 'But *I am not ruined*! I do not *need* to marry anyone.'

'I have been betrothed to Lady Thea for almost her entire life. We have, perhaps, not seen eye to eye on the subject of marriage recently, but under the circumstances I am certain she sees the necessity of accepting my hand.'

Lord Wiveton looked considerably happier.

'Now, look here, Leamington,' Porchester said. 'If the lady does not wish to marry you, then that closes the matter.'

'I do not want to marry any of you.' Thea surged to her feet. 'I do not need to marry anyone. How often do I have to repeat that *nothing happened*?'

'For which we must be truly grateful,' Wiveton said. 'You gentlemen have done us a great service. However, it appears that the Dowager thought all her guests had left, but this was not the case. When I arrived, she and my wife informed me of what had occurred while we were in the main conservatory. I expressed myself loudly in my agitation and two people emerged from one of the garden wings. They *said* they had been lost in admiration of the statuary and had not noticed the time.'

'Who was it?' Hal asked.

'Lady Severns and a Mr Cosgrove. I understand that he is her…er…'

'Frequent companion,' Porchester said smoothly. 'One doubts that any artistic appreciation was involved in their tryst. But the lady is the most notorious gossipmonger in town. I cannot imagine a worse person to have learned of this.'

'Exactly my point,' Wiveton said. 'Fortunately I do not think that they heard all the details, but they will be aware that something is amiss involving my daughter and it is serious enough for my wife to have been in hyst— Er…in an emotional state and the Dowager to be deeply concerned.'

'And it is now almost midnight,' Hal said. 'This is one of the better inns on this road. I would wager that several of us have been recognised. Have any staff been in this room and seen Lady Thea?'

'A serving maid and a pot boy,' she said flatly. Hal thought he could hear a hint of resignation in her tone.

Mr Dudley cleared his throat. 'I will remove myself. My aim in seeking out this cur—' he gestured contemptuously at Linton, who had crawled to the wall and was sitting there nursing his injured arm '—was the bring him to account for a slur on my family's honour. I feel he has been dealt with and, in any case, I can hardly call out an injured man. I shall take a room here for the night and return to London in the morning.'

He bowed to Thea then walked to the door. 'You have my assurance of my utmost discretion, my lady. Your Grace, my lords. I will bid you good-night.'

'Just what are we going to do with that?' Porchester asked, pointing at Linton as the door closed. 'My inclination is to drop him down the nearest well.'

'The family have a Scottish estate, I believe,' Hal said. 'A nice, remote, wet, cold and windy estate. One that is a long way from anything at all entertaining for the likes of Randolph here. Linton, pay attention.'

He looked up, his expression wary.

'You will take yourself off to that estate tomorrow morning. You will stay there for at least one year. I will have checks made to ensure you do stay there. If you do not, or if I hear that you have spoken of this matter, or have done anything to damage Lady Thea's reputation, then I will have you dealt with.'

There was a flicker of hope in the man's eyes. Best to crush it now. 'You forget who I am, Linton. If I want you pressganged into the Navy, believe me, I can have it done. You really would not enjoy life below decks in a man of war. Now get out.'

'But I am wounded. This is my room…'

'I do not care whether your arm is hanging off by a thread or both your legs are broken,' Hal said with soft menace. 'Get out. Now.'

Porchester hauled Linton to his feet, looked around the room, picked up a valise and pushed both it and the man out onto the landing.

'Right,' he said as he closed the door. 'That has disposed of the onlookers. The question remains, Lady Thea, which of us will you marry?'

Thea stood up and smiled at the Earl, and Hal felt a pain in his breastbone that almost stopped his breath. She was going to accept Porchester.

There was a long crack in the wall that had not been there before. It must have happened when her rescuers had dealt with Linton's hired bully.

Thea stared at it blankly. Was she really ruined? Must she marry?

Yes and yes, she realised.

It would have been all right, perhaps, if Lady Severns had not heard enough to put two and two together and probably make forty. And if she had not been seen by the staff of a busy and popular coaching inn. Or even if it had still been broad daylight and she had arrived in an open vehicle. And there was Lady Helena Linton's adder tongue to contend with as well. She already held a grudge, and now Thea was the cause of her brother's exile.

But all of that *was* the case. She could brazen it out, she supposed, but it would cause her mother anguish, her father already looked on the brink of a seizure and there were her brothers to consider.

The Earl of Porchester was an intelligent and interesting man. She trusted him. He would make a good husband and father and, although she could place no confidence in his fidelity, she was certain he would never be unkind or neglectful. And she would be safe with him: she did not love him, only liked him, so he could never break her heart.

On the other hand, Hal could snap it like an over-baked biscuit. He did not love her and she loved him.

Thea took a deep breath. There was really only one possible choice.

She smiled at Marcus Greyson. 'My lord, honoured and appreciative as I am of your offer, I have a prior contract. One which I thought perhaps was broken, but which I feel I should now honour. I will marry the Duke, Papa.'

It was well past midnight now. Thea sat up in the bed she had feared she would have had to share with Randolph Linton and watched the flicker of the dying fire on the shadowed walls. On a mattress at the foot of the bed, the serving maid slept, snoring softly.

Papa had announced to the landlord that, thankfully, he had discovered where her daughter and her escort had arrived in error when they should have been at the Peahen in St Albans to meet him. He had secured a room for himself, lavishly tipped a groom to ride through the night to deliver a note to Lady Wiveton and hired the maid to sleep in Thea's chamber.

They would continue their journey in the morning, he had announced for the benefit of any inn servants who might be listening. Really, it was most incompetent of Cousin Randolph to have mistaken the inn like that.

Hal and Marcus had removed themselves, presumably to inns in St Albans. Marcus had been gallant and gracious, expressed his regret that his suit had not prospered, waved aside her thanks with the comment that he had been honoured to be of some small help.

Hal had said little, merely kissed her hand, shaken her father's and promised to call when they were all back in London.

There had not even been anything unspoken—no pressure of her hand, no understanding look. Her friend Hal Forrest seemed to have vanished and in his place was an unbending and utterly correct duke.

What have I done? But what else could I have done?

Then it stuck her. What else could *he* have done? Left her to marry the Earl of Porchester, of course. That would have been a perfectly acceptable solution—marriage to a man of rank and fortune whom Hal clearly trusted, or he would not have allowed him to join the rescue.

That treacherous flicker that kept giving her hope stirred to life again and she nipped it as firmly as she would a candle flame. Hal was deeply honourable, was her friend and had always been prepared to marry her. Without false modesty he had offered her the choice that would give her the greatest material benefit and the prospect of life with a man whom she already knew very well indeed.

Hal would not suffer for this, she thought. He had been prepared from the beginning to marry her as a matter of convenience. He had been in London long enough to have passed all the eligible young ladies under review and did not appear to have fallen for any of them and she would make a perfectly adequate duchess.

A very good duchess, she corrected herself. Marriage to a high-ranking nobleman was what she had been trained for all her life, although she had not realised just which one. None of what that involved concerned her. Even motherhood, although that gave her a slight qualm, was really daunting. She was fit and healthy and Mama appeared to have managed five pregnancies resulting in healthy children and without her own well-being suffering.

No, it was what was involved in making those children that made her tense, the intimacy of the marriage bed and the day-to-day closeness of domestic life. How did she navigate those without revealing how she felt about Hal? Without him realising and pitying her.

He would be kind, she knew. Perhaps he might try to pretend that he returned her love, and that would be awful, because she was certain she would be able to tell and then she would have to pretend to believe him and they would be caught in a horrible game of emotional playacting.

Thea slid down under the covers and closed her eyes. Hal had come for her. *'I will always—'* he had begun to say when Papa had interrupted her. Had he meant to say that he would always come for her, care for her? Or had he meant that he would always come to the aid of any lady in distress?

The only possible way to survive this uncertainty was to pretend that she did not love Hal, that she only wanted a return to the friendship that had grown between them at Godmama's house. She could forgive him for all those years of neglect, she knew that. It was the deception that she had found impossible to accept, and now she was setting out to deceive him.

Not that Hal would be pleased if she told him the truth, she was certain of it. A one-sided love was an embarrassment that a man would go a long way to avoid, she was sure. She should accept that he and Godmama thought they had acted for the best and put that behind her. She and Hal would begin again, on a fresh, clean, page. She would manage, she told herself. A marriage of convenience would be all right.

Except for the nights, murmured that little voice in her head, the one that purred when she let herself look at Hal and think of them both not as duke and lady, but man and woman. *Except for the bed where everything is stripped away...*

The journey back to London with Papa was not very soothing to Thea's sleep-deprived nerves.

'It all depends on how your mother manages it,' he fretted. 'If she has appeared calm, if the Dowager has dealt with Lady Severns and that cicisbeo of hers, then all will be well. Nobody would believe that you could have been running off with Linton one moment and announcing your betrothal to a duke the next.'

Thea was more worried about Lady Helena and what her desire for revenge might inspire. On the other hand, Hal could very easily blight Helena's reputation and surely she knew that, she reassured herself.

'Absolutely, Papa,' she said. 'No one would believe

that the Duke would offer for me if there was any hint of scandal.'

'Yes, there is that. We must make certain the news is spread far and wide as soon as possible.'

Aristocratic betrothals were not announced on the Court pages of the newspapers, although marriages, births and deaths were. The presumption was that those who needed to know about an engagement would have the information without reading about it in the newssheets. But Mama would inform all her closest friends—in strictest confidence, of course—and they would tell theirs, and within a day the whole of London society would know. And all the fashionable dressmakers, milliners, cordwainers, jewellers and the hairdressers who attended fashionable ladies in the privacy of their own homes would be in a flurry of excitement.

A duke marrying meant, in all probability, an expansion of his household, a refurbishment of his establishments. The owners of elegant furniture and china showrooms would be on alert and those who employed servants of the finest quality would be keeping a nervous eye on their lady's maids, butlers and chefs in case they were lured away. A shower of elegant trade cards would flutter down on both households before the wedding.

Thea told herself that she would enjoy the shopping. There was a trousseau to order and all the arrangements for the wedding to be made. Mama would be in her element.

'Will I be married at Wiverbrook Hall?' she asked. 'Or in London?'

'I imagine that Leamington will want to use Leaming Castle,' her father replied, looking up from his tablets, where he was jotting notes with some difficulty as they jolted over a bad stretch of road. 'Their chapel is famous and the house will accommodate the very large number of guests easily enough.'

Thea had never visited Leaming, but she had seen prints. Once a Norman stronghold, the only trace of the first castle that remained was the grassy mound some distance from the present mansion. It had once been crowned by a stone tower, but now just a few jagged remnants were left.

She recalled that a Tudor Vernier, on being raised to the dukedom, had abandoned the old castle and built a fine moated house some distance away. Subsequent generations had expanded, altered, filled in the moat, added more storeys and built towers, until now Leaming Castle looked more like a palace than a home that anyone actually lived in. And it would be her home now.

Thea told herself that it would be a fascinating place, that she would enjoy exploring it and discovering its history. If, that was, she ever had a moment free, although there would be a very superior steward, a butler and a housekeeper to deal with the small army of staff.

Did she mind not marrying from her home? No, she decided, the place did not matter, only who she was marrying, and a ducal wedding was never going to be an opportunity for a cosy family celebration.

It would all be very interesting, she told herself. Exciting. Challenging. If only that image of a great bed did not keep intruding whenever she tried to imagine what her future held.

Chapter Eighteen

Dealing with the gossip proved easier than Thea had feared, particularly when she had the satisfaction of personally cutting the ground from beneath Lady Severns' feet the day after she returned home.

They were both guests at a Venetian Breakfast, held in the afternoon and, as far as Thea could see, with no connection whatsoever to Venice. Little tables were scattered around all the reception rooms of Lady Trenton's town house, a string quartet playing in one room, a harpist in another. Whenever anyone sat down, footmen produced trays of delicious titbits and glasses of wine, ratafia or lemonade.

Thea, strolling through to find a spot where the harpist and the ensemble were both not audible at the same time, found herself standing behind Lady Severns as she was informing her companions that Lady Thea Campion had eloped with Randolph Linton.

'Her Mama was in hysterics, my dears! And the Dowager Duchess of Langridge was *most* put out.'

'Oh, my goodness,' Thea said, sliding into a vacant seat at the table. 'How these foolish rumours do get about! You are making bricks from straw, dear Lady Severns. Mama was upset because I was supposed to be receiving a certain…er…*gentleman* at home, and I had mistaken the time and been distracted by Mr Linton, who was showing me the sculptures.' She produced what she hoped was a smile halfway between modest and triumphant. 'And here the gentleman in question is. Do excuse me.'

Thea went directly to Hal, who had just entered, and laid one hand on his arm. 'Try to look possessive,' she whispered.

'I can do that.' He laid his hand over hers and gazed down into her eyes. Thea felt something tremble inside her. 'But why?'

'I am scotching Lady Severns' scandal broth,' she said, careless about mixing her metaphors.

'Ah, I see.' He lifted her hand to his lips, then tucked it into the crook of his elbow. 'Let us scotch broth by all means, but also set the cat amongst the pigeons.'

Thea laughed at his nonsense. The tremble had now settled into something more like fluttering, which was not so unpleasant, but very…disturbing.

'Yes, definitely there is fluttering,' Hal said.

'What?' Could he read her mind?

'The pigeons. Look around you.'

Thea fixed what she hoped was a serene smile on her lips and obeyed. Yes, they were being watched and with great interest. People were whispering, some of the matrons were smiling approvingly, and one or two, who must have had ambitions for their own daughters, looked as though they had swallowed wasps with their wine.

'I am glad we have met today,' he said. 'I had intended allowing you some peace and calling tomorrow, but now I can discover when would be convenient for you.'

'For what? I mean, why will you be calling?'

'To start making arrangements, of course. To fix a date for one thing and to decide where we will be married.'

His voice had risen a little and Thea saw Miss Marchmont, whom they were passing, look at them sharply. Yes, she had heard the word *married* and her eyes were wide. Nobody was going to believe Lady Severns' gossip now, and anything Lady Helena might come up with would be dismissed as jealousy by everyone who knew her spiteful tongue.

'Papa thought you would wish for Leaming Castle,' Thea said.

'Would you mind? Do you not wish to be married from home?'

'Papa said the castle was more suitable for so many guests and that the chapel is very fine. And it will be my home afterwards,' she added.

That pleased him, she realised, as he moved his arm to squeeze her hand more tightly against his ribs.

Under her fingers she could feel the beat of his heart, strong and steady. What would it take to make that heartbeat race? she wondered, and felt herself blush.

'Can you do that to order?' Hal had bent his head and was almost whispering.

Really, Thea thought, if they actually embraced here, right in front of the harpist, it would not be more obvious that they were in…were betrothed.

'Do what?'

'Blush so charmingly.' He touched her cheek with his free hand.

Did he want her to burst into flames?

'Oh. No. I am just a trifle discomposed. People are staring at us so.'

'Let them stare. I have no problem with them admiring my duchess.'

Yes, she reminded herself, *that is what he wants, his duchess. His very convenient duchess with the right ancestry, connections and upbringing. There is only one of us here who is in love.*

Did Hal think she had forgotten and forgiven his deception? That he no longer had to atone for that? Not that Thea knew what would constitute an apology that would make her trust him completely again, and trust was the problem for her. He had deceived her completely before. How could she ever believe what he told her about his feelings now?

She would never have to lie to Hal about her own,

she was certain, because there was never going to be a declaration of love for her to respond to.

'Is everything all right?'

A quick upwards glance showed her the concern on Hal's face. 'Yes, of course.'

'Only you sighed just now. Such a very deep, sad-sounding sigh.'

'My new shoes pinch,' Thea improvised. 'You would sigh too if your feet hurt.'

'Is it necessary to suffer for fashion's sake?' he asked quizzically.

'Sometimes I think so, but then I imagine having to wear the styles of Mama's youth, or Grandmama's, and I am devoutly glad no hoops are involved, let alone wigs and powder and patches and feathers.'

'Hoops are still worn for Court Drawing Rooms,' he reminded her. 'And ostrich plumes.'

'I know,' Thea said with a shudder. 'And it is so ridiculous—the hoops are still required, but the waists have risen with fashion, so the hoops are right under one's arms and one cuts such a ludicrous figure.'

'I hear the Prince Regent has vowed to do away with hoops when he ascends to the throne.'

'How distasteful that he anticipates his own father's death by speaking of plans for when he succeeds him,' Thea said.

'I agree. It is doubtless verging on treason to say so, but I have never encountered a more selfish or self-centred person in my life.'

'I agree. So we can begin our married life in the Tower of London for our opinions,' she said with a laugh, her spirits restored a little. It felt good to have her friend Hal to share jokes or silly fantasies with again.

Not that friendship would get her very far in the marriage bed, Thea thought, her spirits taking another sudden plunge.

There had been something upsetting Thea the day before at that ridiculous Venetian Breakfast. Hal realised that he was fidgeting with his gloves as the carriage sat unmoving in Piccadilly's customary jam of traffic.

The congestion was caused by an incoming coach from the west of England arriving at the White Horse Cellar, he guessed. That was enough of a show to regularly draw crowds of onlookers, one of the 'sights' of London that visitors would include on their itineraries.

He pulled off his gloves and laid them on his knee, smoothing them into order as he thought back. Thea was no longer angry with him, he was sure of that. At times the day before it was as though they were back at Holme Lacey and were friends again, able to share a joke or laugh at the ridiculous.

There had been moments too when he thought she might be feeling some of the physical attraction that he most certainly was. That delicate blush... He did not think she was afraid of him, of that side of marriage, which was a relief, both because he wanted her to feel safe, but also because, selfishly, he was finding it increasingly difficult not to sweep her into his arms and…

No. Because then she became cool, just a little formal and there was a distance between them he could not explain. Perhaps she had not forgiven him after all, did not trust him completely. He had no idea how to deal with that, except by being totally honest with her at all times. And taking great care not to rush things, to give way to his own feelings.

But she had spoken of Leaming Castle as *home*. That meant a lot. He would have to make certain she felt like that once they were married.

The carriage was moving again and must have been for several minutes, he realised, glancing out of the window. He was almost at her door and it was time to make a fresh start.

The family were waiting for him in more force than he had expected. All four of Thea's brothers were on parade, the strain of behaving themselves visible on the faces of the two youngest. But they shook hands politely and stood quietly for a few minutes of small talk.

Hal was certain he saw movement in the pocket of the youngest—Ernest, was it?—a mouse or a frog most likely. He caught Thea's eye and tipped his head in the direction of the youngster and saw her spot the same thing. Her lips twitched.

'I think the boys can run along now Hal has met them, don't you, Mama?' she asked.

'Yes, of course. Say goodbye, boys.'

They all bowed and obeyed, although the oldest one, Piers, showed some resentment at being labelled a 'boy' and classed with his young brothers. Hal could see himself filling the role of elder brother to that cub before long.

Lady Wiveton steered them all towards a grouping of chairs and a sofa with, beside one of them, a notebook and pencil.

Lists, Hal thought. *Here we go.*

'Now, the date for the wedding is the first thing we must agree upon,' his future mother-in-law declared once they were all seated. 'A Spring wedding would be delightful. April, perhaps?'

'I had thought November,' Hal countered.

'November? But it is almost that now.'

'Yes, a month's time, I think. The twenty-seventh,' Hal said agreeably, as though she was not staring at him, aghast. 'Then Lady Thea will have enough time to be used to the castle before Christmas. I intend celebrating Christmas and the New Year in style.'

He looked at Thea, waiting to see whether she was as horrified as her mother—in which case he had no intention of insisting—or whether, as he suspected, she would be pleased to avoid months of fuss and preparation.

'That sounds delightful, Mama,' she said. 'Christmas in a castle—just imagine.'

'I am imagining making all the preparations, assembling your trousseau—all in a month,' Lady Wiveton replied tartly.

'I cannot assist with the trousseau,' Hal admitted. 'But I can with everything else. I have an excellent steward, butler and housekeeper at Leaming who await your orders. I will employ a secretary to attend you here daily, or as suits you. He can relay your wishes to the castle, write invitations, run errands. Whatever you require. I would not dream of putting you to trouble over this.

'And,' he added, when he saw a certain yielding in the Countess's expression, 'I hope you will be able to join us for the festive season with as many of your family as wish to come. I am sure the boys will enjoy living in a castle for a while.'

'I am certain that with all that help we could manage perfectly, Mama,' Thea coaxed.

Hal was conscious of considerable relief. At least his bride-to-be was not snatching at excuses to postpone the wedding for months. Was she becoming fond of him? What a ridiculous euphemism, he told himself. He knew she liked him as a friend, he suspected she desired him—as much as a well-bred young lady might—but was she falling in love with him?

As soon as the words formed in his mind he pushed them away. Love would complicate things. Love was… It involved too many emotions. Besides, he did not want Thea to love him because he was sure he was not in love with her. Whatever that felt like…

He produced some folded sheets of paper from his inside pocket. 'Here are the names of the senior staff at the castle,' he explained, handing them to Lady Wiveton. 'I have included a note of the number of guest bedchambers, both in the castle and in the Dower House, which is presently unoccupied. I shall now go and see about finding some suitable candidates for your secretary, Lady Wiveton, and will send you details so you may interview them at your convenience.

'Before I leave, may I beg the indulgence of a few minutes alone with Lady Thea?'

Lady Wiveton looked up from the papers he had given her. 'Yes, yes, of course, Duke.'

'Oh, please call me Hal,' he said with a warm smile.

She positively fluttered. 'Thea dear, the small sitting room would be perfect for you to, er, converse with Hal. But perhaps for not more than fifteen minutes,' she added.

'Yes, Mama.' Thea stood and waited while he shook hands with her parents, then led him out, across to the rear of the hall and into a room that he guessed was used by herself and her mother for reading, sewing and relaxing in the absence of visitors.

Thea moved a sewing basket off an armchair and sat down opposite.

Hal sat, crossed one leg over the other and leaned back. 'Are you content?'

'With the date? Yes, perfectly. I confess that I am not looking forward to Mama's endless planning and her campaign of shopping and the less time that takes, the better.'

'I meant that, of course, but also with our marriage, Thea.'

Her smile vanished. 'You wish not to proceed?'

'I very much wish to proceed. But do you? You do not seem to be entirely happy about this.'

'What do you expect?' she retorted, startling him. 'We had decided to forget that preposterous betrothal and now, thanks to the plotting of a venal brother and his spiteful sister, and the fear of a flock of sharp-tongued gossips, we are forced into marriage.'

'You have not forgiven me, then? Thea, I meant it for the best when I hid my identity from you and I badly misjudged matters, but I swear, on my honour, never to deceive you again.'

'There is a problem with forgiveness,' she said, almost to herself. 'On being told that he is forgiven, the sinner, shall we say, feels cleansed and much better. The injured party still has the memory and the hurt of the fault, or the betrayal or the lie. Forgiveness does not make that go away.

'Understanding helps. I believe you when you say you thought it for the best. But then I am left with the knowledge that I am marrying a man who has made such an error. Of course I accept your word of honour, that will always be the case. But how can I trust your future judgement of what will wound me? I must learn to do that. Learn to trust.'

Hal felt himself flinch. That hurt. Badly. The fact that he had let himself believe that forgiveness made things better for both of them was like a slap in the face. What had he been about, letting himself wonder about love, when what he needed was a wife who could offer him forgiveness? And that was a long way from love.

'I had been thoughtless,' he admitted. 'I did not see. I did not see *you*, only a woman who would make me the perfect wife and who, surely, would want to marry me once I had apologised.'

Thea made a sound that sounded suspiciously like a snort, and he saw she was shaking her head and smiling, just a little.

'What have I said now?'

She was laughing at him, although there was still something lurking at the back of her eyes that made him certain that she was not entirely happy. 'That is such a male way of thinking.'

'Well, I am a male,' he said, baffled now. How else was he supposed to think?

'I had noticed,' Thea murmured demurely, then blushed.

That was his cue to sweep her up in his arms and

kiss her until all resistance crumbled, Hal thought. Then he heard voices outside. Perhaps not now.

'I think I had better leave,' he said, 'or I am going to scandalise your mama.'

That really did make her blush. He found it left him with a warm glow too.

Chapter Nineteen

Hal was beginning to think that if he never attended another At Home for some society hostess to show off her new conservatory, or her latest portrait, or the entire refurbishment of her reception rooms in the Egyptian style, as was the occasion for this one, then he would be a happy man.

On the other hand it did give him the opportunity to see Thea looking dazzling as she was that afternoon. When she saw him across the Templeton's drawing room she blushed, just as she had the day before.

'Walk with me,' he said when he reached her side and found himself ridiculously pleased to see that colour in her cheeks. 'I am sure there are many more couches with crocodile legs to admire.'

She laughed, but she slipped her hand under his elbow and allowed him to steer her through the rooms, further and further away from where their hostess was holding court.

Hal glanced around. They were alone in an empty parlour. Ideal.

'I see we are quite alone,' he said, 'I would very much like to kiss you, Thea. If you permit.'

'Permit?' Thea seemed confused by the question. 'We are to be married. I had assumed...'

'That I would demand my marital rights? Or whatever a betrothed man might want? I would never *demand* anything of you, Thea.'

He turned her, gathered her close, close enough for him to feel the brush of her breasts against his chest.

Thea said, 'I have been kissed before, you know.'

Of course she had. She was enchanting and she had already been out for one Season. No doubt any number of men, from young bucks to serious suitors, had claimed a kiss.

'So have I,' Hal said, straight-faced, and was rewarded by that smile again.

'I guessed,' she whispered and met his lips as he bent his head. He kept himself in check, did not demand or press, kept his hands still once he held her, but she tasted so sweet, even through closed lips, and he could not resist sliding his tongue between the swell of the upper and lower.

With a little gasp she opened to him and her tongue flickered out, as tentative as a mouse from a hole when it thought the cat might be about. Hal knew he desired her, but that instinctively sensual response, the heady taste of her, all Champagne and woman and nerves, ran through him like a lightning strike.

Then he heard voices coming closer and broke

his hold. 'Quickly, sit down.' He pushed her into the nearest chair, threw himself onto the sofa opposite it and crossed his legs, wishing he could dump one of the cushions into his lap. That had been exceedingly arousing...

Thea gave her hair a quick pat, smoothed her gown and said brightly, 'I must disagree with you, Duke. I think Herr Mozart superior to Mr Handel, except for church music. I confess I find his oratorios very moving,' she added as another couple strolled in, looked highly disconcerted at finding the room occupied and went out again.

Hal, who was finding the thought of oratorios as effective as thoughts of iced water for dampening the evidence of arousal, stood up and offered Thea his hand. 'Perhaps we should return. And, I have to say, you handled that like a true duchess.'

'The kiss?' There was that demurely teasing tone again.

'The interruption,' he said mock-severely and inwardly sighed with relief. That kiss had been... Best not to think about it again, not here. But Thea's teasing was almost better—he had his friend back again.

Hal desired her, Thea thought, still slightly dazed as she chatted about trivialities with a small group of acquaintances.

Somehow she was managing to maintain a façade of perfect normality, or at least she assumed she was, as no one was laughing at her or staring blankly at whatever it was she had just said.

Underneath she was in a turmoil of emotions she could not disentangle, not here. Hal really seemed to want to marry *her*, not Lady Thea Campion. Yesterday he seemed to understand why she was upset and doubtful and just now he had certainly wanted to kiss her, and more than kiss her. She might be a virgin, but she knew, in theory, what happened between a man and a woman between the sheets and she had, for a few startling seconds, been pressed very closely to his body.

And, goodness, that kiss. She unfurled her fan and flapped it inelegantly. 'So hot,' she said brightly, then noticed that all her friends seemed perfectly comfortable.

'Is it?' Jane Fielding said, 'I hadn't noticed. Now, all of you, tell me what you plan to wear for the Duke of Leamington's ball.' She cut Thea a meaningful look. 'I am sure you have your gown all planned, Thea.'

'Oh, I…er… Amber with a gold net,' Thea said.

It was enough to break down what remained of their polite reserve and the questions came thick and fast. Was she really betrothed to the Duke? Were they madly in love? When was the wedding to be? Where? Had he given her a ring yet?

'Yes, it is true, we are betrothed. We will marry next month at Leaming Castle and, of course, you are all invited,' Thea said, avoiding saying anything about feelings or rings.

The thought of invitations to such a wedding in the near future set the others chattering and gave her a moment to feel a pang about the ring.

Or the fact there was no ring. Thea stamped resolutely on the small hurt. She must be careful or she would be back to feeling resentful over his neglect again. She should think about the kiss instead and that was no hardship, except that it made disturbing pulses beat where, really, they had no business agitating her in polite company.

She had told Hal she had been kissed before, and she had. But those had been quite different. Some had been unwelcome, one or two disgusting and a few so respectfully polite that they might as well have been handshakes.

But this… She took a deep breath. All Hal had done was to hold her, perfectly respectfully, and press his lips to hers and then there had been the pressure of his tongue and something in her had answered, had opened to him, and there he had been, the taste of him, the heat of him, the desire in him for her.

Did she feel like this because she loved him? Partly, she told herself, determined to be honest. But also there had been what she realised was simple desire for an attractive man who made her yearn for his touch.

But that of course applied as much to him. She had never thought herself a beauty, but she knew without vanity that she was considered attractive. And men's desires were far less complicated than women's. Show a man an attractive woman—show him an *available* woman—and they appeared to react instinctively. That kiss had been nothing special for Hal, she realised with a sinking sensation in her midriff. He'd had his arms full of a female who was shortly going to be his, that was all.

'There you are, Thea.' Her mother spared a smile and a gracious inclination of her head towards her friends. 'It is time we should leave. The Duke is coming to dinner tonight.'

He is?

Thea said her goodbyes, thanked her hostess and followed her mother to their carriage.

'He is? Hal coming to dinner, I mean?'

'Yes, I encountered him just now and he said he would call tomorrow, so I invited him to dine tonight as we are *en famille*. But we must get back and warn Jean-Paul. I simply cannot recall what I ordered for this evening. It should be enough,' she said, frowning, 'but Jean-Paul can throw such tantrums.'

'The food is worth it,' Thea soothed.

Hal again. Tonight.

This time Hal did not have to ask permission to be left alone with her. No sooner had Drage announced him and he had greeted his hostess and host than Mama left, Papa in tow. 'I simply must see how they are doing in the kitchen. Wiveton, do tell those wretched boys to hurry up.'

'Alone at last,' Hal remarked. He was still holding her hand from their initial greeting.

'Yes,' Thea said. She smiled, refusing to be flustered, which was easy as she was not expecting any heart-stopping moments of passion, not now she had realised how little a kiss meant. 'Won't you sit down?' She did so herself, gesturing to the sofa opposite.

'In a moment. First I have to remedy an omission.' He went down on one knee by her chair and produced a green leather box from his pocket. 'I should have given this to you before, but when I took it from the safe I found one of the stones was loose. So here, at last, is the ring I should have given you four days ago.'

He opened the box and she gasped.

'Traditionally the Leamington bride's ring is a sapphire, but I thought that the green of emeralds would suit you better.' He took the ring from its case and lifted her left hand. 'May I?'

Thea nodded, lost for words as she gazed at the deep shimmering colour. It slipped on her finger, a perfect fit. 'So lovely. Thank you, Hal.'

'The big stone is from a jewel Queen Elizabeth gave to the second Duke. The setting was massive, so the fourth Duke had it made into a lady's ring. I was right, it does suit you.'

It looked as though it had always been on her finger, Thea thought, turning her hand so the candlelight sent green fire flashing deep inside the stone. It was lovely, and a thoughtful choice, when tradition should have sent him unthinkingly to the sapphire.

'Thank you,' she said again. 'It is exactly what I would have chosen myself.'

He looked pleased, dipping his head to kiss her fingers before he rose and sat down.

Of course he is pleased. He is not uncaring, he simply does not love me.

And why did that matter now when she had never expected a love match?

Because I love him, Thea answered herself. And thoughtful, sensitive gestures like this defiance of family tradition did not help her subdue that emotion as she must do for her own sanity.

Her parents were delighted with the ring. At least, Mama declared herself in ecstasies over the beauty of it and Papa simply looked relieved that the betrothal was cemented by this very visible object.

Thea, who had thought herself the possessor of a very adequate—and fashionable—wardrobe, was bemused by the amount of shopping Mama thought necessary for her trousseau.

And she was marrying a duke, for goodness sake, a man who was possessed of a number of fine, fully furnished dwellings, so why was it necessary for her and Mama to visit his town house and go through the rooms, Mama's new temporary secretary at their heels with a notebook, to decide what she wanted changed?

She said as much, standing in the middle of a very elegant drawing room, Hal's town butler, Mayhew, in attendance.

'This is all perfect. And beautifully kept,' she added with a smile for Mayhew, who looked deeply gratified. 'Why would I want to change anything?'

'Surely you wish to put your own stamp, your own style, on the house,' Mama said. 'Hal would not have asked you to do this if he did not expect that.'

'It would be a great deal of disruption, to say nothing of pointless expense, to make changes just for some whim of mine,' Thea said firmly, earning another approving look from Mayhew. 'When I have lived in each house for a while, I may have suggestions for changes, but for now, it is premature.'

'Well, at least look at your suite, even if you do not want to make changes to the reception rooms.' Mama led the way to the hall.

Thea thought mutinously that she would much prefer to survey her own future bedchamber by herself, and certainly not in company with her mother, Mayhew and Mr Scott, the earnest young secretary, notebook in hand, pencil poised, pince-nez clamped to the end of his nose. However, one could hardly say so, let alone explain why, so she obediently toured the ground-floor sitting room, which was pale green and pink with one wall of Chinese paper, its flowers and exotic birds giving the space the air of a garden room.

'This is delightful. There is nothing I would change here,' she said firmly.

Upstairs, the Duchess's Suite, as Mayhew announced it, opening the door with a flourish, consisted of another sitting room, the bedchamber, a dressing room and a bathing chamber.

The sitting room was a little formal, but that could wait and she certainly was not going to criticise it now. The bedchamber, which appeared to be half filled with *The Bed*, as she could not help thinking of it, was far too frilly for her taste. Perhaps when all the bouffant and decorated soft furnishings were stripped back, *The Bed* would not loom so.

She would feel ridiculous, sitting in the middle of it, encased in pink frills, white tulle and what looked like an acre of fine Brussels lace. But at least she would not have to spend her wedding night in it, which was one mercy. Again, that could wait.

The dressing room was a masterpiece of mahogany fittings with enough room to store three duchesses' wardrobes. That certainly did not require any changes and she suspected that Jennie would be thrilled.

Mama, however, had discovered the bathing chamber, and was exclaiming in delight at the large bath, the pretty washstand and, behind a tactful screen, a wonderful innovation.

'The latest design utilising Mr Joseph Bramah's

valve closet,' Mayhew murmured from the doorway, then effaced himself, leaving the ladies to view this marvel in sanitary engineering in privacy.

Thea would have been happy to leave on that discovery, but Mama insisted that they tour the kitchens and meet the chef and the housekeeper.

Thea had asked Mr Scott to make a note of the names of the servants they encountered so she could be certain to learn them all quickly. Mama maintained that it improved domestic discipline if one knew all one's servants. Thea preferred to think that everyone was happier if they were treated like human beings.

The afternoon was taken up with a visit from Hal, bearing flowers not only for Thea, but also for her mother, which Thea considered showed cunning.

'The flowers are lovely, not that you need to turn Mama up sweet,' she told him, lapsing into some of Piers's regrettable slang. 'Simply being a duke is quite enough to ensure that she is a happy mother-in-law.'

He tutted in pretend disapproval, whether at her cynicism or her language, she wasn't certain. 'Have you any thoughts on what you would like changed in the town house?' he asked.

'I thought it better to wait until I was used to it before making any suggestions,' Thea said. 'Everything seems delightful and very efficiently run.'

But The Bed must go...

'Thank you, and that does seem sensible,' Hal said.

'I hope you will like the castle and the other houses as well.'

It would be a brave new duchess who took a dislike to Leaming Castle, Thea thought. 'How many are there?' she asked.

'Six, in addition to the town house, the castle, the Dower House and the shooting lodge in Leicestershire,' he said.

'Oh. How lovely.' Her family owned this house, Wiverbrook Hall, a small dower house and an elegant villa in Brighton. 'I should have found that out for myself. Do you have a seaside villa?'

'No, but we can remedy that.' Hal looked interested. 'Where would you like? Brighton?'

'It does get very crowded in the summer season, especially now that the Prince Regent seems determined to expand his home there. Papa was talking of selling ours and looking elsewhere.'

'We can have a summer expedition and put all the coastal resorts under review,' Hal said. 'What do you think?'

'I think I would enjoy that very much.' Thea found herself ridiculously excited by the idea and realised that all the emotional worries she had over this marriage had stopped her thinking about some of the more practical, everyday advantages. Perhaps if she focused on interesting tours, visits to the seaside, wonderful indoor plumbing and the pleasure of Hal's company, she would be less anxious.

'Excellent. I have brought my preliminary list of wedding guests and thought it might be a good idea to sit down with you and your mother to see where we have duplications, or it there are any problems. It would be good to have some idea of how many guests will need to be accommodated.'

'What a good idea.' Thea, daunted by the length of the list he produced, told herself firmly that it was about time she started thinking like a duchess and learned how to manage a castle full of guests with aplomb.

Mama, of course, was in her element, with Mr Scott by her side marking off on her draft guest list the names that were already on Hal's.

'Eighty-five,' the secretary announced. 'That is for the ceremony and the wedding breakfast. Of those, Your Grace, you have indicated that sixty-two will require accommodation. Then the suggested list for the ball the evening prior to the ceremony is two hundred, including those invited for the day.'

'You can accommodate sixty-two guests and their staff in the castle?' Thea asked, trying to sound unconcerned.

'We will use the Dower House as well, and the single men can go to the Leaming Arms in the village, I have written to ensure all their rooms are free,' Hal said. 'Now, do you feel this is a complete list, Lady Wiveton, or shall we leave it another week to make certain?'

'No, with your additions, Duke, I feel that is quite complete.'

'Thea?' he asked. 'Are your attendants already included? Is there anyone else?'

'Yes, they are, and no, thank you.' She found she was quite calm about this enormous gathering because there was no room for panic in her mind—it already had far too much to worry about.

She was going to marry a man who did not love her, and she would lie in his bed, raise his children and spend the rest of her life with him. *As long as we both do live.* She remembered the wedding service. It said something about love, as well. She could manage that, but she could not see how Hal could promise to experience an emotion he did not feel, however much the church ordered him to.

Set next to that, she could manage a wedding and a house party that included all of the Royal Dukes, if she had to.

'No Royal Dukes?' she said, meaning it as a joke.

Her mother went pale. 'Should we?'

Hal laughed. 'I do not think so. It would mean them bestirring themselves to travel, for one thing. I have invited them to my ball—which I am alarmed to realise is the day after tomorrow—and I imagine we will be honoured by the presence of two or three of them.'

'Including the Prince Regent?' Mama asked faintly.

'He is the most likely. We might see York or Kent as well.'

'Who is your hostess to be?' Thea asked. It wouldn't be her, even though she was betrothed to him.

'I have asked my cousin Augusta, Lady Brinklow,' he said. 'Brinklow's in Paris, working on the various treaties. All you ladies have to do is attend and enjoy yourselves.'

Mama appeared pleased by that, and Thea knew she would revel in receiving the congratulations of her wide acquaintance on securing such a brilliant match for her daughter.

Thea was less certain of how she felt. She would have no role to keep her mind occupied; instead, she would be stared at, talked about, assessed critically and would have to cope with a stream of comments, not all of them kindly, given that she was removing the most eligible gentleman of the Season from the Marriage Mart.

Hal was hardly out of the door before Mama began to fret about her gown.

'We already have the perfect gown,' Thea said.

'Yes, but *Royal Dukes. The Prince Regent.*'

'I am certain that if I am well-dressed, which I will be, they will not take the slightest interest in my gown.' Unless the neckline was too low, Thea thought, remembering her sole encounter with one of those dukes—York—all pop eyes and a very obvious interest in cleavages. And the Prince Regent was reputed to be the worst of them.

'Yes,' Mama agreed. 'But everyone will see you meeting the princes. You must look perfect.'

Thea assumed an expression of concerned interest and let her mind go blank. She loved both her parents, in as far as anyone could who was brought up with so little informal contact and with no expressions of affection given or expected on either side. But she had to admit, being free from Mama's constant anxiety that everything was perfect, would be a blessed relief.

Chapter Twenty

'Your Royal Highness.' Thea swept down into a Court curtsey and rose without a tremor, thankful for thighs strengthened by frequent riding.

'Charming, charming.' The Prince Regent pinched her chin and she managed to keep her smile fixed. 'Well done, Leamington, you dog. Expected you to come back from the Congress with some Viennese beauty, but you've chosen one of our English roses, eh? What?'

'Indeed, sir.' Hal, who had been escorting the Regent for twenty minutes by that point, also had a smile that was somewhat strained. 'May I introduce you to—' He guided the Regent off in the direction of a number of officers in full dress uniform and Thea let out a sigh of relief.

The Duke of Sussex was making his ponderous way in her direction, and she slipped behind a group of gossiping matrons, hoping that he would be distracted by someone older and, as her mother would put it, *riper*, than she. All the royal brothers appeared to find lavish curves attractive, so Thea felt she should be safe from any overly warm attentions. She might no longer merit Twig as a nickname, but she most certainly was not voluptuous.

'What has made you smile?' Hal asked, making her jump.

'I was just thinking that there are some advantages to being your Twig—I am not at all the type to attract the Royal Dukes. What have you done with the Regent?'

'Left him with a general, two colonels and a handful of lesser officers, telling them all about how he personally overcame Bonaparte. And you are still my Twig, are you? Does that mean I am forgiven for teasing you all those years ago, despite the fact that you bear absolutely no resemblance to one any more?'

'I did not mean *your* Twig,' Thea said, flustered. 'I meant… Never mind. Yes, of course you are forgiven.'

I suppose. It still rankled, she realised, despite the fact that she had a perfectly good figure now.

'I believe the next dance is ours,' Hal said, tucking her hand under his elbow and strolling towards the ballroom. 'The first was very staid, but this is a waltz and so is the third I am going to claim—shocking, I know. I will have to marry you.'

Thea laughed at that, and was still chuckling as they reached the dance floor and Hal took her in his arms. A quick glance around had her sobering quickly.

'Everyone is staring at us,' she whispered.

'They are staring at you in admiration and envying me my good fortune,' Hal said as the first notes were played and he swept her into the dance.

Thea made herself relax and allow the music to take her. Hal led strongly, but not forcefully, and it was easy to let go of the inhibitions that would usually keep her at a respectable distance from her partner's body in a potentially shocking dance like this. But now she felt the pressure of his thigh against hers in a tight turn, the heat of his gloved hand through the silk of her gown at her waist. Her skirts swirled around his legs and, when she looked up, his breath was warm on her face. And his eyes…

Was that desire she read there? It was intense, hot and stirred something inside her. Those naughty, blush-making flutterings that she sometimes felt when he was close swept through her and she trembled in his arms so that he tightened his hold. Which only made them worse.

Ladies were not supposed to feel desire. That was for men who had those physical needs that it was the duty of a wife to submit to. In return she received the blessing of children.

Thea, desperately trying to keep her footing, had long suspected this was nonsense, but now she was certain of it. Women—virginal young ladies—experienced desire.

If Hal had dragged her off the floor, out of the ballroom and up the great flight of stairs to his bedchamber here and now, she would have gone.

Did this mean that the marriage night might be… pleasurable? Dare she hope that it might? It seemed unlikely that such a thing could be, because the mechanics of it had always struck her as quite bizarre and childhood tales of storks and gooseberry bushes had seemed just as logical an explanation of where babies came from.

'What are you thinking about to make you smile in that mysterious way?' Hal asked her.

'Oh…gooseberries,' she said.

'Really?' Those dark brows arched upwards. 'I have never had a dance partner whose mind was on soft fruit when I held them in my arms.' His tone was light, but she could tell he was not really amused.

'I am embarrassed to admit that I was noticing one or two of my acquaintances who are as green as gooseberries over my good fortune,' she said, pleased with herself for getting out of that so easily.

'I am flattered,' Hal said, but his voice was dry.

Of course, she realised, he must be sick and tired of being wanted for what he was, not who he was. He could be as bad-tempered as a bear with toothache, as foolish as any air-headed young buck and look like a toad and he would still be fawned upon and courted.

'They do not know you,' Thea said as the music came to a close. She curtseyed to his bow. 'If they did, they would desire Hal Forrest as much as they want the Duke of Leamington.'

She swallowed when she heard her own words. Had she betrayed too much, given away her feelings for him?

'That, my dear Thea, is the nicest thing you have ever said to me.' Hal lifted her hand and kissed it.

'Which is not saying much,' she countered with a laugh. 'Not when you consider that I have been scolding you for your youthful misdeeds and running away rather than marrying you.'

'But you are not running now, are you, Thea?' he asked, still holding her hand, seemingly uncaring of the fact that they were causing other couples to detour around them to get off the dance floor.

'Certainly not,' she said, trying to read his expression and failing. 'Not that I have the breath to do more than stroll after that dance.'

She had meant it as a mild joke, but there was that look in his eyes again and she realised Hal was reading rather more into that than she had meant to say. Even though it was true.

'Here is my next partner,' she said. 'I am going to have to beg that we sit this dance out.'

As the gentleman who came to claim her hand was an amiable cousin of her mother who had only been doing his duty by dancing, he did not need much persuasion to retreat to seats on the sidelines where he could admire her ring and they could exchange family gossip comfortably.

'Your mama is in alt over this match,' Cousin Ernest observed. 'Add the celebrations at Leaming Castle into the bargain and I am amazed she can string two words together coherently for all the triumph and excitement.'

'Fortunately the Duke wished for an early wedding,' Thea said.

'Thus saving the sanity of all concerned,' he observed with a rich chuckle. 'And you are in love with the fellow, which is pleasant. I don't like to see young girls married off without a thought to how compatible they are going to be with their husbands. Makes for a lot of quiet unhappiness.'

'Naturally, I hold the Duke in high esteem and find his company most pleasant,' Thea managed, flustered. Was she that obvious? 'One does not look for a love match. Mama says that is *so* bourgeois and a result of reading too many novels.'

'Poppycock. And do not look so anxious, my dear. You are not wearing your heart on your sleeve for all to see. It takes an old romantic like me to see how you feel about him, and there are not many of us in this cynical world.'

He reached out, squeezed her hand and then lifted it to admire her ring. 'An interesting choice, and very much more flattering to you than the traditional Leamington ring, if I recall it correctly.'

'Yes, it was very thoughtful of the Duke.'

'Thoughtful? More than that, my dear. Dukes are not given to breaking family traditions just to be thoughtful. We might have a love match on our hands.'

'Oh, no,' Thea protested. She couldn't afford to hope, did not dare indulge that daydream, because the truth would be far too painful. 'We are friends, that is all. Hal knows me, perhaps better than might often be the case.'

Cousin Ernest released her hand. 'What a very sensible young woman you are.' It did not sound as though he meant it as a compliment. 'And here comes your next dance partner to claim you. It has been delightful having this talk. I expect I shall see you next at Leaming Castle.'

He stood as she did and, on impulse, Thea kissed his cheek. 'Thank you, Cousin Ernest.'

What for, she was not certain, she realised as she smiled brightly at Lord Hopewell, a cheerful young man whose red hair burned even brighter than her own youthful locks had done.

'I will tread on your toes, I expect,' he apologised in advance as they took their places in a set for a country dance. 'We could sit out if you would rather not risk it. I just find these things confusing. I always seem to be heading in the wrong direction.'

So do I, Thea thought. *And mostly in the direction of false hopes and foolish wishes.*

'Never mind,' she reassured her partner. 'I know this one, so I'll steer you if needs be.'

'Thank heavens,' he said fervently as the dance began and she tugged his hand to point him in the right direction.

Looking back, it seemed to Thea that Hal's ball had been a positive oasis of calm and normality compared with what followed as the days rushed past before the wedding.

Hal left for Leaming Castle immediately after the ball, taking with him virtually the entire staff of his London house with the exception of two footmen and two grooms, whom he left to assist the Wiveton household with fetching and carrying and running errands.

Mama was delighted with this consideration and with the arrival of a clerk whose sole duty was to write wedding invitations in exquisite copperplate. There were those for the house guests; those for guests living locally who would attend for the day, divided into those who would be there for the ceremony and those arriving afterwards for the wedding breakfast and those for the reception to be held a week after the wedding, which would include tenants, local gentry and professional men and their wives.

Two representatives of Rundell, Bridge and Rundell, jewellers to the royal family, arrived with caskets of family gems and three hefty bodyguards, in order to ensure that everything that Thea might wish to wear was of the correct size and in perfect condition.

'The coronet,' Mr Worthington declared, opening a velvet box to reveal the silver gilt coronet with its eight strawberry leaves, signifying a duke. Papa's earl's coronet had eight too, but they were small and were separated by silver balls. 'I thought you might wish to examine it, my lady, although of course you will not need it until the next State Opening of Parliament. Or in the event of a coronation.'

'Quite,' Thea said faintly as it was placed on her head and declared a perfect fit.

Like Cinderella's slipper, she thought rather wildly. But her prince had not fallen wildly in love with her after dancing with her at a ball.

She looked at herself in the glass and shivered. Who was that woman with the pale face and the wide eyes and the hair that clashed nastily with the red velvet inner cap of the coronet?

'Yes, it is rather heavy, I fear,' Mr Worthington said, lifting it off and placing it reverently back in its box. 'Now the rings.'

Then there were the appointments with the *modistes* for what Thea privately considered a ridiculous number of gowns, considering that they would be spending the rest of the year at the castle, returning to London in the Spring for the opening of the Parliamentary session, the first opportunity for her to wear the coronet.

The wedding dress was Mama's prime consideration and, for some reason, she was determined on palest pink. Thea, emerging from a shopping-induced daze, put her foot down. 'Cream,' she insisted. 'And green.'

Mercifully, Madam Lanchester agreed with her and, as she was the most exclusive *modiste* in town, Mama was forced to yield.

Thea's married friends, taking pity on her, persuaded her mother that she must rest and spent two days with Thea shopping for lingerie and shoes.

Embarrassed, but determined to be the perfect bride for Hal, Thea was persuaded into deliciously fine Indian muslin underwear, corsets that did amazing things for her bosom, ridiculous little slippers with lace or feathers and nightgowns and peignoirs that had her blushing.

'I can't wear that,' she protested in one shop off St James's Street. 'It is transparent.'

'No, it only looks as though it might be.' Lavinia Royce, Lady Finedon, held up nightgown and peignoir together. 'See? I have a set just like this, only in pale blue. Geoffrey went wild when he saw it,' she added in a whisper.

The other three nodded. 'The Duke will be utterly enslaved,' Georgia Jameson assured her.

Thea bought it. And everything else her friends recommended. She could only hope it would not look to Hal as though she was trying too hard.

It was very strange, she thought, letting the silk

gauze sift through her fingers. After years of being schooled in very proper behaviour and in only allowing the mildest flirtations, now she found herself expected to enslave a man in the bedchamber. How on earth did she do that? Would Hal look at her and see the skinny Twig he had first known, all dressed up in some ridiculous charade?

Or would those grey eyes look at her with that exciting, frightening heat in them? Might he possibly desire her, not just in the heat of a ballroom with Champagne drunk and flirtation in the air, but when they were alone? Might he desire her…for ever?

Chapter Twenty-One

Finally the waiting was over and, on the twelfth of the month, the cavalcade of carriages set out from Chesterfield Street. Thea travelled with Mama and Papa, and the carriage following held Papa's valet, Symington, as well as Jennie and Maunday, both fiercely protective of dressing cases and jewellery boxes.

Then there were the staff returning to Hal's household and finally the two loaded coaches with Thea's trousseau and Mama's gowns and accessories.

It might have been November, but the sun shone and the sky was blue, belying the crisp bite of the air. Thea told herself that it was a good omen, to go to her future home, to her husband, in sunshine.

She had a new velvet travelling cloak, a sumptuous new muff and a ridiculously flattering bonnet in green velvet to match the cloak. At least she looked the part, she decided, as the carriage rattled over London Bridge, the first landmark on their route into Kent.

The bridge was jammed, of course, as it always

was, being the only crossing for travellers going into Kent and, as they were heading for Canterbury, it just had to be endured. Then they were clear and driving through Southwark, taking the route that Chaucer's pilgrims had, hundreds of years before. Thea told herself to take an interest in the passing scene, all new as she had never travelled this way before, and then she would arrive at the castle relaxed and calm.

That tactic worked until Canterbury when John the coachman turned off the Dover road and headed south-west through green fields, high hedges and coppices brown and leafless against the still-blue sky.

Then they were driving alongside a high wall that seemed to stretch for miles and Papa said, satisfaction in his voice, 'We are almost there.'

Thea told herself to breathe, to stay calm. She was not going to be sick, she told her rebellious stomach firmly.

Look how lovely the park is. Look at the deer. Look at the trees and the lake. Breathe.

'That must be the old castle,' Papa said, and she craned to look, saw a fleeting glimpse of a mound with jagged teeth of ruined walls atop it.

Then the road curved and Thea caught her breath. The castle had been built in Tudor times, but every duke since then had added to it, played with the plan, added and subtracted. All had chosen the glorious pale

Caen stone that Canterbury Cathedral's builders had used, and somehow that unified the whole.

It wasn't tall, three stories except for the occasional tower, but it was wide, and it took Thea's breath away. How was she ever going to find her way about this place? And how could it ever become her home?

She was jolted out of her panic by the carriage stopping and the door opening. Her view out was blocked by Papa, who descended first, then turned to give his hand to Mama, and then it was her turn.

No going back now.

Thea put out her hand, expecting it to be taken by a footman, but there was Hal.

'Welcome home, my lady,' he said as she stepped out and down onto the gravel. Onto solid earth, although Thea was certain it was shifting under her feet.

'Thank you,' she said and smiled, then let herself be led towards the front entrance. The sight of the staff ranged on either side forming a guard of honour almost took her remaining breath away. There seemed to be hundreds of them, with the outdoor staff first—gardeners, boys, clutching their caps, grooms, three stately coachmen, their long whips at attention, then the humblest of the indoor staff, tweenies and scullery maids, the boot boys…

Thea smiled and tried to catch the eye of everyone as she passed, but it was impossible. Up the steps now, past housemaids who looked as though they had been starched along with their aprons, footmen, the butler, housekeeper, chef—and finally an imposing man in black, his bald head polished to a shine as bright as his shoes. The steward, she guessed, controller of all of this.

'Graves, my lady,' he said with a bow. 'Welcome to Leaming Castle.'

Thea had herself under control now and training took over. 'Thank you, Mr Graves. And please give my thanks to everyone for such a welcome.'

Beside her she felt Hal relax and realised he had been holding his breath too, concerned about how she might cope with this. He laid his free hand over hers, resting on his arm, and together they stepped into the hall.

The *Great Hall*, surely, because this was where the old Tudor house seemed almost untouched.

'How magnificent,' she breathed. 'I half expect to see Queen Elizabeth herself descend that staircase between all those carved beasts.'

Hal laughed. 'It is the devil to heat, even with two fireplaces, and the carving keeps the housemaids constantly employed, but it does have a certain something. And you, my lady, look perfect here.'

The fluttering butterflies settled down again, leaving her strangely calm. And happy.

'I may have to stay here,' she said, smiling up at him. 'I am never going to find my way about this vast building.'

'I will give you a ball of string as Ariadne did Theseus so you can lay a trail through the labyrinth. It is not as bad as it looks, I promise, because it is not very deep. Now, here is Mrs Abel to show you and your parents to your rooms. I thought you would wish to be with them until the wedding.'

'That is thoughtful, thank you,' Thea said. She was not so concerned about being close to Mama, simply relieved that she was not to be installed in the Duchess's Suite yet. With the Duke next door and *The Bed*.

But now there was the next member of the household to get to know, and she turned to the housekeeper, who was curtseying. 'Good afternoon, Mrs Abel. I am relying upon you to help me navigate this wonderful house that you keep so beautifully.'

Beaming, the housekeeper led her and her parents away, and Thea felt a sense of relief that one of the most important people in her new life seemed amiable and efficient. Managing this castle was going to be considerably easier than learning to live with its duke, she suspected.

The two days before the wedding seemed to Thea to pass in a blur, with something of the mad logic of a dream.

She was the future duchess, but she was a guest as well, and that was unsettling. Then Mama's nerves were wound as tight as a clock spring and she was anything but restful company. Thea escaped as often as she could to Mrs Abel's comfortable sitting room, where the housekeeper began the long process of familiarising Thea with her new world.

Jennie—Eames, as she was now comfortable styling herself—was fiercely territorial, and Thea had to intervene in a pitched battle with Maunday before hairbrushes and scent bottles were thrown. When they were alone Jennie, broke down in tears, confessing that she was terrified that she would not be good enough for a duchess, especially on her wedding day, and she had to be soothed and encouraged and then Maunday warned to concentrate on her own mistress and leave Eames alone.

'I know better than to tell a lady that she looks tired,' Hal said when they found themselves alone in the library—the Old Library as opposed to the New Library—on the afternoon before the wedding.

'But I look tired?' Thea flopped down on a window seat. 'Look, more guests are arriving.'

'I will go down in a moment. You most definitely do not need to. Go and rest,' Hal said.

He stood beside her, the back of his hand against her cheek, moving slightly as though enjoying the texture of her skin. Then he dropped to one knee, leaned in and murmured, 'I have seen less of you in my own home than I did when we were in London.'

The kiss was gentle, but strangely intense and Thea could feel the tension in Hal's body. He was holding himself in check, she realised and found to her shock that they were kissing open-mouthed, tongues tangling, caressing. If this was Hal being restrained, then what would it be like when—

Thea lost track of time, of place. All that was real was the hard masculinity pressed against her, wanting her, the taste of him, the sense that Hal was holding himself back for one reason, to take care of her.

When he stood up abruptly, stepped back once, twice, she had difficulty stopping herself jumping up and taking hold to drag him back.

'Hal,' she managed, clutching at a curtain with one hand.

'I am sorry,' he said. 'I had no wish to alarm you.'

'*Alarm* me?'

But he was already striding away down the length of the room.

Thea swallowed and sat up straight as she tried to get her hair and her gown into order. At least it was quite clear that whatever Hal felt for her emotionally, he most certainly desired her.

The sensation of something powerful and feminine unfurled inside her. She had no idea what to do with this power, but she was aching to use it now.

The wedding was to be at noon. At eleven, Thea found herself strangely calm, as though she had gone beyond being tired, beyond being nervous, into a state of unreal tranquillity.

Last night's dinner, meeting so many guests—most, thankfully, familiar—had been an ordeal, but had left her so tired that she had slept dreamlessly, it seemed, for hours.

Around her the feminine bustle of maids, of Mama, of the four friends she had chosen to be her attendants, was simply background. In an hour, she would walk down the aisle of the chapel to Hal and become his wife. She would marry the man she loved.

The man who liked her and desired her, she reminded herself as the gown was dropped over her head and the other women gasped and sighed and Mama burst into tears, again.

'Don't look in the mirror yet,' Lavinia and Gloria chorused. 'Not until your hair is done.'

Someone had thrown a shawl over the dressing table glass, so she sat looking at its lacework while Eames finished her hair, helped her with earrings and necklace and then stood back with a sigh of satisfaction.

'Look now,' her friends urged, clustered around the long mirror on its stand.

Thea looked.

Yes, there is the Duchess of Leamington. Here is Hal's bride.

The chapel at Leaming had been built by the Jacobean duke who had seen the one at Hampton Court and been determined to outdo it. Now it absorbed all the guests as though it had been designed for just this wedding, the hushed murmur of their anticipation filling it with echoes.

Hal stood at the altar steps with his old friend, Colonel Jack Wylde, back from Waterloo with a limp and an interesting scar on his left cheek that he assured Hal was ideal for attracting young ladies. Now he stood stock-still as though waiting for a cavalry charge, the wedding ring safely in his fob pocket.

Perhaps waiting for the French cavalry was less stressful than this, Hal thought. He felt as though some of the holly leaves that were part of the decorations had taken up residence under his shirt, so he fixed a serene expression on his face and set himself to study the chapel.

The team of gardeners and housemaids had done a wonderful job, given that it was November. Berried evergreens were lightened by golden ribbons, and stately cream-coloured candles and bows of creamy organza on the pew-ends made the space look bridal rather than a celebration of Christmas.

Jack unbent enough to mutter from the corner of his mouth, 'You are supposed to be facing front, not looking yearningly at the door as though you want to bolt.'

Now he knew why he had chosen Jack to stand with him. Suppressing a laugh, Hal turned to face the altar and Miles Haversham, the Castle's chaplain. 'I suppose you would see it as your duty to bring me down and haul me back?'

'No such thing. I am reliably informed that if the bridegroom flees, it is the duty of the best man to marry the bride. And I have to say, that is a delightful prospect.'

Then the organist stopped playing something quiet and vague and struck up something triumphantly processional.

Hal turned, all thoughts driven from his head by the sight of Thea on her father's arm beginning her slow walk towards him. Tall, slender, clad in cream and touches of green, his family's emeralds glowing at her throat, in her ears, on her hand, she came to him unveiled, her face serious, her eyes wide. In her hands a spray of orchids trembled.

That tremble steadied him. This was not a vision of some goddess; this was a real woman. His woman. She was nervous and he would let none of his own fears show, because now she was his to protect.

He held out his hand and smiled and he saw something run through her, relief perhaps, and her lips curved into an answering smile.

As she reached the steps, she turned and passed her flowers to one of the young women behind her and then her hand was in his, warm and steady as though all her nerves and doubts had fled.

'Dearly beloved, we are gathered here together—'

He knew he should be facing forward, solemnly attentive to what Haversham was saying, but he could not keep his gaze from Thea's face and, it seemed, she felt compelled to hold that gaze with her own.

I love her. I am in love with Thea.

As that hit him the chaplain's words swam in and out of his comprehension. 'An honourable estate… not to be enterprised, nor taken in hand, unadvisedly, lightly…but reverently, discreetly…soberly…'

He had taken marriage lightly at first. Just another duty to be performed, no need to exert himself with his bride already chosen. That was a sobering thought, because this did not feel like a light thing now. Not now he realised how he felt about this woman.

'…the causes for which Matrimony was ordained. Firstly, the procreation of children…'

There was a little blush on Thea's cheeks.

'Secondly…a remedy against sin…'

He had been very close indeed to sinning the day before in the library on that window seat. Still he could not drag his eyes away from Thea's face.

I love you.

And that was something his almost-wife did not want to hear, surely. To have the burden of his feelings. At any moment they would be asked to promise to love each other, as though that was something that could be ordered, an obligation. She was already marrying him because of obligation—that old betrothal, the need to protect the family name in the face of scandal—and he would not heap more on her. If she ever came to feel for him what he realised he felt for her, perhaps he would be able to tell. Until then, he would show her how he felt in everything except words, he vowed silently.

* * *

'Thirdly…for the mutual society, help and comfort, that the one ought to have of the other…'

That she could offer without blushing, Thea thought, wondering at the intensity in Hal's eyes. There was no doubt that he took this ceremony seriously, that it meant something to him beyond the legalisation of their marriage.

I love you. I will help you and comfort you, she promised silently. *Always.*

'…or else hereafter for ever hold his peace.'

There was the sensation that the whole congregation was holding its breath that Thea had noticed at other weddings. But, of course, nobody jumped to their feet to protest.

But now Hal had looked from her to the chaplain, although her hand was still secure in his. Soon, very soon, she must find her voice and make her vows. Say them strongly and firmly as she truly meant them.

'Wilt though love her,' the chaplain was asking Hal. 'Comfort her, honour her…'

How can they ask someone to vow to love? she wondered.

Just as Hal said, 'I do.'

Now it was her turn. 'Wilt thou have this man? To thy wedded husband…'

'I will,' Thea said and heard her own voice, steady and certain in the still, chilly air.

'Who giveth this woman to be married to this man?'

'I do,' she heard her father say, and he stepped back, leaving her with Hal, giving her to her new life.

'I take thee, Thea Caroline Anne, to my married wife,' Hal said, clasping her right hand in his.

'I take thee, Avery Henry de Forrest Castleton,' she repeated after the chaplain, speaking steadily until, '…and thereto I give thee my troth.'

The tall man in uniform, his cheek bearing the scars of battle, handed the ring to Hal, and Hal slid it onto her finger. 'With this ring, I thee wed.'

It was not a dream as she had half feared it was. This was reality, and any moment now she would be married to Hal.

'I pronounce that they be man and wife together.'

And there, it was done. Her own deep sigh was echoed around the chapel.

Thea knelt beside her husband as prayers were said and the chaplain delivered a blessing.

'Amen,' she said.

Please let this marriage be happy for both of us. Please let me love him and not betray myself.

Hal helped her to her feet and they followed the chaplain into the vestry to sign the register. As the best man and her own attendants signed as witnesses, he kissed her.

'My duchess,' Hal murmured against her lips. 'My most beautiful duchess. I swear I will do all in my power to make you happy.'

When he lifted his head, she went on tiptoe to

kiss him back. 'I know you will,' she whispered. 'I trust you.'

I love you.

The words he would not want to hear, the words that would be like a shackle.

Chapter Twenty-Two

The sea-green silk of the nightgown slithered over her skin like a caress. Thea shivered.

'Are you cold, my—I mean, Your Grace? Best wear this as well.' Eames held up the matching peignoir. 'I can put some more coals on the fire.'

'No, the room is warm enough, thank you, Jennie. It was just that the silk was cool and my skin was rather warm.'

'I watched some of the dancing from the little balcony high up. The minstrels' gallery, they call it. It looked lovely.'

'It was,' Thea said, determinedly cheerful. She had been wracked with nerves, but it wouldn't do to say so. 'We must hold a Servants' Ball very soon to celebrate all the hard work everyone has done.'

It *had* been lovely, she told herself. Everyone had been so happy for them, the castle had looked wonderful, the food and the music better than any London ball she had ever attended.

Hal had been attentive and clearly proud of her and he seemed pleased, if, sometimes, a little distracted. Perhaps he, too, had been thinking of what was to happen next.

In the dressing table mirror she could see the reflection of the room behind. The Duchess's bedchamber. And The Bed. This one, thankfully, was not draped in virginal white or covered in frills, but had elegant pale green and white side curtains and coverlet, heaps of pillows, a prettily inlaid headboard.

The entire suite, what she had taken in of it, seemed fresh and pretty and…comfortable. She had been dreading either an overly feminine boudoir or an imposing chamber with heavy furniture and massive paintings.

'It's a lovely room, isn't it, Your Grace?' Eames's chatter began to cut through her thoughts again. 'Mrs Abel told me that His Grace had it redecorated especially for you.'

'Lovely,' Thea echoed. How thoughtful. How like Hal.

'There now.' Eames stood back. 'You look perfect, Your Grace. Is there anything else? I'll just turn the bed down.'

'Thank you. No, there is nothing else. Good night, Jennie.'

Now what was she supposed to do? Get into bed or sit by the fire? Bed, Thea decided. She slipped off the peignoir and climbed into the bed, which now seemed enormous.

Lie down? But that might look as though she had just gone to sleep. Sit up? Read?

With her eyes on the door that apparently led directly into the ducal bedchamber, Thea sat and listened. Absolutely no sound penetrated the heavy oak panels. Perhaps he was still downstairs with the guests? Perhaps he had gone to his own bed and was asleep…

The door opened and Hal stood there. 'May I come in?'

'Yes, please do.' That sounded calm and pleasant.

Hal closed the door behind him and she saw his gaze flick to the peignoir, draped across the fireside chair, then back to her. 'You look very lovely, but rather lonely in that big bed.'

'There is certainly room for two.'

He was wearing a heavy robe in a dark green, and his hands went to the cord tying it as he approached. 'Would you prefer it if I snuffed out all the candles?' As he spoke, he pinched the flame of the one on the dressing table beside him. That left the flickering firelight and three two-branch candelabra around the room.

'No,' Thea said. 'No, I want to…to see you.'

It was hard to tell in the subdued light, but his eyes seemed to darken.

'As you wish.' The knot fell open and he shrugged out of the robe.

Thea kept her eyes fixed on Hal's face. She hadn't meant…*all* of him. Not just yet.

His mouth quirked, but it was as though he was laughing at himself, not her. 'Is this better?' he asked as he slid between the sheets.

'Yes,' she admitted and found she could smile too.

'Are you tired? Are you certain you want me to stay?'

'No. Yes. I wish… I wish you would kiss me, Hal.'

So he did, taking her in his arms, his body hard and hot through the thin silk of her nightgown. As it had when he had kissed her before, her body knew what was happening, even if she was overwhelmed by sensation and strangeness and new feelings that seemed to be taking over.

At some point she realised that her nightgown had gone and that she was naked against Hal's bare flesh, realised that marble statues of naked Greeks and Romans bore very little resemblance to what appeared to happen to an English duke in bed with his wife, and then she was lost again.

Sometimes—when he took one nipple between his teeth and tugged gently, when his fingers brushed through intimate curls, explored deeper, when she realised with horror that she was wet there where he was creating whirlpools of pleasure—she felt shy, apprehensive, almost fearful, but then she thought about how much she loved Hal, how wonderful this all felt, and she let herself relax into the moment.

Her body seemed to know what to do too when his weight came over her and she drew him close. There was a moment of panic when it all seemed too much, a second or so of pain, then they were one and she was being rocked up, up into velvet darkness broken by flashes of light, heard him say her name with an urgency that called for a response, if only she knew how to make it and then her world unravelled into a spiral of pleasure and darkness and joy.

How long was it before she came to herself? Thea had no idea. She blinked her eyes open and the candles were still alight, although the fire had burned lower.

She was lying on her back and there was a heavy weight across her midriff, which she identified after a moment as Hal's arm. He was sprawled beside her, face down, deeply asleep, his breath slow and even.

Slowly she found herself able to think clearly, to remember some of what had happened. Not all of it, because much was simply a blur of pleasure. Hal, she realised, had been gentle and careful and had *given*, not just taken, as whispers she had heard had told her so many men did. Mama, in her careful 'little talk,' had warned her that the marriage bed was at best a duty for the woman, something to be endured or tolerated, depending on how considerate one's husband was.

Clearly, it could also be a joy, if one was married to a man one loved and he was kind and thoughtful.

Only she did not want someone who had to be kind to her. She wanted to be loved as she loved him. Why had she thought she could bear this? Thea asked herself. It *hurt*. She felt the first hot tear trickle down her cheek and bit her lip. She did not think she could stop the tears, but she must not wake Hal. Not for a moment must he guess that she was hurting, that she loved him.

Hal woke to a room in darkness. Beside him he could hear Thea's soft breathing and realised that his arm was lying heavy across her. To extricate himself without waking her, given that he was face down, was not easy, but it seemed that she was deeply unconscious.

When he was free, he stretched out his right hand and pressed the repeater button on the little carriage clock beside the bed. Five faint tinkling notes told him the past hour. Far too early to wake Thea and, besides, whatever his body was telling him it wanted, now was not the time to make love to her again so soon.

Make love. Yes, that was what it had felt like. And she had responded to him with such instinctive passion, with such innocent trust, that he felt humbled. He would tell her today that he loved her, he decided.

Have the courage to believe in that trust. Even if she did not feel quite the same, she would be kind. He winced at that thought, then remembered how important trust was for her. He would not deceive her about his feelings.

Cautiously he slid out of bed, then padded across the deep Chinese rug to the window. Just a little light. He wanted to sit and watch her wake up, however long it took.

When he came back to her side of the bed, the thin dawn light sending his shadow in front of him, he did not see it at first. But when he sat by the bed, leaned in closely to look at her sleeping face, he saw the tear tracks down her cheeks, the way a wisp of hair had stuck in them, the shadows under her eyes.

When he laid his hand on the pillow next to her, it was damp. His wife had lain there and cried herself silently to sleep.

She had trusted him, she had responded to him, she had given herself utterly—and in the aftermath, when he'd slept and she had felt safe, she had wept.

Why? He could hardly ask her, put another burden on her to find acceptable lies and half-truths. He'd thought she had found happiness in their lovemaking, but it seemed he'd been wrong.

Hal stood up and backed away from the bed. His heel caught in his discarded robe and he stumbled, caught at a chest of drawers, and Thea murmured something, turned her head, then lay still again. He picked up the robe, drew the curtains closed again and walked out, shutting the connecting door behind him with the faintest of clicks.

Or perhaps that was the sound of his heart cracking.

Thea woke to see light between a thin gap in the curtains. It was early still, she realised, listening. Although she was unfamiliar with the great house, it did not sound as if anyone was about yet, although doubtless, down in the kitchens, a sleepy scullery maid was labouring over the fires.

She was alone, she discovered, not surprised, and rather glad of it. It would be difficult to encounter Hal again after last night, wonderful though it had been. Wonderful and heartbreaking. She would face it better when she was dressed, she was sure.

When she sat up, she discovered that she was sore and embarrassingly sticky, and her face felt strange. When she touched it she realised that it too was sticky, from her tears. That at least must be remedied before anyone saw her. She slid out of bed and went into the dressing room where a pitcher of water stood on the dressing table.

It was cold, but she washed and felt better for it. Even so, a bath would help with those interesting twinges, not all of which, she realised, were actually painful. Some of them were tantalising little echoes of new pleasures.

Thea climbed back into bed, shook out her damp

and crumpled pillow, and lay down again. It would be better next time, she resolved. She had shed her tears, done her mourning for a love that would never be hers. But she had so much: a wonderful husband who was clearly determined to be good to her, an exciting new life, a fascinating new home.

She would manage to live this new life, and she would show Hal how she felt when he came to her bed again, even if she could not say the words.

When Thea came down to breakfast at nine o'clock, she realised that it was not only her new husband that she had to face but a number of house guests. How had she forgotten?

Foolish question, she told herself. She knew perfectly well why everything except Hal had gone out of her head.

He was already down, of course, presiding over a very casual breakfast as guests emerged sleepily in their own time after what had clearly been a long night of dancing. Staff were hurrying in and out, clearing dishes and bringing fresh ones to the buffet.

Heads turned as she entered and she fixed a smile on her lips, forbade herself to blush, and returned greetings with composure. A footman began to pull out the chair at the foot of the long table for her, but Hal was before her.

'Good morning, my dear.'

'Good morning. Thank you.' Yes, she was blushing, but nobody was staring or sniggering, although there were one or two sentimental sighs. Her mother looked happier than Thea had ever seen her.

Mercifully, there had been no acceptances for Hal's open offer to stay for as long as guests wished after the wedding. The uncertain weather, the lure of the Season and, she guessed, tact had all of them declaring that they must be on their way. Half, it seemed, would be leaving that morning, the rest after an early luncheon. Even Mama and Papa and the boys were leaving that morning.

Thea caught the eye of Pirton, the butler, and saw his slight nod. Yes, he already had that information. Grooms and footmen would be on hand at the right time, and the midday meal would be sufficient.

Her duties as hostess would occupy her very fully until the last of them had gone, by which time, she hoped, she could handle being alone with her husband with reasonable composure.

'Alone at last,' Thea said, and she and Hal stood at the foot of the front steps, waving goodbye to the final carriage.

'Yes,' he said with what sounded like as much relief as she felt. 'You managed magnificently, Thea. Anyone would think you had been managing a great occasion and dozens of guests all your life.'

'I hardly had to do a thing. You have the most competent staff here,' she added as they went back inside out of the cold. She spoke loudly enough for Pirton, standing at attention by the door, to hear. 'I thought we ought to have a Servants' Ball, to celebrate and to thank everyone.'

'That is an excellent thought. Pirton?'

'Your Grace?'

'When was the last Servants' Ball here?'

'Two years before the late Duke passed away, Your Grace.'

'Then it is about time we held another. Discuss it with Mrs Abel and then consult Her Grace when you have some preliminary ideas.'

'What would you like to do now?' Hal asked her as Pirton left.

'I am not sure,' she confessed.

Go back to bed with you, was the honest answer, but he showed no signs of wanting to do that.

'I must have some long conversations with Mrs Abel before long, but I do not want to distract her while she has so much to do in the wake of the wedding.'

'Would you like me to show you some of the Castle?'

'Yes, please. I would like that very much.'

Thea enjoyed exploring, even more because it was with Hal. The castle was a fascinating mixture of old and new, some of it strange, but little of it ugly. They began on the ground floor, much of which was already familiar—the Great Hall, the ballroom, the dining room, two of three formal drawing rooms.

Once away from those and the constant unobtrusive presence of the staff, Thea thought Hal might take more interest in her and less in his tour. Not that he was not attentive to her and interesting to listen to, but he did not appear to want to kiss her.

Perhaps last night was enough, she mused as she admired the New Library—which had window seats that looked as comfortable for a kiss as the one in the Old Library had. She wished there was someone she could talk to who knew about male desire. Surely he would want to make love to her again soon? Unless she had disappointed him and he was not eager to repeat the experience.

He hadn't seemed disappointed.

She would see at bedtime. He had not really had an opportunity to see the nightgown and peignoir, and her friends had assured her they would be very inflammatory.

When she rose from the dinner table and said, 'I will leave you to your port,' he followed her into the Chinese Drawing Room—the smallest and most comfortable, the one she seemed to prefer. It was ridiculous, the way every little sign that she was feeling more at home, that she had found something that she liked, made his heart lift.

'Do not feel you have to wait up for me,' he said.

'You must be very tired after the past few days. I will leave you in peace tonight.'

Patience, patience, he told himself.

If only he knew how fast to dare go, how the devil he would know how to let her see his feeling without them being a burden to her.

She looked up, seemingly startled. Had he spoken aloud? No, Thea just looked a little puzzled.

He did kiss her then, a quick pressure of his lips to hers, as gentle and undemanding as he could make it, even as his body screamed at him for it. Her cheek was soft and warm as he touched it. 'Good night, Thea. Sleep well.'

Thea did not sleep well. Nor did she on the next two nights when her husband *thoughtfully* left her to rest. On the third night he did come to her, but although he seemed to be taking trouble to give her pleasure, he did not remain in bed afterwards.

Then another lonely night, and on the next, when he did come to her door, she informed him that it was not convenient as her courses had started.

Which meant she was not with child, although he did not appear to mind about that and merely kissed her cheek and left her alone for a week.

When he did politely enquire whether he might join her, she opened the door to him with relief mixed with a strong desire to throw her book at him.

But what did she expect? she scolded herself as the

door closed behind him an hour later. Hal did not love her. His visits now were as much duty as pleasure. Probably he would find a mistress in the New Year. And it was almost Christmas. Her family would be arriving on the twenty-third and on the twenty-seventh there would be the Servants' Ball. A great deal to plan for and think about. She would not have time to be… To worry about anything else.

Chapter Twenty-Three

There had been so much to learn about the house and the household, so many courtesy visits to receive and return in the neighbourhood, that Thea had found no time to do more than glance out of the windows at the gardens. Besides, the weather had been cold and windy and unpleasant enough for her to take short, brisk walks for the sake of the exercise and to clear her head.

Then, on the nineteenth of December, the weather changed to a light dusting of snow and, by the morning of the twenty-first, to still, frosty perfection.

'How beautiful,' she said, standing at the window of the small breakfast room they were using now that it was so much colder. 'I shall explore the gardens this morning.'

'You will?' Hal sounded surprised.

'Why, yes. I am sure they will look delightful in this weather, and it really is time I looked at them properly.'

Hal cut into his bacon, looking, she thought, as though he were trying to work something out. 'I will come with you. Show you around.'

'Why, thank you. I would enjoy that, if you are not too busy.'

'I would never be too busy for you, Thea,' he said seriously.

Then why not spend more time in my bed? she thought.

But she smiled. 'At ten, then, while the sun is shining? It changes so quickly at this time of year.'

They met in the hall on the hour, and it seemed to Thea that Hal was making rather a fuss over whether she was warm enough and whether her boots had soles that would not slip on the frosty ground.

There were formal lawns at the front with statues and urns set about them. She was familiar with that view, the one she had from the windows of her suite, so they walked around to the right where there was a small shrubbery with paths that led to an ornamental pond.

That had affronted-looking ducks sliding on the ice, and she made Hal promise to have the gardeners break it for them.

'The maze is down there.' He pointed. 'But I am not negotiating that in this cold. We will save it until the Spring. This path leads to the South Lawn and the terrace.'

Thea walked with him, her hands tucked into her

muff. The South Lawn was one great sweep of grass running down from the terrace to a ha-ha from where the vista of the park opened up.

There was another shrubbery at the far corner, and Thea began to walk towards that.

'It is too cold…you should come in now.' Hal put his hand under her elbow and began to steer her towards the house and the French doors that led inside.

'Not yet, I haven't seen it all.' She tugged free and kept walking, in no mood suddenly, to be ordered about.

'Thea.'

'No.'

He waited until she reached the edge of the terrace and started down the steps before he strode after her. 'Thea.'

'It is warmer in here,' she said from just inside the shrubbery. 'Come on, show me what is on the other side.'

'No.' Hal caught up with her, stood in front and tried to turn her back.

'For goodness sake! I am not cold. I am not fragile. I want to see the gardens. *My* gardens.'

'I would very much prefer that you turn back now,' he said tightly.

'Really? Just as you would prefer to come to my bed occasionally and retreat back to your own room immediately? I suppose that I have to learn to live with that, but I do not have to put up with being barred from one quarter of the garden for no reason.'

'There is a perfectly good reason,' he began. 'One that I do not intend to stand here discussing.'

'Oh, I was so wrong. You are just as objectionable as you were as a boy, ordering me about, mocking me.'

'I would not mock you! Thea—'

She saw a flash of red on the ground and snatched up the twig with its one brave scarlet leaf left clinging to the end and brandished it at him. 'I am just your Twig again, aren't I? You have married me and you have bedded me and I suppose you are finding me a good enough duchess, but you don't… You don't want *me*.'

'Damn it, Thea.' He snatched the twig from her and tossed it aside. 'I love you.'

'What? What did you say?'

'I. Love. You. I love you, Thea.'

She stared at him, saw the truth in his face, the hurt that they were fighting.

'But why don't you come to me and… Why isn't it like it was the first time?'

'Because you don't love me. You cried yourself to sleep that night. I saw your face in the morning, felt the pillow soaked with your tears. I had done that.'

'No.' She shook her head. 'No. You had done nothing to make me cry. Only make me happy.'

Thea turned, blundered out of the shrubbery, hardly aware of where she was going, and found herself teetering on the edge of a five-foot drop. Strong hands grasped her shoulders, pulled her back, and she found herself clasped to Hal's chest.

'I made you happy?'

'I love you,' she managed to say through a mouthful of woollen scarf. 'I have for so long. And you made me feel so wonderful that night. And then I woke up and remembered that you didn't love me.'

'But I do.' He held her away from his body, his hands firm on her shoulders. 'I love you and you—you love me?'

'It would seem so,' she said with a shaky laugh that was swallowed up by his kiss.

When he finally released her, pulled her in tight again, she said, 'I thought you didn't really want me when you came to me as you did, and you never stayed. It is more than a week since the last time,' she added, recovering enough to be indignant.

'Well, yes,' Hal said. 'But it isn't a good time. I mean, it is that time, isn't it?'

'No.' Then she started to think, to count. 'No. But… but it should be. Hal, do you think I might be—'

'It is too soon.' He had gone pale, she saw, and his eyes held just a touch of panic. 'We can't assume… Doctor. That's it. Come inside and I'll send for the doctor. Thea, you almost fell just now.'

'There is no need to fuss,' she said, suddenly feeling utterly serene. And certain. Hal loved her and she was carrying his child. 'If I am, I am not sick. But what did I almost fall into?'

She turned, although his hands held her back from the edge. 'Oh. You are having an Italian garden built?' Then she looked closer. 'No, it isn't. All those plants are roses, and there is a pool. And a fountain? And arbours in all the corners. Is that jasmine and honeysuckle? I can't tell with all the leaves gone.'

'Yes. Roses and jasmine and honeysuckle. There will be lavender and sweet bay too.'

'You are having my romantic garden built for me and you wanted it to be a secret until it was finished. Oh, Hal, I do love you so.' She kissed him, then turned back. 'But this hasn't been done in the last week or so. This is work that has been stopped because of the weather. Hal, when did you order this to begin?'

'The day before you left Godmama's house for London,' he confessed.

'But you thought I would not marry you. You did not love me then.'

'I hoped. And I think I loved you from the moment I set eyes on you, I just didn't realise it until I saw you walking down the aisle towards me.'

'Oh, Hal.' She reached up her arms around his neck and kissed him with all the love she had in her as he scooped her up into his arms and began to walk back to the house. Their castle.

'You, my precious duchess, are going to be loved with everything I have. Do you believe me?'

'Yes, my love,' she said, laughing up at him. 'You see, I will say *yes* to a duke. If he is the right one.'

* * * * *

*If you enjoyed this story,
be sure to read
Louise Allen's
previous Historical romances*

His Convenient Duchess
A Rogue for the Dutiful Duchess
Becoming the Earl's Convenient Wife
How Not to Propose to a Duke
Tempted by Her Enemy Marquis

MILLS & BOON®

Coming next month

COURTING SCANDAL WITH THE DUKE
Ann Lethbridge

His ire rose once more. 'Listen to me, you little fool, you are one whisper away from ruin. Do you not understand this?'

She backed up until the trunk halted her progress, clearly surprised by his anger.

She frowned at him. 'What does it matter to you?'

What indeed? It shouldn't matter at all, but for some reason it did. 'You asked me for advice. Now I am giving it.'

'Then what are you suggesting?'

'It all depends on whether or not you were recognised.' He removed his hat and ran a hand through his hair. 'Why the devil would anyone think going to a gentleman's club would not be a problem?'

Defiance filled her gaze. A dare. A challenge. 'In Paris a lady is welcome everywhere.'

He stepped closer, forcing her to raise her gaze to his face, reminding her that for all that she was tall, he was taller. Larger.

Her soft lips parted on a breath. Her eyelids dropped a fraction. Her chest rose and fell with short sharp breaths.

His heart pounded in his chest. His blood, a moment before warm with anger, now ran like fire through his veins. Desire.

Only by ironclad will did he restrain from unbearable temptation.

'I—'

She raised her palm, face out as if holding him at bay.

He took a breath.

Her hand pressed against his chest, then slid upwards, around his nape, and she went up on tiptoes and pressed her mouth to his.

Luscious, soft lips moving slowly.

He pulled her close, responding to her touch in a blinding instant, ravishing her mouth, stroking her back, pulling her close and hard against his body.

For a moment his mind was blank, but his body was alive as it had never been before. Out of control.

Continue reading

COURTING SCANDAL WITH THE DUKE
Ann Lethbridge

Available next month
millsandboon.co.uk

Copyright © 2025 Michéle Ann Young

COMING SOON!

We really hope you enjoyed reading this book.
If you're looking for more romance
be sure to head to the shops when
new books are available on

Thursday 25th September

To see which titles are coming soon, please visit
millsandboon.co.uk/nextmonth

MILLS & BOON

MILLS & BOON TRUE LOVE IS HAVING A MAKEOVER!

Introducing

Love Always

Swoon-worthy romances, where love takes center stage. Same heartwarming stories, stylish new look!

Look out for our brand new look
COMING SEPTEMBER 2025
MILLS & BOON

FOUR BRAND NEW BOOKS FROM
MILLS & BOON MODERN

Indulge in desire, drama, and breathtaking romance – where passion knows no bounds!

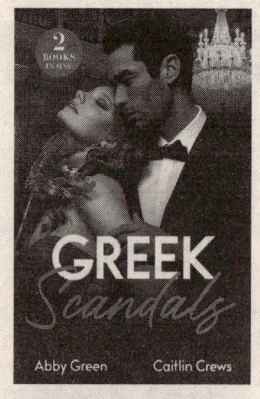

BILLION-DOLLAR TEMPTATIONS
Melanie Milburne Kali Anthony

GREEK Scandals
Abby Green Caitlin Crews

SEXY RICH BOSSES
Maya Blake Tara Pammi

One Night, Nine Months
Heidi Rice Emmy Grayson

OUT NOW

Eight Modern stories published every month, find them all at:

millsandboon.co.uk

OUT NOW!

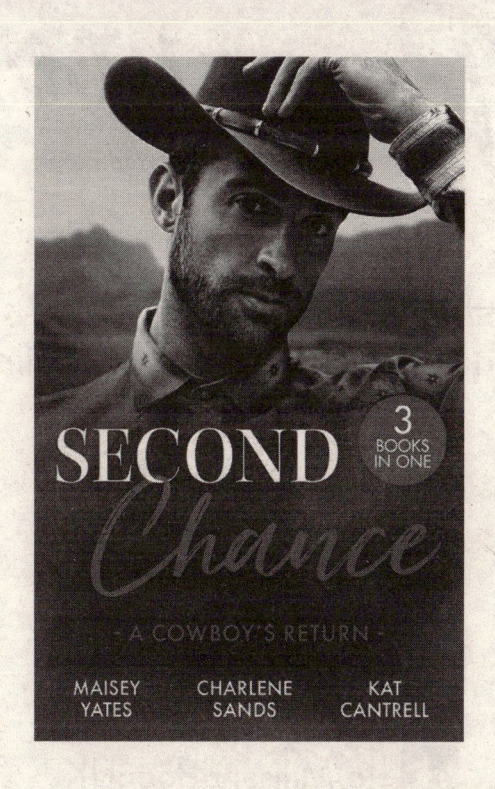

SECOND Chance

A COWBOY'S RETURN

3 BOOKS IN ONE

MAISEY YATES   CHARLENE SANDS   KAT CANTRELL

Available at
millsandboon.co.uk

MILLS & BOON

LET'S TALK
Romance

For exclusive extracts, competitions and special offers, find us online:

- **f** MillsandBoon
- **X** @MillsandBoon
- **◉** @MillsandBoonUK
- **♪** @MillsandBoonUK

Get in touch on 01413 063 232

For all the latest titles coming soon, visit
millsandboon.co.uk/nextmonth